KEEPING MY
PACK

LANE WHITT

Cover Design: © L.J. Anderson, Mayhem Cover Creations
Formatting by Mayhem Cover Creations

ISBN-13: 978-1534786936
ISBN-10: 1534786937

DEDICATION

For Amanda, Zoe and Ryan. My own loosely formed pack that has been there for me for support and encouragement. Each of you inspires me every day.

TABLE OF CONTENTS

ACKNOWLEDGMENTS

Thank you to all the readers who have left reviews, sent me messages, and shared your love for the first book. Thanks to the all the other Reverse-Harem authors who have welcomed me into our small group of supportive and dedicated readers. You guys are amazing and so talented, and I'm honored to be a part of it.

CHAPTER ONE

My name is Kitten. I am a prisoner. I love eight men. Two of them are dead. I will never see any of them ever again. My name is Kitten. I am a prisoner. I love eight men. Two of them are dead. I will never see any of them ever again. My name is Kitten. I am a prisoner. I love eight men. Two of them are dead. I want to see them again more than anything.

NO! I shout at myself. You said it wrong. Now we have to start all over again. My name is Kitten... Wait. When did we start referring to ourselves as we? There, you did it again. No... I did it again. Just me. I've been here too long. Having conversations with yourself means you're crazy right? God. I hope I'm one of those crazy people who are blissfully ignorant, not the tormented kind. You've never been that lucky. If I tell myself to shut up, will I listen?

"You're getting worse." I look up into bland gray eyes. The same eyes I have seen every day for…well, who knows how long. The sad- looking face staring back at me is yet another reason I have completely lost my marbles. Remy visits me, or I guess his ghost does. He always asks the same question.

"What do you want most, Kitten?" I just stare at him, drinking in each one of his features while I can. I used to answer him. I used to shout out all the things I wanted. You. To go home. To escape. The list is endless, really; I want anything other than to be here. No one's life is easy, mine certainly never was, but I don't think humanity was built for this type of torture. No one should have to go through this. I've asked myself countless times whether or not I really want to survive it. The only thing that keeps me going sometimes is that thought that six of the eight men I love are somewhere on the other side of that door. That thought crushes me until I find it hard to breathe. If it weren't for me, then Remy and Tristan would still be alive; they'd still be happy. If it weren't for them, I wouldn't expect anything other than the life I'm being forced to live. I could give in. But because of them, I never will.

I reach my hand out to ghost Remy, watching as he drifts away like a cloud of smoke. It never hurts any less when he leaves. His departure is a reminder that he only exists in my messed-up mind now. The strong, faithful leader of my pack of wolves is no more. It's a knife to my heart.

I hear the chains on the outside of the door rattle, telling me it's time to try to escape again. I try every time someone comes in, but I never make it past the white bathroom. They expect it now, and I don't hold out hope of escape anymore. I do it for two reasons. Remy won't return until I try again and, really, what else am I doing? I get beaten and whipped each time, of course, but I've become numb to it. I think my brain knows that it hurts, but it's just a routine now. The same routine, every day, again and again.

The chains rattle, I try to escape, I'm beaten and left with breakfast food. The chains rattle, I try to escape, I'm whipped, and Adam comes in with a sandwich and talks. The chains rattle, I try to escape, I'm beaten, then led to the white bathroom where I shave, shower, and dress for dinner.

It's the dinners I hate the most. Uncle and Adam are always seated at an elegantly-laid table. The room is stuffy, with old portraits in gold frames lining the walls. The dishes are delicate and easily breakable. Guards line the back wall, with two stationed on either side of the entranceway. Each night I take my seat across from Adam, with Uncle taking the position at the head of the table. They pretend like I'm not a prisoner, but a guest here. They talk pleasantly to me and each other. After that first night, I know not to touch any of the food. I never do. Food sickens me now. I don't need it to live; they supply their blood whenever they think I'm about to die of starvation. Eating the food means Adam gets to touch me. I'll never forget that first night.

I walk into the stuffy room; several men are standing about the room, but what grabs my attention are the two who are seated. Both Adam and Uncle are donning full suits. Uncle looks like he belongs in one while Adam looks like his is trying to strangle him. They both stand

and smile at me. I squeak and try to flee the room. Two men who I didn't notice before are behind me, blocking my exit. They don't touch me, just gesture for me to turn around and sit.

"Don't be afraid. Here…come sit," Adam says in an amused tone. Like I just did something funny.

I glance behind me at the two mountains of men. They aren't moving. I swallow thickly and tentatively move towards Adam, where he stands behind an empty chair. He pushes it in as I sit.

"You are a guest at my table, and I expect you to act as such," Uncle tells me. I don't know what to say, so I say nothing.

I glance around me, wondering how far away from the door we are. I wish there were windows in here. Uncle and Adam start a conversation about God knows what. I don't want to talk to them. I'm confused about what is going on here. After a short time, three men dressed in weird suits enter the room, carrying silver trays. Somehow, they manage to place the trays in front of each of us at the exact same time. The man who has my silver tray lifts the dome thing, revealing a bowl of soup. Soup? You'd think rich people would eat better than this. Even so, my stomach rumbles loudly. I like soup.

Adam laughs, drawing my attention. "I take it you like the soup. Go ahead, eat up." I briefly wonder if they poisoned mine, but if they wanted me dead, I would be already. I stare at the array of silverware sitting next to my tray. Does it matter which one I use? A spoon is a spoon, right? I take the biggest one, more food per bite. Makes sense to me.

I devour my soup in minutes, licking the bowl clean.

I should be grateful for my tiny bowl of soup, but my stomach begs me for more. When the man comes to take my tray, I catch a satisfied smile on Adam's face. He shares a look with Uncle. They must also like the soup.

"Adam tells me you are a relatively accomplished figure skater. Is this correct?" Uncle asks.

When I don't answer, he continues anyway. "Any other accomplishments? Talents?"

I stare at him while the men take away their trays as well. Uncle slams his hand down on the table, making the silverware jump. "Answer me!" he shouts.

"No," I answer hastily.

"Figures." His tone is dripping with contempt.

"At least she has beauty," Adam chuckles nervously.

"And good blood running through her veins," Uncle agrees.

I answer the few questions directed my way after that. They both seem content that I don't speak much. It turns out that the soup was just one of many courses served. Salad, lamb something or other, chicken stuffed with cheese, pudding. I hated to admit it but the meal was pretty good; not to Tristan's standards, but good.

"Now then, now that you have eaten, the fun can begin. That wasn't so hard, now was it, Kitten?" Adam asks as he wipes his mouth and stands.

"Katerina," Uncle corrects. He slides his chair back but makes no move to stand.

"Of course, Alpha Ivaskov, Katerina," Adam soothes. When I realize that he is rounding the table to come to me, I stand and back away.

The guards block the exit again as strong arms grip both of mine behind me. I gasp at the harshness and suddenness of it. A look over my shoulder tells me that one of the men that was standing against the wall now holds me.

"*Tsk, tsk,*" Adam chides as he comes to a stop in front of me. "I told you the rules: you eat, and I touch. That was a fine meal you devoured like a fat kid in a candy shop; I deserve way more than one. Don't you agree, Uncle?" I glance over at the older man from the corner of my eye. He looks bored.

Uncle carelessly waves a hand at Adam. "Do what you will, boy." An attendant brings out a box and Uncle takes a cigar out of it, the attendant lighting it for him.

"It doesn't have to be this way, you know," Adam whispers. "I could make it feel nice for you; you could learn to enjoy it." His fingers trail along my jaw to my cheek. I close my eyes, trying to imagine it's one of my guys. But I can't. It's not them, and my body knows it.

"Let her go," Uncle commands the guard holding me. "If she's to be your mate, boy, you'd better well learn to handle her yourself. Can't have men present every time you wish to fuck her, now can you?" The older man laughs harshly at his own joke, others in the room joining him. Adam gets a hard glint in his eye at his words.

The guard releases me and Adam instantly backs me against the table. His hips pin me in place as one of his hands wraps around my hair and pulls hard enough to make tears come to my eyes. With my head jerked back, my neck is exposed, and he takes full advantage. I feel his slimy tongue running down my throat before I feel his teeth scrape against my pulse.

A loud growl makes him jerk his head away from me. "No consuming her blood before you're mated, boy!"

Uncle shouts at him.

Adam's face is angrier than it was before. He takes a step away sighing impatiently. "Fine then," he says just as he grips the front of my dress with both hands and tears the fabric in half, down to my waist.

I gasp and try to make my escape again, only to be shoved face first into the table, bent over. I try to push myself up, but he's stronger than me.

"There you go son, make her submit," Uncle says in an excited voice. "Make that bitch take it."

I struggle for a while as others in the room laugh at the scene in front of them. I eventually have to give up, tired. Adam runs a hand up and down the length of my spine. "There you go. My submissive whore all laid out for me, just as you should be." His voice is a husky whisper, which, oddly, scares me more than when he yells.

I feel utterly helpless, made worse by so many witnesses. They could stop him, but they choose not to. I suppose I should be used to that, but I'll always hold out hope that there is good in people, somewhere. The man who claims to be my family is sitting there in his chair, avidly watching this happen to his supposed blood. Maybe there are some people beyond hope. Maybe this is the point Reed was trying to make.

"Uncle," I call out to him in a shaky voice.

I hear a groan before he responds. "What?"

"You call yourself my uncle. Is this true? Am I really your niece?" I ask him, desperate for him to stop this, to save me.

"Yes. Now shut up, you're ruining the show." More laughter and chuckles sound around the room.

Tears prick my eyes, but I have to keep trying. "How you can sit there, watching this happen to your niece? You're an Alpha; you can stop this!" I yell hysterically. I hear his chuckle, and it makes me angry. "How can you possibly protect your pack if this is how you treat family!" I shout before a sob wracks my body.

Before I know what is happening, Adam is shoved back, and Uncle has one arm around my hips, turning me around to face him while his other hand is wrapped around my throat. "You will watch your words, or so help me, girl, I will snap your neck." He spits in my face.

"No, you won't," I whisper defiantly.

He turns me to face Adam. My exposed breasts seem to have all of his attention. Adam steps forward, his hands going to my chest. I rock my body side to side, trying to get out of this hold. Uncle won't release me, and Adam doesn't retract his hands. Instead, he moves his body closer, pinning me against both of the monsters.

"Don't stop struggling now, little girl; I was enjoying it quite a bit. This is all you will ever be, just a whore, a little breeder slut for Adam, and whenever he's through with you, whoever else I choose," Uncle whispers in my ear as he grinds himself against me.

Tears streak down my face. Angry tears. My faith in justice in this cruel world is gone. "Why aren't you stopping this?" I shout to the guards and attendants stationed throughout the room. "There are more of you than them!" I don't know if they can understand me through my sobs, but I don't care.

I notice a few of them drop their eyes in shame. "Oh, no. Don't you dare look away! You know it's wrong! But I'm not your wife, not your daughter, or your mother, not even your friend, so you don't have to care, right?" I break into wracking sobs as Adam uses his fingers to inch up my dress.

With nowhere to cover my face, as Adam's shoulder is in front of me and Uncle's shoulder is behind me, I turn my head and glare at the guard by the door. "You should be ashamed of yourself. You are not a man. A man would stop this. You and everyone else here are cowards. Useless, the lot of you!" The man hangs his head, looking at the floor. I look around, noticing that almost every one of them is doing the same. Except for one attendant who is doing something weird with eyes. He's looking at me, then at the table next to me. Again and again, he does this.

I finally look to where his eyes keep going. There, on the table, is a knife! It's a butter knife, but a weapon all the same. I let my hands drop from where I've been uselessly trying to push Adam away. I let them hang there for a moment so neither one of the monsters will think I'm up to something. Not that I think they would; they both seem to be giving my body all of their attention.

Ignoring the feel of their hands on me, I reach out quickly, gripping the butter knife as hard as I can. Adam just managed to get the bottom of my dress up over my butt, eliciting a loud growl from Uncle as he squeezes the life out of me and grinds harder against my backside. Adam's hand is running up the inside of my thigh.

"Adam," I whisper. His eyes look clouded when they glance up into mine. That's all I needed. I bring my hand up and put all the strength I can behind it. A sickening popping sounds as the knife penetrates his right eyeball. Moving quickly, I pull the knife back out and swiftly jam it down into Uncle's thigh. They both stumble back, shouting in pain. I run as fast as I can to the doorway, noticing that the attendant takes a step in front of one of the guards who are reaching for me.

That's all I remember from my first dinner. When I woke up, I was back in the concrete room, my body broken worse than ever before. A long time passed before anyone opened the door. No food, water, blood, anything. It was during those days when Remy started showing up. He'd ask me what I wanted most, and I'd tell him. I'd beg and cry for him to stay with me. He never would, and eventually, I was made to go to dinners again. I was only given a spoon after that, but it didn't matter. I didn't eat. I didn't talk. Just to keep it lively, every now and then I try to attack them again. I haven't been able to hurt them as badly as before, but still, I get satisfaction every time I see an expensive plate shatter over Adam's head or a hot bowl of soup land on Uncle. They wanted an animal, and now, I have become one.

CHAPTER TWO

KELLAN

It's been nine weeks since I last laid eyes on Kitten. There's a constant ache in my chest, a tight feeling as if someone is squeezing the life right out of me. As a doctor, I know it's just my worry for her taking a physical form. The worry for her, worry for my brothers, and worry for myself.

I've done my best to try to hold this family together while searching for her. Remington feels so much guilt for losing her that he's losing his ability to lead as an Alpha. Ash wants to punish the people who took her so badly that he's taking his anger out on the rest of us. We mostly just stay as far away from him as we can. My twin is beyond devastated, which is understandable since he had just told her he loved her, before she was taken. Finn has become a robot, doing his tasks in a mechanical fashion. I just don't know how much longer we can go on like this.

My brothers and I were used to the quiet and

mundane life we led before Kitten came into our lives. I'm not sure any of us realized we were growing dead inside over the years. Seeing them, how they were with her, how *we* were with her, brought us back to ourselves and it was exhilarating. Now, I notice the absence of Tristan's laughter, the sometimes-annoying-chatter of Logan as he discusses the do's and oh hell no's of the fashion industry. I feel how much Finn has retreated into himself and father away from me over the decades. I see how badly Ash needs someone to protect for him to feel whole. As for me, I feel as though I had forgotten that caring for others is not always done with physical examinations and medical procedures. For a while there, when we had her, I had had thoughts of giving her a bath, of rubbing lotion into her beautiful skin to keep it creamy and smooth. Of making her a hot cup of tea and massaging her tiny feet after a bad day. Just little things to show her that I cared for her and enjoyed having her around. The thought of never getting to share my feelings with her is almost more than I can stand.

"Stop combing your fucking hair already! That shit's getting on my last damn nerve!" Logan shouts at Jace.

"If you don't like it, look somewhere else," Jace sneers back.

"That's all you fucking care about, isn't it? How good you look! You're the most conceited asshole I've ever met!" Logan snatches the comb from Jace's hand and tosses it.

Great, round four-hundred-and-thirty-three has started. I finish changing my socks and slip my boots back on, preparing for when this goes badly, because it will. It always does. These two have been at each other's throats since the start. I'd like to think it's because they have similar personalities, but I know it's because they both feel helpless, and neither one is used to that feeling.

"Hey! You dickheads want to look like peasants when we finally reach Kitten, be my guest. I'm not going to look like shit when we get our girl back!" Jace goes after the comb and Logan shoves at his shoulder, pushing him back.

Logan gets dangerously close to Jace's face, the challenge clearly written in his stance and his ocean-blue eyes. "What kind of a freak of nature are you?"

Jace chuffs in derision. "Seriously? Pot...meet kettle." He points between the both of them.

"Good to know that you're doing your part there, Jace; keeping the hair on your head in place has really done wonders in helping us find her so far," Logan sneers.

Jace looks indignant as his chin lifts and his back straightens. "And just what are you doing to help find her? Nagging at me won't bring her back either."

Logan gets red in the face, looking for all the world like he might explode. His skin ripples as his wolf fights to surface. "What am I doing? What am I doing? Nothing! Abso-fucking-lutely NOTHING! Just like the rest of you. We're following shit leads, city to city, state to state, and house to goddamned house, but she isn't ever there. She isn't fucking anywhere!"

I wince internally at that. She has to be somewhere, right? Kitten is a lovely young woman; even the worst of our kind surely wouldn't end her life, right? We're reasonably sure that wolves are responsible for her kidnapping. Finn had stayed up for days tracing every number on the phone we got from the first attempt at taking Kitten away. Ash had pounded away on the prisoner for information, but with confirmation from Tristan, it became apparent the man was told very little from his employers. That didn't help to change his fate in the end, though. What we did get was a starting place, one that has led us to practically living out of our cars and running on little to no sleep. No time, energy, or expense has been spared as we've searched for her. It can't all be for nothing, right? She has to be alive, right?

"Just stop fighting, guys. Turning on each other isn't going to do us any good." Reed speaks up from next to Finn, who is tapping away on his laptop. With each new location, Finn gets right to work tracking anyone down who has had any contact with our current target. He assesses their call patterns, emails, bank records, anything he can get his hands on to see if anything sticks out like a red flag and might lead us to Kitten, or at least someone who knows where she is.

I smile at Reed as he once again tries to play peacekeeper with our family's two divas while still trying to keep an eye on what Finn is doing. I have to say that Reed has really surprised me through all of this. I can tell he's slid back into being the emotional introvert he was before Kitten arrived, but he's been the most level-headed of all of us. I worry about him if we don't find her, though he has every confidence that we will and has never once doubted it. His conviction is admirable, if a little intense, and I fear that it's all that is keeping him, and us, from total despair.

A plume of dust rising over the hill a short distance away is the only warning we have before the large black SUV makes its way down the gravel drive toward us.

Remy and Ash had gone to check out a compound of outlying Ivaskov pack members. No matter what we do, the information always points back at them. The guys have been gone for longer than usual, and I have to hope that means someone finally talked and not that Ash flew off the handle again. We need a good lead, and we need it desperately before we all fall apart.

"Gather 'round!" Remy barks, throwing open the passenger door and sliding out before Ash has even put the car in park.

My heart pounds frantically in my chest. Do they know where she is?

Remy motions Finn to step closer before he speaks. "While we were investigating, we came across a man who had information about a young woman being held by their Alpha. A servant there has been trying to reach out, hoping to get in contact with Maksim Ivaskov, their former Alpha, to get the woman some help. He said her scent when she first came in was similar to an Ivaskov, but it has since changed and neither he nor the man we spoke to knew what it meant."

"Maksim is 'The Grandfather' from the book," Finn states, jumping to his feet.

"That's great news! Where? Let's go get her!" Reed exclaims, heading toward the car.

"Their fucking Alpha?" Logan growls in disgust.

Several other shouts go up at once as we all start talking over each other. I feel excitement course through me, and it takes significant effort to keep my wolf from coming out in celebration. A glance at my brothers tells me that they are feeling it, too. I've never scented an Ivaskov, but if Kitten is one of them, that must mean that she is safe. This must all be a misunderstanding. Just a family looking to get back one of theirs, not realizing that she belongs to us now. Maybe they thought she was in danger.

Remy holds his hands out in front of him in a shushing gesture. "Quiet down! Now, I know you are all excited, I am, too, but you need to understand what this means. We can't just rush the door of an Alpha of royal bloodlines. If she is one of them, and they wish to keep her from us, then getting her back will prove more complicated than just asking."

"What are you saying?" Tristan asks, confused. "I don't care if they're her family. They threw her away and left her to fend for herself, then kidnapped her and almost killed two of us to do it. Those people don't deserve her! She belongs with us!"

Remy clasps him on the shoulder in understanding and Tristan takes a deep breath, scrubbing his hand down his face. Once attention returns to him, Remy continues, "Our best bet will be to track down this Maksim guy. Apparently most of the Ivaskov pack is still loyal to him, not his son. If we can convince him she belongs with us, he might be able to generate support with the current Alpha or back us up if we have to take the Alpha house by force. It's a risk, and we might lose our advantage of surprise, but it would be better to have him on our side."

"So we're just going to leave Kitten where she is then? C'mon, man! You can't be serious," Logan sneers at Remy.

"Don't!" Ash barks, getting in Logan's face. "You think we want to leave her there longer than we have to? We might be stronger than them, but taking on an entire army by ourselves is no joke. It may not be necessary, and Kitten could get hurt in the crossfire!" Logan seems to deflate at that statement.

"So we find this Maksim…then what? How long do we have to wait to get Kitten? How do we even know she's the girl being held by the Alpha in the first place?" Finn asks. He's still using his robot voice, but his eyes are showing some life in there.

"That's a good point." Ash rumbles thoughtfully while shooting Remy a look.

"This guy seems to think that Maksim is hiding out in his cabin in the mountains. How about we give him three days from when we find him to get us the support we need? It may just be a phone call to the Alpha or a civilized meeting that needs to happen; I don't know. If he doesn't come through, we go after her anyway." Remy looks at each of us, seeming unsure of himself. I hate seeing him this way.

"Sounds like a plan to me, Remington," I speak up, clasping his broad shoulder and giving him my support.

"I find that acceptable." Finn nods.

"Let's go find this prick!" Logan claps excitedly.

The others agree with words or gestures, and I offer to help pack up before jumping in the passenger seat with Tristan driving and Finn in the back, continuing whatever he was doing on his computer. I try to think about what Kitten may be doing at this very moment, wondering if she's okay and adjusting to her new surroundings. My wolf is still restless, and doubt fills me even as I try to imagine her smiling face as she twirls around in a new dress in her new home. I don't know if I don't believe the image because I don't want her to be happy without us, or if my instincts have been right all along, and something is seriously wrong, but at least we have a damn good plan for finding her now.

JACE

It was decided that it would be faster to fly to Maksim than it was to drive. While some of the other men may do this on a regular basis for work, I have never enjoyed being trapped in these metal machines. Every time I've been in one so far, I've had Kellan knock me out with drugs. Unfortunately for me, he refuses to do so this time, stating that we should all be on alert. Alert is not what I'm currently feeling. I believe queasy would be more apt. Why humans ever invented these things is beyond me. What's wrong with a good ship, or train, or car?

"You holding up okay, man?" Reed asks from the seat next to mine. I give him a short nod, turning my attention back out the window. With all the new-fangled gadgetry these deathtraps have nowadays, sometimes the pilots don't even realize when the plane is losing altitude. I'm determined to keep watch for that exact reason. Flying is only made more bearable when one of my brothers is in control of the plane, and I know Ash has checked all of the mechanics. As we are in a bit of a rush, we had just booked the earliest commercial flight available.

"Move your arm, dickweed," I hear Logan groan from the seats in front of us.

"No! You move. Your fat arm is on my armrest,"

Tristan shoots back. I can't help but grin at their antics. Another downside to these flying beasts: they definitely weren't designed with your average wolf in mind. Even in first class, the seats are tiny. Ash had damn near bitten the head off the human woman who dared tell him he was too large and had to purchase a second seat, if not a third.

The plane lurches, and I resume my watch out of the window. No mountain crashes for me. Nope, no way. Damn planes.

REMINGTON

I roll my eyes as yet more branches scratch at the rented SUV. The trees surrounding this winding drive are aggressively trying to take back this dirt road. According to the directions we were given, we turned on to Maksim's driveway eight minutes ago. I'm wondering, not for the first time, if we have been led on a wild goose chase. Thankfully, it's only moments before I see what looks to be the peak of a roof through a break in the trees. Well, at least there's a building here.

Slamming my door shut, I turn to Kellan as he climbs from the second car where he rode with Reed, Jace, and Tristan. "We might as well all go in," I tell him as he leans next to me while we look over the small cabin in front of us.

The front door opens with a groan, and a polished-looking older male greets us with a frown. A quick sniff determines he is, in fact, a wolf.

"I have to warn you, if you're here to kill me, I'm not worth the fallout that comes afterward." The man's deeply accented voice calls out from his position in front of the door. I have to admit that he's got some balls to greet eight changed wolves head-on.

"We're not here to kill you," I tell him, directing his attention to me. His eyes meet mine, and it's almost enough to steal my breath away. Pale green with tiny streaks of gold, exactly like Kitten's. I push through the pang of sadness that overcomes me and continue. "We're here to speak with a man named Maksim Ivaskov. That's you. We need your help."

Maksim scoffs, but I notice his posture relaxes the tiniest amount. "And why would I help you?"

Reed takes a step forward, causing me to release a growl at him. He should know better than to step out of line. I suppose this is what comes from being off my game for so long. "Besides us not killing you in the most painful of ways, you'll help us because you'll be helping your family." Reed's voice chokes off at the end, and Kellan takes a step closer to his twin, their arms now touching.

Maksim takes his sweet time looking over each one of us carefully before coming to some decision. "Maybe we should take this inside. Be sure to leave your shoes at the door; I don't want you making a mess of my rugs. I'll put some tea on." With that, he stiffly turns and walks into the cabin without another word.

My men look at each other, confused by the old man's behavior, but I just sigh and start unlacing my boots. Clearly, Russian habits die hard.

Shoes left in the mudroom and now settled into the sitting room with Jace, Tristan, and Kellan taking one couch, Reed and Finn taking the loveseat and Logan, Ash, and myself seated on the couch opposite of the other one, Maksim returns with a tray of tea cups and takes his seat in a recliner. When none of us makes a move for the tea, his eyes narrow. I mentally roll my eyes and pick up one of the small cups. The other men follow my lead silently until Ash's rhino fingers crush the delicate china and he curses at the hot liquid burning his hand.

Maksim speaks over Logan's sniggering. "Now what's this about my family?"

Finn meets my eyes, asking for permission to answer, and I nod my head at him. "To be fair to you, sir, we're not positive that Kitten is, in fact, your family. What we do know is that she was abandoned as a baby, with a blanket sporting the Ivaskov family crest. She was being watched by men that we believe were responsible for an attack that led us to find a history of sorts on your family, and right before she was abducted a police officer asked for a Katerina Ivaskov with Kitten's description, implying her father was looking for her. With that information and your eyes matching the exact unique coloring of hers, it's a safe bet that you *are* related. Factor in her age and the lengths that her kidnappers went through to obtain her, and that leads me to believe that Kitten is your granddaughter."

I watch Maksim's response carefully. For all I know, he could have been in on her abduction. From what I see, which is a mix of hopefulness, anger, sadness, and curiosity, I'd have to say that he had no idea Kitten existed.

He takes a deep pull of tea before slouching back in his chair. "Well, son, you don't beat around the bush, do you?" he says to Finn. Finn's cheeks tint a light shade of pink, but he only shrugs a shoulder and looks to me. I know that look: he no longer wishes to speak.

Leaning forward with his elbows on his knees, Maksim's expression changes to that of someone who means business. "Do you have anything of hers with you?" he asks no one in particular. Ash grunts but reluctantly shoves a hand into his pocket, producing that damn stuffed animal he carries around and talks to when he thinks no one is paying attention.

Ash reaches out to hand it over to the older man before he snatches it back and looks at Maksim suspiciously. "What do you need it for?" he asks gruffly.

Maksim has an amused glint in his eyes as he drolly responds, "I won't hurt your stuffed animal. But apparently there's a lot you boys don't know about wolves. If this Kitten is my granddaughter, I will be able to tell from her scent. All born wolves carry the scent of their fathers before they are mated." I sniff the air again, but I get nothing of Kitten from this man's scent.

Maksim must notice this. "It's one of the only advantages born wolves have over you changed wolves," he explains. He sniffs at the stuffed animal for a moment before running his hand over the fabric and sniffing again. He gives the toy back to Ash, who snatches it quickly and places it back safely in his pocket.

Maksim covers his face with both hands, speaking softly to himself in Russian. We all watch him carefully, waiting for the verdict.

"So...?" Logan blurts out, his knee bouncing so fast it's blurry.

When Maksim looks up, he appears to have aged twenty years. He gives me a curt nod. "And you believe someone in my pack has her." It's not a question, and he doesn't seem happy about it.

"Yes," I answer anyway.

Logan jumps up and punches the air. "Yes! That means he's gonna help us get her back, right? Right, Rem?" He turns to me, blue eyes excited and looking a tad crazy.

Maksim stands abruptly, clapping his hands together loudly. "Alright, boys, fuck the tea. I need all the information you can give me. We'll get this mess sorted."

One thing I love about Russians is their ability to come up with a crazy-ass plan in a matter of minutes. We had shared all of the information we have about Kitten's upbringing and combed over every detail about her time with us. In turn, Maksim had told us that his son, Mikel Ivaskov, was Kitten's father. That's whose scent he caught from the toy. He had gotten quite emotional as he spoke of his son, who was murdered in his own pack house. Maksim had always suspected his second son, Marcus, but was never able to prove it. Marcus inherited the Alpha title, and Maksim is confident that if he does indeed have Kitten, nothing good could come of it.

His first call was to the man Ash and I spoke to at the compound. It just so happened that the inside man with the Alpha and Kitten was Mikel's most trusted advisor and a friend of Maksim's. Through a series of messages, Maksim was able to learn that the Alpha is currently at his summer home in Alaska, not at the pack house in Colorado. It's as we first suspected and Kitten is not being treated as a guest, but as a prisoner. Much to all of our grief, the man said he hasn't actually seen Kitten in weeks, but he knows she's still in the house. The current Alpha is a sadistic bastard and had a dungeon of sorts built in the basement, where he's been known to torture human women. He'll die for taking her from me in the first place, but if my beautifully innocent woman has been anywhere near that basement, it won't be the quick and painless death he will wish for.

Maksim is currently out in the SUV with Finn, sending a message to the guy whose name is Albert Rosen. I was unsure about trusting him since he now works for Marcus, but Maksim was quick to reassure us that he only does so because Marcus threatened to kill off his family.

"How did it go?" Reed asks nervously as Maksim and Finn step back into the room.

"Perfectly. I was able to confirm with Albert that there are a few men in the house who can be trusted to know about Kitten's real status. Now that they know we're coming, they'll look out for her. He told us to hurry. From what Albert told me, he doesn't plan on keeping her alive much longer," Maksim says as he rushes past us and into a bedroom. I follow after him.

"What do you mean, her *real* status?" I question him.

Maksim pauses in his mad rush to throw clothing and other items into a suitcase. His back straightens, and he gives me an unreadable look. "You really don't know, do you?"

"Know what?" I bark at him. Shit just got real, and he wants to play fucking mind games?

"Marcus isn't holding Kitten just because she's his brother's daughter, a brother he hated and probably murdered in cold blood. He has her because she threatens his reign as Alpha, something he's always wanted. Wolf law states that Alpha will always follow direct descendants, Father to son, son to grandson. Marcus only became Alpha because his brother died without any heirs, and he was my son. I refused to make any more heirs without my mate, who I lost during The Suffering."

"But she's a female! Females can't be named Alpha, of any pack." I shake my head at him. Even I know that about the born wolves. It still doesn't make sense.

"Look, son, I don't have time to explain how wolf society works right now, but the short and sweet of it is that Kitten herself can't be named Alpha, but her mate can be until she gives birth to an Alpha son. Even if she never has a son, the title stays with her until she dies. Now, get your men ready to leave. That girl isn't only my granddaughter, but also the key to ending Marcus' reign of terror on my pack and the potential collapse of wolf society as a whole."

I watch, stunned, as he uses a knee to get the over-stuffed suitcase to close. In the back of my mind, I suppose I knew Kitten was important if she was Maksim's granddaughter but...this? This is a lot to take in. It also means she's in even more danger than we could have predicted. That thought snaps me out of my shock and gets me moving toward the others. I hear Maksim begin a phone call behind me to one of his contacts as I stomp my way over to Ash in the living room.

"Time to get our girl, brother," I tell him as I clasp his broad shoulder. I see the swirl of emotion in his eyes, my own probably reflecting the same. I hold back a chuckle as Ash rushes Logan and Tristan and throws them both over his shoulders, running for the door.

CHAPTER THREE

KITTEN

I hear shouting from the other side of the door. I try to sigh at the interruption but end up coughing dryly instead. I wish they would just leave me be. I've been lying here, exactly like this for a long time now. I haven't spoken to anyone in what feels like weeks, though maybe it's only been days or even hours. Time is an elusive thing when you can't see the sun. I don't try to escape anymore, and I don't go to their stupid dinners. It all seems pointless. Everything is pointless. I won't get to eat; I can't escape. Talking to them is pointless, too. They don't say anything I want to hear, and there's nothing I can say to make them let me go. I've found that lying in one spot and not moving is what makes me the happiest now. Uncle beats me no matter what I do, but if I don't move I can barely feel it anymore. I've become numb to the pain. I like closing my eyes and pretending I'm with the boys. In my mind, we're living out a peaceful life where I feel cared for, cherished, and even loved.

My dry, cracked lips sting as I smile at the thought.

The shouting gets louder and even though I don't want to, I can't help but hear them.

"I just need more time!" Adam shouts, sounding panicked.

"You couldn't get that girl under control if I gave you a hundred years to do it! I told you, the agreement is off, Vanderson! She'd rather lie there and die than let you put one finger on her. It's not going to work. I gave it a shot; now it's time to move on!" Uncle shouts back at him.

"But...but you can't do this! You promised I'd be Alpha! You promised she'd be mine! I can get her under control. Just look at her; I already got her to stop fighting us. We can still breed her and sell the pups to the highest bidders. I just need more time!"

"Oh, we're still doing that. I've just found another way to go about it. One where we don't have to put up with the defiant little shit and I can finally be rid of her. The humans have been doing this for decades; it should be fine," Uncle says dismissively.

"But this could kill her! She's supposed to be mine, damn it! I can't very well go making my own pack without a mate and heirs." Adam's voice gets high-pitched and whiny, making my ears hurt.

"Remember who you're speaking to, boy. If the little bitch lives, I'll let you have her. Deal?" Uncle asks.

"Fine," Adam huffs.

The metal door creaks open, and I hear what I think is squeaky wheels. I don't care to turn my head and look. I'm not sure what they're up to but it sounds like whatever it may be will be the end of my time here, one way or another. A part of me wants to fight them, to try to stop them from doing anything to me. I won't, though. If nothing else, all this time alone has given me a chance to think about my life. How insignificant I was from the very beginning. My entire life has meant nothing; I have done nothing of any worth. I've been surviving, not living, and I'm tired now. The best thing I have ever done was to meet the boys and because of me, two of them are dead. I ruined their family by trying to be a part of it. Even if I lived forever, I'd never forgive myself for that, so I might as well die today.

Cold hands grip my ankles the same time warm ones go under my arms, and I'm lifted up off my spot on the floor. I almost protest this but decide to close my eyes and picture the guys in their wolf forms again. I wish I could have had more time with them. I didn't know the right words to say or the right things to do to let them know how much I care about them. I never told them how special they were, never told them that all out of all of the people I've ever met, they were my favorites. I didn't get to tell the others how sorry I am for killing Remy and Tristan.

"You should give her your blood again before we do this. Make sure she's in perfect condition so we'll have more time if this goes badly. I've never done this procedure myself." A voice I've never heard before speaks from above me.

A hand grips my face and puts pressure on my jaw, causing my mouth to open reflexively. Moments later I taste the coppery tang of blood as it hits my tongue. Uncle presses his wrist harder on my mouth, forcing me to swallow and my lips to bleed as they crack. The new man begins to speak again, but I can't hear him as blood rushes through my ears, and the healing process begins. Somehow it hurts more to heal than it does to be broken in the first place. A searing heat starts up on every cut and bruise, and I can feel in great detail as my skin, muscles, and veins knit themselves back together. The bones are the worst, though. With them, not only do I feel the heat but also an incredible pressure that makes me think I just might shatter before it ends.

By the time the blood had done its job, I'm panting heavily, and a new coat of sweat covers my body. I hate being fully healed most of all. When I'm already broken, there's only so much he can do; with being healed, I know I'm going to be broken all over again.

Before I can relax for even one moment, a new pain shoots through my tummy. It's so painful that my brain can't even process what's happening. My mouth opens to scream, but nothing comes out. The pain makes my vision spotty and steals my breath from me. I slam my head back on the table or whatever I've been put on, and arch my back until I hear, more than feel, something break. I feel my fingernails rip off as I claw at whatever is hurting me. I have never felt such pain. Smoke fills my nose as soon as I'm able to get a short breath and with it is such a sickening smell that I instantly want to retch.

I turn my head to do just that, and I see a guy ambling toward me through my blurry vision. As I try to focus on him, I see him lift a hand to his face, a finger going over his lips. There's a loud *boom*, and everything around me shakes. Or I do; it's hard to tell.

"Wha…" Adam starts before he howls in pain.

"Shit. No, please don't! H-he made me do it!" I hear someone shout.

Before I can turn my head to see what happened, I feel a new pain in my chest. My eyes snap down to see Uncle standing over me. Something big and shiny is in his hands, holding onto something…in my chest. The polished surface of the blade reflects my confused and panicked eyes before thick, dark red blood bubbles to the surface and covers the rest of the knife that is not inside of me. Inside of me. Covered in blood. My blood. I had thought that I was ready to die, but as I know I only have moments left, I can't help but wish that I would live.

My eyes shoot to my uncle's, to the only member of my family I ever knew. My eyes ask the question my mouth cannot. The same question I've been asking myself since the day of the accident. "Why?"

CHAPTER FOUR

LOGAN

I bounce on the balls of my feet as I crack my neck from side to side, getting myself pumped up. This is it. Through those woods is Kitten. I just gotta get there. And fuck me, am I gonna get there. Ten weeks. Ten weeks she's been kept from me. Ten weeks we've searched for her. Kitten is mine. She's ours, and today we take her home, where she belongs. Not one of these motherfuckers is gonna stop me. They can't catch me; they can't touch me.

"Logan!" Remy shouts, breaking my concentration.

"Huh?" I answer.

"Remember the plan. Wait for my signal before you take off." He gives me a stern look.

"I know, I know." I wave him off.

Remy gets distracted by Maksim as they start talking about details and all that shit. I continue bouncing as I take a look around, trying to picture how this plan will work. For the past four days, Maksim has been building up a force strong enough to take on the guards the jackass Alpha has stationed here. His hope is that once the guards see it's pack members against pack members, they'll give in without a fight. While that sounds all hunky-fucking-dory and all, I'm happy Remy insisted they be prepared to fight. While my brothers and I may be stronger than all these bitches put together, we'll never reach the house if we have to fight them on our own.

Ash steps next to me, putting his giant paw on my shoulder and stopping my bouncing. He keeps his eyes trained on Remy and Maksim as he leans close to speak in my ear. "Whatever happens, Logan, get there. Get to Kitten. We'll make sure you get back out. You're going in first."

My head rears back a bit at his words. This wasn't the plan we went over on the plane; the plan Maksim created, and Remy said we'd follow. I meet Ash's dark eyes and tilt my head to Remy.

Ash nods once. "He's on board," he says before walking over to Tristan, probably giving him new orders as well.

Huh, so we've got our own plan it seems. My faith in Remy is once again restored. Maksim is a good guy and all, but his priority appears to be causing the least amount of collateral damage. Our goal is simple: Get Kitten and go home, fuck the rest. I like this plan more.

I see some of the reinforcements shifting into their wolves and getting into position. The plan is for them to run ahead and distract the guards patrolling at the gate and the front of the house. Behind them are a few men with grenade-launchers, designed to send the house into chaos and send their fighters out to meet us in the yard rather than the house. Wolves are better at fighting when we have room. While the first line of wolves corrals their fighters, the rest of our wolves and those in human form will enter the house and secure it room by room, locking the whole place down. That's when I'm supposed to enter and search for Kitten, who is supposedly in the basement.

Thank god I don't have to wait for all that shit to go down first. I assume my brothers are getting their own instructions before we set off, but Ash said to focus on my job, so that's what I do.

Ages later, Maksim gives the order and wolves take off in the direction of the house. I glance at Remy, and he holds up three fingers; my signal. I count to three...okay two, before I take off after them. Adrenaline zips through my veins as my toes dig into the hard-packed ground, shooting me forward. I hear Remy's half-assed shout for me to come back, but there's no command in it. I pump my arms higher to go faster as I effortlessly glide through the trees and brush. In no time at all, I'm through the woods and entering a clearing with the gate straight ahead.

I must've passed those other wolves because these shithead guards are sure surprised to see me. I smirk at them as they open fire, their slow as fuck bullets no match for my speed. I sense a few of them shifting but couldn't care less. An oak tree sits fairly close to the gates, and I throw myself into it, feet first. I kick off the trunk of the tree, using my momentum to propel myself over the gate. I tuck and roll and am up on my feet faster than they can redirect their weapons at me. I let out a laugh and start singing breathlessly. "Can't catch me, I'm the

Gingerbre…ooof!"

A gray and black wolf manages to tackle me, but I'm able to flip him over and get the upper hand. "Don't you know better than to interrupt a man when he's gloating?!" Each word is accompanied with a fist to his face. His head flops to the side, but he's still alive. That should please Maksim. The grenade rockets fire in the distance and I'm out of time with this douche. I shift to make myself a smaller target.

Humans, wolves, and…is that a hooker?…stream from the house as a fire starts up on the left side. I fight the flow of desperate people trying to escape, biting at anyone stupid enough to get in my way. My paws scrabble for purchase on the hardwood flooring, and I try first to sniff Kitten out. I catch a snippet of her scent coming from a room on this floor and enter an empty dining room that seriously needs a makeover. I let out an irritated growl and exit the room at full speed thanks to the ugly carpet.

Too late I realize someone else is running down the hall, and my paws don't have brakes. I take out Tristan's legs right from under him, and he does a flip before landing on his back. I snicker for about two seconds before a huge black wolf appears, and my eyes widen. Oh…fuck. Ash's fat ass slams into me, and I get to know the wall intimately as I become one with it. I grumble at him as I get back on my feet, and he nudges a dazed Tristan to stand.

The three of us continue down the hall to a door with a padlock. I'd bet my left nut that it leads to the basement. I bark at the door, and Tristan yanks the lock hard enough to tear a hole clean through the door. He runs down the stairs first, and I try my damnedest not to trip down them. Ash…the ass…throws himself down the steps, and we have to untangle ourselves at the bottom. I nip at his leg, but he doesn't return it. Instead, he sniffs deeply and runs full force into a closed door straight ahead. The air down here smells of Kitten, but the scent is off, like something has been added to it.

The steel door flies off the hinges as Ash uses the full force of his weight to crash through it. I enter behind him, and my heart sinks at what I see.

"NO. No, no, nonononononono, no!" Tristan cries as he falls to his knees behind me.

Ash lets out the loudest howl I've ever heard. It's full of anger, grief, and pain so sharp it rattles me to my bones. I let out a whimper as I lie down and have to cover my ears with my paws.

My eyes close for just a moment, and I pray to any God willing to listen that the scene before me is just a figment of my imagination, and everything will be okay when I open them again. An image that will haunt me for the rest of my days. Kitten, so pale and dirty spread out on an operating table, a knife plunged into her chest.

Ash's furious low growling snaps me out of my stupor, and I'm just in time to catch that Vanderson prick trying to back out of the doorway as Ash stalks him like the totally fucked prey he is. I leap in front of the opening, crouching, and baring my teeth at the fucker. His eyes go wide with fear, and he retreats to the corner where he begins to hyperventilate.

I keep him in my peripheral vision as I take in the rest of the scene around me. A man lays dead on the ground near Kitten's body, while another man struggles with some dude in a white coat. A slightly younger version of Maksim has backed up against the wall and has an amused smirk on his lips. Tristan has made his way to Kitten, and I hear him cooing to her, but I can't concentrate on what he's saying.

I turn my attention back to the smirking bastard and growl, snapping my teeth in his direction. He's the one who was standing over Kitten, his hand gripping the knife embedded in her chest. I take a step forward, but Ash barks at me, his eyes telling me he wants him to himself.

Before I can protest, I hear several pairs of footsteps echo down the hall, and I know it'll be my brothers responding to Ash's howl. Growls, shouts, and snarling fill the air as the rest of my family comes to a stop behind me. I step out of the way so they can enter the room, Maksim following in behind them.

There's a moment of stillness as if the chamber itself has paused for a breath. The only sound being Tristan, pleading for Kitten to come back to him. I focus on the anguish in his voice as a way to avoid my own. Something inside of me is telling me I'm in shock, but I ignore that as well. I force myself to look at the girl on the table and tell myself that it's not her. It's not Kitten up there. The filthy, blood-covered body with the strange scent can't be my girl. My girl is pretty as a picture, with soft, pale skin, a killer smile, and eyes full of lightning and life.

Shouting gets my attention and makes me aware of the chaos going on around me. Maksim is yelling in Russian as he shakes his son by the shoulders, slamming him repeatedly against the wall, while the other man cackles with insanity. Ash has decided that Adam is his new favorite chew toy, and has the boy's shoulder between his teeth as he shakes his head back and forth, trying to tear him apart. Kellan and Finn are slapping around the guy in the white coat, asking him what they did and how to fix it. The rest of my brothers have surrounded Kitten and are prodding her with their noses, and whimpering or licking at her hands as they join with Tristan, trying to revive her.

Maksim turns abruptly, pushing his son to the ground and shoving Reed out of his way to get to Kitten. Reed latches onto his leg, as he's in wolf form, but the older man barely notices him. I watch in sick fascination as Maksim's teeth sink into his own wrist, and he shoves it into Kitten's lifeless mouth. My cry of outrage is lost among others. His desperate eyes implore Tristan, and I don't realize why until it's too late. Maksim lifts Kitten's arm, bringing her wrist to Tristan's mouth. A look of desperation and determination falls over his face as he makes his decision.

"Tristan, no!" Kellan shouts.

"It doesn't matter! She's dead!" Marcus laughs before his airflow is cut off by Remy pouncing on his back. He starts to speak again, but the giant red wolf silences him once more by taking his neck between his teeth.

"It's not too late! Change her now!" Maksim demands angrily.

"It could kill her!" Kellan pleads.

"She'll die anyway!" Tristan barks back.

His canines elongate, and he bites into her wrist forcefully.

"No! Tristan, stop! You don't know what you're doing!" Kellan calls out as he's now struggling from both Jace and Finn restraining him, the man in the white coat forgotten.

Maksim pushes Reed away from him and glares at him before slumping to the ground, presumably to let his leg heal where Reed tore through it.

"He missed her heart, the idiot. If you all calm down, you can still hear it. It's faint, but it's there. My blood can heal her, not fast enough on its own, but Tristan's bite may be able to change her in time. It's her only option," Maksim defends himself.

A tear falls down Tristan's cheek as he carefully places Kitten's arm back down by her side. He unbuttons his shirt and places it on her, tucking the edges under her protruding ribs. She's even slimmer than she was before. It's obvious that she was starved as well as tortured. I've never been happier to have the ability to be a wolf than I am right now. Wolves can't cry, only whimper and whine, and right now, I feel like bawling my fucking eyes out.

"How long should it take?" Finn chokes out in a raspy voice. His eyes roam over Kitten, head to foot, then back again, checking for any changes. "Should she be moving yet? Tristan, check her pulse, is it picking up?" My ears perk with the same hope I hear in his voice.

"It could be a while," Maksim murmurs. "She's been through a lot, and she's been given too much blood recently. It will take time for my blood to heal her and then Tristan's bonding bite to move through her," he explains.

The man in the white coat shifts his position and all attention snaps to him. Ash moves to roar in his face, and Maksim wipes a hand down his face. "Let's get the princess moved upstairs. Leave them all here for now.

Don't kill them yet. If she dies, I want the pleasure myself, and if she lives, she may want to do it herself."

CHAPTER FIVE

ASH

We got my little one up the stairs and into a bathroom where I placed her carefully in the tub. The man in the penguin suit turned out to be Albert Rosen, the Russian's contact, and the soon-to-be-dead-Alpha's servant. Kellan instructed me to carry her carefully, so the blade didn't shift in her chest. I thought we should take it out immediately, but Remy was right when he said we should get her away from those assholes.

Keeping my eyes on her is the only thing keeping me calm right now. Knowing her abusers live only a short distance away while she may die is almost more than I can take. But she needs me, and she's never leaving my sight again, not even in death.

A hand lands lightly on my shoulder and my head jerks around to snap at it, my skin rippling with the need to shift.

"Easy, Ash. It's just me. Let me get the knife out of her so the wound can close." Kellan's deep green eyes are wary, and they should be. I'm barely holding on to control of my wolf. Behind him, Logan trips, shoving Kellan forward a step. He moves too quickly for my liking, and my wolf takes over immediately. My body starts to shift, my chest rumbling with a warning of imminent attack.

"Ash!" Kellan says firmly. "I need you, man. You have a crucial job right now. I need you to listen carefully to Kitten's heartbeat, okay?" My wolf calms a bit with his words. I have a job to do. He needs me to help Kitten.

I take a deep breath and reverse the shift. Kellan moves carefully, but swiftly, lowering himself down next to me, keeping his eyes on me the whole time. He places his hand on the hilt of the blade and slowly pulls it up. I've been in bloody battles, seen good friends killed right in front of me, but I can't make myself watch what he's doing now. I close my eyes and bow my head, my hearing focused on the faint and erratic sound of my girl's heart.

Time passes, I'm not sure how much, but Tristan's soft voice that I've only ever heard him use on Kitten brings me back to the room.

"It's done, Ash. Why don't you come out into the hallway with the rest of us so Kellan can clean her up a bit?" he asks.

I shake my head, staring blankly at the lip of the tub, unable to look at the woman inside of it for fear of what I'll see. Is blood gushing out of the wound? Has she gone paler than she already was?

"No," I say gruffly. "I have to stay. She needs me."

"Just leave him be," Remy sighs, leading everyone

but Kellan and me out and closing the door behind them.

I listen, more than watch, as Kellan fills a small bowl in the sink and brings it and a washcloth over to the tub. He talks to her as he cleans her. Mostly telling her where he's washing next.

"Let's get that pretty face all shined up, yeah? There we go. Now behind those ears, always have to wash behind the ears. You have the neck of a swan, you know that?" He prattles on. I half wonder if this is a doctor thing, or if he's doing it for my benefit so I know what's going on. He doesn't mention her wounds or her womanly areas, so he either doesn't clean them or just doesn't speak about them.

"Now time for those little piggies; no giggling now." He tries for playful, but his voice sounds sad nonetheless.

"No," I grumble, snatching the washcloth from him. "I'll do it."

I hold my hand out for the bowl, then take it over to the sink to wash it out, filling it with fresh water. I get a new cloth and sit next to the tub, with my back facing the rest of her body. Her tiny feet are caked with dirt and grime, her little toe missing a nail, and she has half-healed scrapes, even there.

I focus on my task, scrubbing every inch of her small feet, then doing it all over again. Tears threaten to fall, but I hold them back. I refuse to cry. It's tough, though. I failed these toes. I promised to protect them and now here they are, all messed up and broken and hurt.

"Her toes will heal, Ash. Kitten will heal. You didn't fail her; she'll tell you that herself soon," Kellan whispers. My body goes stiff as I realize I was talking out loud. "I have to turn the showerhead on now, okay? We need to spray her down, and I need you to help me with her hair, okay? Can you do that, Ash?"

I grunt at him and set the bowl aside. Taking a deep breath, I turn around and focus on her face. Without all the dirt and blood, she looks like she's sleeping. Her face is paler and thinner than the last time I watched her sleep, but she looks less like the murder victim she did earlier. Kellan starts the spray and adjusts the temperature to warm, bringing down the removable showerhead. I gently lift Kitten and place my arm behind her shoulders. I bring her close to me and put my other hand behind her head. My face goes to her neck, and I hug her to me. She smells different, but it's still her. I cry silently as Kellan continues to wash her. I'll never admit to it, but fuck if I could stop it from happening.

Eventually, Kellan dries her hair with a towel, and I help him wrap her in a dry one and carry her with me out to the hallway. Maybe it's just wishful thinking, but I could swear her heartbeat now has a steady rhythm.

REED

Remy was quick to put us to work as soon as we stepped outside of the bathroom. I know there's a lot to be done around here, but knowing that Kitten could die at any moment and I won't be there to say goodbye, has put me on edge. The whole time she's been missing, I've been trying to think with my rational mind, or at least channel Finn and *his* rational mind. I tried to tell myself that my brothers and I barely knew her, that she wasn't a part of our lives for very long and we'd all be okay if we couldn't find her. I knew I loved her from the moment she told me about her past. Even if she weren't beautiful on the outside, her soul still would be. Her kindness and ability to forgive spoke to me on a spiritual level, and I knew her shiny, happy aura was just what our family needed. She was delicate as a butterfly and strong as a lioness. Stubborn as a mule, too, if you ask me, but oddly that only added to her appeal. Oh, and when the girl paints, mmm...so lovely. Her mind is a million miles away, her eyes telling a story of an old soul, earned by a hard life, even in one so young.

But I digress. What I was trying to tell myself is that my family's love for Kitten was not normal. I had sought to rationalize our relationship and my feelings for her, but I was kidding myself. We were never normal before her and even less so after she arrived in our lives. Telling myself I couldn't possibly truly love Kitten in such a short amount of time is like the waves of the ocean telling the sand on the beach that it will never return.

I go about my task of clearing the upper floors, with one ear out for the bathroom door two stories below. The grenade- launchers did a fairly good job of clearing out the top level, but I've found more than few men and women too strung out on drugs to care that the house was on fire. With so many humans here, I have to wonder what they've seen and if we can even let them all go. Marcus was obviously careless and didn't give a damn about protecting his wolves from the humans, or all wolves actually. If humans knew we were real, they'd hunt us down and either kill us or experiment on us. Or worse, lock us up in some zoo for other humans to ogle us.

I open the last door on this floor at the end of the

hallway. It's as big the master bedroom was at the other end, but this room holds none of Marcus' scent. The bombs have shattered the glass out of the windows in here, along with the mirror hanging over the dresser. It reeks of stale sex, alcohol, and human blood, but underneath that, I smell the fading scent of Kitten.

Before my heart can break at the thought of her being with a man other than my brothers and me, I calm myself and remember that I could still smell her innocence on her. I concentrate on where her smell is coming from and find myself opening the closet door and rummaging through a small cardboard box. Inside, I find a few pairs of her underwear, her scent mostly faded from them, and the jewelry I know she was wearing when she was taken.

I quickly pocket the gifts my brothers gave her and turn to punch at the wall until my entire arm goes numb. I'm not usually a violent person, but I just can't stand the thought of Kitten being with these monsters. This was obviously Adam's room and who knows how long the sick bastard has been getting off on her used panties. For once, I completely understand Ash and Remy's physical need to hurt someone. I throw the underwear in the trash by the door on the way out.

Heading down the stairs to the second story, I almost laugh at the sight of Jace and Logan trying to keep the scantily-clad, highly-drugged women off of them. I'm sure they think they're being alluring, but even if they didn't look freshly had, they'd be barking up the wrong trees. Before Kitten came into our lives, Jace only made himself available to ice queens and women who at least played hard to get. Logan, on the other hand, only touched a woman after multiple drinks and I'm sure made love with his eyes closed. I had thought him gay for a while before having a conversation with him about how none of us would judge him if he were into men. He'd laughed heartily at that, but explained his reasons for his behavior, and I understood him better after that.

"No touchy-touchy," Logan chides a particularly aggressive woman. I go to help but cringe away from her once I notice the clear fluid running down her leg.

"Uh, I'll just leave you guys to it," I say, inching my way around the herd.

"Reed! You fucker, get back here and help us get them downstairs!" Logan calls out angrily.

It's tempting to run away, but I can see the two of them are stressed and outnumbered.

"Fine," I grumble. "There's pot brownies dusted with coke in the dining room!" I say loudly and excitedly.

The hoard murmurs and chirps excitedly before racing each other down to the first floor in a mass of stumbling limbs and glitter.

Jace blows out a breath as he runs his hands through his hair. "Thank fuck."

I smirk at my brothers as they lean against the wall and regroup themselves. "First rule of drug addicts, boys: they're always on the hunt for their next fix."

"I don't even know if I want to go down there now," Jace says as he adjusts his lipstick-smeared and rumpled shirt.

"Our girl is down there, and Kellan is probably almost done." I try for playful, but my tone comes out dangerous anyway.

Logan kicks himself away from the wall and throws

an arm over my shoulders. "C'mere, you beautiful bastard. You will forever be known to me as the skank-wrangler from this point on." A laugh bursts out of me, my mood lightening immediately.

TRISTAN

The house is in organized chaos as Maksim and Albert separate the faithful followers of Marcus from those who were just following Alpha orders, and getting the human females calm enough to get into vehicles and shipped off to recover elsewhere. Since the humans were drugged, there's little chance they'll remember any wolves or, at worst, chalk it up to hallucinations. The few followers of Marcus are being directed into a different room in the basement for holding until we can figure out what to do with them.

A howl starts up in the distance, and I swing my head to the side to listen better. My heart pounds into overtime as I recognize Remy's urgency in the howl. Shoving people out of my way, I make it to the back door and leap down the concrete steps leading to the lawn and sprint my way over to the detached pool house.

I swallow thickly as I slow to approach Remy, who stands just outside the open door. I meet his pale eyes, thinking the worst, but I see no new pain there. "Is she alright?" I ask.

"Same as before, though Kellan assures me she's improving," he answers before shifting his eyes behind me to greet the rest of my brothers who came running as I had.

I duck through the door and am relieved to see Kitten, sans all the gore, with a blanket tucked around her, appearing to be sleeping. I attempt to run my hand along her gorgeous, clean hair but the wolf lying across her legs snaps at my hand.

"What the fuck, Ash?" I narrow my eyes at him.

"It's probably best to leave him be, for now. He's having a difficult time reining in his emotions, and guarding her seems to be keeping him from killing people," Kellan explains as he eyes the feral-looking Ash warily.

"What! No way, uh-uh fucker. She's ours, too; we missed her too," Logan demands stubbornly behind me.

Ash moves quickly as he jumps to his feet, his jaw snapping dangerously as he barks wildly at all of us.

"Enough!" Remy shouts, his booming voice carrying so loudly that it hurts my ears. Ash huffs, his dark eyes narrowing at Remy as he turns his large body around on the small chaise longue and lays himself over Kitten once again. His nose nuzzles under her arm until he manages to get her hand on his head. He gave us his back, but I'm not stupid enough to think that he's ignoring us now.

"Fucking caveman Neanderthal asshole mother fucker," Logan grumbles as he finds a seat on the couch next to Kellan.

Remington closes the door with a bang. "Enough bitching and fighting for today, guys. Maksim and Albert will join us once everything is under control at the main house. Why don't we use this time to get cleaned up and settled down? I've ordered our vehicles to be brought to us, so we'll have our clothes and things momentarily."

Jace, of course, calls dibs on the first shower, and I

make myself at home in the small kitchen located right off the living area. Maybe now the ungrateful bastards will eat something, since we have Kitten back, sort of. There's not a whole lot to work with, but I manage to put together enough simple grilled cheese sandwiches for all of us, cut up some apple and pear slices, and make a couple pitchers of iced tea from the powdered can. It's not my best, but the guys eat greedily, and that makes me happy. Even Ash barked until someone tossed a few sandwiches at him, which he swallowed whole.

I grin to myself as I find a bowl in the cabinets and fill it with the iced tea. I add a few of the ice cubes, remembering when Kitten thought Finn was a dog and gave him water on the rocks because she likes ice water so dogs must like it, too. I meet Finn's eyes as I set the bowl in front of Ash, and he smirks back at me, remembering, too.

About an hour goes by with no change in Kitten before Maksim and Albert show up. They choose to stand on the far wall after Ash gives them a warning growl. Nice to know the possessive wolf is giving us more rights than strangers.

"Get everyone settled out there?" Remy asks the newcomers.

Maksim nods his head tiredly. "For the most part. Albert has been here and knows who's who and where they stand, so that helped. The others were reluctant to leave after I explained just who they were helping keep captive. They wished to stay and see after her health and beg forgiveness."

Remy raises an eyebrow at this. "And I hope you told them to fuck off, because no one is getting close to her again."

Maksim frowns but nods his head. "Something of the sort, but you do realize that these people are her pack members, right?"

Remy jumps to his feet, getting in the older man's face. "Your blood may run through her veins, but make no mistake: she is ours, and we will be taking her with us when we leave."

To his credit, Maksim doesn't even flinch. "My granddaughter may do as she pleases once she wakes. If she chooses to be with you and your men, so be it. That doesn't change the fact that she is the princess of the most feared and respected wolf pack in the world. She has responsibilities here, and once word travels of her existence she'll be in even greater danger than she was before without the protection of her pack," he argues calmly.

Remy, on the other hand, is furious. "Is that a threat?"

Maksim's eyes flash in anger. "Not from me, no. The Ivaskov pack will know better than to try to harm her again, but we have enemies, and I imagine even more so now that we will be dethroning our alpha and taking prisoners within our own pack."

Remy takes a step back, looking for all the world like Maksim just grew three heads. "Am I supposed to say sorry? They kidnapped and tortured one of mine!"

"No! You stubborn imbecile, you're supposed to see that she belongs with us, with or without you! It's what's best for her, for her safety and because we are family!" Maksim shouts, his hands going out to his sides in the universal 'isn't it obvious' gesture.

Remy scoffs. "Her family? Her family is responsible for what happened to her."

Kellan jumps to his feet and pushes his way between the two men. "Let's cool this down a bit, shall we? A girl is lying over there, trying to recover from a fatal injury, and she doesn't need any outside stress."

That gets their attention, and they both back off. Kellan looks relieved as he continues, "The issue of what Kitten wants or needs can be revisited once she is no longer fighting for her life and she can speak for herself. If the two of you, or all of us for that matter, would like to discuss our options no matter what she chooses, then we can do so in a quiet, peaceful manner."

"Yeah, that." I smile and nod my head, pointing at Kellan in agreement.

"Fine," Maksim agrees through gritted teeth. "May I sit?" He looks to Ash with an expression of annoyance. Ash grumbles but jerks his head to the side, indicating the group of chairs furthest away from Kitten.

Remy remains standing but moves to stand in front of everyone, much like he does at home when he's leading a meeting. "I just want it said that I don't oppose Kitten finding a place within your pack if that's what she wants. I'm telling you now, though, where she goes, we go." His eyes scan the room, and each member of our family gives a nod of agreement.

Albert stares at Remy in confusion for a moment, before turning to look at Maksim. "They still don't seem to understand," he tells the former Alpha, shaking his head.

"Understand what exactly?" Finn speaks up.

"It is not *our* pack; it is hers. She's the heir. Without

a mate, she cannot rule the pack, and that of wolf society as a whole, on her own, but she will be given a counsel until her mate is found or arranged. Once she has a mate, then he will be named Alpha until she births a son and the son is deemed mature enough to rule."

I blink at him in shock. I guess I should have known it already, seeing as how Remy explained something similar after we first met with Maksim, but I suppose I figured they'd be wrong, and truth be told, I wasn't actually paying attention. My focus was on finding her at the time.

"Holy shit! So she's like, a *princess* princess," Logan says dazedly. He must not have been paying attention either.

"Yes, exactly," Albert smiles, happy to be finally understood.

Remy stares at Maksim in a silent challenge, his arms crossed over his chest. He doesn't appear to be shocked or surprised at all, but he's still skeptical. "Even if she awakens and Tristan's bite changed her, you have no way of knowing if she'll be able to shift, or bear any pups."

Albert raises his hand and waves it frantically in the air like an eager child in a classroom. Remy nods his head to him, and he stands proudly. "I have a theory on who Princess Kitten's mother is. I spent a lot of time with the former Alpha, Mikel, and we journeyed the globe on scientific missions. Her father was obsessed with finding a way to create more females. Either by safely turning humans, or curing the virus that prevents our remaining females from giving birth entirely or only a few children in an entire lifetime."

"Your point being?" Jace says distractedly as he

inspects his fingernails. He looks bored, but the set of his shoulders tells me he's anything but.

"What that means," Albert continues, "is that I can look over his research and see what he found. Kitten's existence obviously means he found something. The last year he was with us, he was very distracted and hardly spent any time with his pack. He took frequent trips to Australia, and on the occasions I accompanied him, we met with some fascinating people."

Maksim turns outraged eyes to Albert. "Interesting how? And why is this the first I'm hearing of it?"

Albert looks to the floor, appearing every bit the kicked puppy. "If...if you don't mind, sirs, I would like to hold off on giving that information until I have spoken with the princess in private. I answer to only her for the time being." He shifts nervously from foot to foot.

Maksim jumps to his feet and grips him by the collar of his shirt. "No," Remy says calmly, making Maksim pause. "We'll respect his loyalty, for now. If it's something we need to know, Kitten will tell us herself."

I barely stop myself from clapping for my hot-headed brother, but I also know that he fully expects Kitten to tell him everything and won't take no for an answer.

"However, you still have yet to make your point." Remy eyes Albert in a way that should tell him to hurry it up.

"My point is that, if the girl is what I suspect she is, she should not only be able to shift but will also be the most fertile female wolves have seen since The Suffering." He smiles like he just found a pot of gold at the end of a rainbow.

That news should excite me, but I find myself

swallowing what feels like lead. So not only is the girl my brothers and I have claimed as ours a princess of a pack that clearly needs her, but she also might be a pup-making machine that most wolves would kill for. She's always been special to me, but knowing just how special she really is, is a bit overwhelming. I see now that getting her back is less of a final solution and more of a start into the unknown. There will always be someone out there trying to take her away from us.

"Does this mean she will have to choose one of us for a mate?" I ask Remy, my nervousness showing. Are we already back to this?

Remy frowns in thought, but Maksim is the one to answer. "The odds of any of you being her mate are slim to none. Each wolf is born with a predestined mate in the world. You all have been around for much longer than she has; it's not impossible, just not likely. Besides, not one of you is a natural wolf." He holds back the sneer at the end, but barely.

"She's not a born wolf either," Kellan points out. "Nor is she fully a changed wolf. She had Ivaskov blood already."

A quick look to Albert reveals a knowing smirk, but he doesn't chime in.

The girl in question lets out a whimper and all eyes turn to her. The room goes completely silent except for the thumping of Ash's excited tail at the base of the longue. I creep closer to her, afraid to move too quickly as if that will cause her to return to her slumber. The others must have the same idea as we form a circle around our girl. There's movement behind her closed eyelids, and her whole body starts to tremble. It's more than I can take.

I pick up one dainty hand and wrap it in my own. "It's okay, sweet girl. Everything's going to be okay now," I tell her softly.

Her head turns slightly in my direction, and my heart beats a little faster. A few moments later, pale green eyes with flashes of golden lightning are looking up at me. They are a tad subdued, but that's to be expected. I smile brightly at her until she gasps in horror and starts crying violently. I panic and look to Kellen, my free hand indicating the crying and pleading for him to fix it. He shakes his head at me and makes the talking motion with his own hand.

Okay, so talk to her. I can do that. I put my smile back in place and begin to rub her back. She shudders away from my touch, and I'll admit that hurt. A lot.

"Kitten. It's me, Tristan. You're okay now, sweetness. No one's going to hurt you anymore," I tell her.

"No. No, no no no no no," she says through her sobs. I'm at a loss for what to do, so I just sit beside her, my heart breaking for her.

Ash jumps up and races from the room, then back again once he realizes he can't open the door to outside, and grips Logan's arm in his mouth and the both of them run outside. Moments later and they're back, Ash resuming his position over Kitten and Logan shaking his head amusedly.

"Not him, too. I can't take any more," Kitten whispers, keeping her eyes firmly shut now. Maybe she's only half awake?

"Kitten, please, honey, wake up. Let me see those pretty eyes again," I plead with her. She doesn't move. I lay my head on the side of her shoulder and sigh. She just needs some time.

Shocked gasps meet my ears a split second before I feel a sharp bite in my neck. My first reaction is to pull away, but a small yet strong arm reaches out to pull me closer. A second later and you couldn't get me to pull away if you tried. I let out a moan of sheer bliss as the sting of the bite is replaced with unadulterated pleasure. My blood heats and courses through my body ten times faster than it should, and all of my focus is on those sharp teeth and tiny tongue licking at my neck like an ambrosia-flavored lollipop. Christ on a cracker, I've never been so turned on in all my life!

All too soon, Kitten pulls back, and I'm left shaking my head, wondering what the hell happened. I feel stoned, and there are tiny pinpricks on my skin wherever I'm touching Kitten. I look back to her and see her licking her lips lazily, as she appears to be falling back to sleep. Her face is no longer scrunched up in distress or pain as it was before, and if I didn't know better I'd say she's stoned off her ass as well. I feel a nudging at my shoulder, and I dazedly look over to see Ash eating a stuffed animal. Wait, no, he's trying to get me to take it. I take the thing and stare at it for a minute. Ash whines and tilts his head at Kitten. Oh, I get it.

"Kitten," I slur, "Ash wants you to have his baby."

There's a snort and a few laughs before I realize what I said. Then I start giggling, too. That is until she snaps her eyes open, sees the toy, and snatches it out of my hands. She grips it tightly with both arms to her chest and purrs contentedly before her body relaxes and drifts to sleep once more.

"Okay, someone explain what the fuck just happened, because that's the weirdest shit I've ever seen," Logan demands. Sadly, all this talking is a real buzzkill, and my vision clears away the lovely fog of lust.

I pull away from Kitten to take a seat on the couch. My legs are wobbly, but I manage the short trip.

Each of the guys looks just as stunned and confused as I am, but Albert's face is blank, like he's just watching a show on TV, and Maksim looks damn near outraged.

Logan taps his foot in agitation, never one to like being ignored for long. "Hell if I know." I shrug at him.

"It appears our princess has chosen a mate and claimed him," Albert answers.

"Really?" I gape at him before a smile overtakes my face. "I guess it's only natural. She loves food, and I'm a maker of food; it was only a matter of time before she fell head over heels in love with me," I explain, okay, well, gloat, but damn does it feel good to know she's wanted me as much as I've wanted her.

"That's not what a claiming is about," Albert explains. "It doesn't mean she loves you, though it doesn't mean that she doesn't. Love and emotions are for the human side of her to figure out. Claiming comes from the wolf part of her deciding that your wolf is a good match for her. Chances are she isn't even aware that she did it at all."

I frown at him for taking away some of my happiness. "So it doesn't count?" I asked, more confused than I was before.

He raises a brow at me. "Oh, it counts. You bit her to change her, but either way, she bit you back, so you are mated now."

"What if she didn't want to be mated to me? Or I didn't want to be mated to her, not that this is the case," I say quickly.

"She wouldn't have bitten you if she didn't want you or deemed you unworthy. As for you, though you didn't intend to claim her with your bite, it had the same effect. If your wolf did not wish to mate with her, it would not have allowed her to bite you back, regardless of your feelings for her." He tilts his head at me like I'm stupid for not knowing something so basic.

The room falls into an awkward silence, with my brothers finding random things to do rather than make eye contact with me. I feel uncomfortable as well. I mean, I'm happy she chose me, but what does that mean for the rest of them? What does it mean even for me? Maksim's anger makes sense now at least. He's none too thrilled that the hope of all wolfkind just picked a changed wolf as her mate to dirty up the Ivaskov name.

The sun is close to setting when Ash yips excitedly and again, his tail thumps loudly as we wait for Kitten to wake up. The circle is formed around her once more, but this time a little more loosely as everyone is left to see where we now stand.

I move to my knees beside her and brush her hair away from her face. "Are you awake, beautiful girl?" I ask.

Kitten yawns and blinks her eyes sleepily. "I think so," she rasps.

"I'll get her some water," Kellan offers quickly.

She looks up at me with a small frown. "Am I dead? Do you wake up from being alive and into death?" she asks, confused.

I chuckle low. "You're not dead, Kitten."

Her frown deepens. "I have to be, or else you wouldn't be here because you're dead," she explains, and now I'm the one frowning. I look across to Remy, and she follows my line of sight. "See? He's dead, too, so we all must be dead," she says with a firm nod of her head, like it's decided now.

Behind Remy, Reed raises his hand. "I'm not dead." Kitten glances at him before staring up at the ceiling and huffing out a breath.

We give her a moment to think and then she grips the stuffed wolf with both hands and holds it up to look at it. I see a small smile creep over her face, and she brings it down to sniff at it before tucking it away happily at her side. She pats her chest and stomach before her eyes go wide and she starts screaming.

Everyone jumps back, looking around for the threat, but it's still just us in here. The screaming stops and she begins to sob once again. "What is it, Kitten? What's wrong?" I ask her urgently.

"My legs!" she wails. "They took my legs! I don't have legs!" she says hysterically.

Logan bursts into laughter and doubles over, holding his stomach. "I'm sorry! I know it's not funny, but, oh my God, she's so fucking adorable." He speaks through his endless laughter, wiping away tears from his eyes.

I roll my eyes at the idiot but quickly turn back to the distraught girl in front of me. "You have legs, Kitten. Ash's big ass has just been sitting on you for hours now, so they've probably gone to sleep."

She sniffs cutely and looks down to her legs, or actually, she looks down at Ash sitting on them. He barks a hello and raises his head to lick away her tears, causing her to giggle and dig her hands in his fur.

I relax and sit back on my heels, just taking in her smiling face. She turns to me, and her expression becomes more serious. She reaches out a hand and brushes a lock of my hair away from my face before cupping my jaw, her eyes roving over every inch of me. I hold still and let her inspect me, enjoying the tiny pinpricks her touch is creating.

"I thought you were dead," she tells me.

"Nope, never dead, sweetie. You thought I was dead this whole time?"

She nods her head and looks over to Remy. Her other hand stretches out, and he's quick to fall to his knees and lean into the touch. His eyes close as he places his own hand over hers, turning his head and placing a kiss on her palm.

"We didn't die in the crash," he explains. "But we were incapacitated, and for that, I am so sorry. I wasn't able to stop them from taking you, and I will never forgive myself for allowing that to happen. I have no right to ask your forgiveness, but I hope that one day I will be able to earn back your trust."

Kitten blinks at him a couple of times and shakes her head. "There's nothing to forgive, nothing to be sorry about. You didn't take me, you didn't hurt me, and actually, you helped me stay alive."

"How so?" Remy speaks through his emotion.

"You visited me, your ghost did, or maybe I was just crazy. You kept asking me what I wanted," she replies.

Maksim clears his throat. "I hate to cut this reunion short, but now that you have awoken, my dear, many things need to be discussed." He speaks kindly and gently, but Kitten's eyes go cold as soon as she notices the two outsiders.

She swiftly sits up, dislodging Ash, and swings her feet to the floor. "Get out!" she growls at them.

Neither of them makes a move to leave, and Kitten shakes in fury. "I said out," she repeats through gritted teeth. Ash jumps in front of her and bares his teeth at them.

"You heard the girl," Remy says with a smirk. "She looks angry; I'd listen to her. We'll call you back in when she's ready."

With that, Maksim and Albert make hasty bows before backing to the door and closing it lightly.

Kitten deflates as soon the door closes, and she rubs a hand down her face. She pauses to take a closer look at that hand then shifts her attention to Remy. "So, can we go home now?" she asks sweetly.

CHAPTER SIX

KITTEN

The guys each took turns explaining what they could to me. They said things about my father and mother and a grandfather that I'm sure I'll process later. I have no desire to meet any more of my family; one was more than enough.

The guys, in that unspoken language of theirs, decided that they each needed one on one time with me because, shortly after the explanations stopped, I was left in the small house alone with Reed. He had sat on the oddly-shaped couch next to me and just stared at me. I stared back, taking in his multi-colored eyes, dirty blonde locks, and thin lips set in a contented smile.

"I missed you," I whisper after some time has passed. It's true; I did miss him and the rest of the guys. The short amount of time I spent with them were the best days of my life.

Apparently that was all he needed, as I was scooped

up and placed on his lap almost before I had finished speaking. My body tensed immediately, and I hated myself for it. This was Reed; he'd never hurt me, but it's just my reaction to touch now I supposed.

He had eventually laid his head on my shoulder and hugged me as hard as he could, telling me how he never gave up hope of finding me. Somewhere in my head, a part of me whispered that I should be crying, that I should be overly emotional at being in my sad boy's arms again, but the tears never came.

Finn entered seconds after Reed left, and the first thing he did was tell me he loves me. Actually, he said it five times. I, of course, said it back. If my recent experiences taught me anything, it's to let the people in my life know how I feel about them. I want to tell them all how much I love them, how my love for each of them is different, yet the same, but there's a new part of me now, a part that is afraid, a part that doesn't know how to be the old me anymore.

I let him take my hands in his own as he kneeled before me, and he explained that he thought he'd never get to tell me that ever again. I promised him that we'd tell each other how much we loved one another until we tired of hearing the words. Finn had laughed at that, and said that would never happen. As he took a step outside, I was sure to tell him that I loved him once more. He left, looking the happiest I have ever seen him.

Logan bounded into the room and pounced on the couch next to me, bringing a girly squeal from me that I wasn't sure I was capable of anymore. He buried his face in my neck, and I think cussed me out because he had said every swear word there ever was and a few I've never heard of. He told me that they had managed to bring most of my stuff with them and that he'd find me an outfit so I could get out of the towel/blanket combo I was wearing. He also told me he was cutting my hair. Didn't ask, just told me. It's okay, though, because it means he's really here and he still cares. He can play with hair all he wants if it means I get more time with him, time I had thought I'd never get. He left with glowing blue eyes, and I was sad to see him go. I had forgotten how much energy he could pump into a room with just one smile or wicked look.

Tristan came in next, wearing a tight smile, both hands shoved in his pockets. He seemed a little off, and it made me feel weird, so I gave him a lame wave of my hand. He must have noticed how odd he was being because he blushed slightly and mockingly waved back before taking a seat beside me. We both gasped as our arms met and static electricity zoomed over our skin. His eyes went wide, and he scooted away from me slightly. I glanced at his feet to see if he maybe walked across the carpet in socks, but he was wearing shoes. When he started to tell me how scary it was for him when he woke up after the crash and I was gone, I ignored the shock in favor of trying to comfort him. He eventually looked up at me from under his lashes, that wayward lock of hair falling into his chocolate eyes, and chuckled at how ridiculous it was that I was comforting him when it should be the other way around. Tristan left with a light peck on my lips, and the electricity was toned down, but still shocking nonetheless.

When Ash came in and sat exceedingly close to me, quiet as usual, I had to wonder if he was going to sit on me again. I asked him questions about his mood, and he'd grunt in the negative or positive. Somewhere along the line he'd started to tuck the blankets around me again, even laying me back gently so he could get my shoulders nice and snug as well. His eyes seemed to roam over me, taking in every detail, and my face heated at the intensity of his gaze. Without a word and with a decisive nod of his head, he stood and made his way to the door so the next one of my guys could come in. I was left feeling a bit baffled by his actions until I attempted to sit up. I rolled my eyes and giggled to myself; he'd made me a burrito again.

Kellan had chuckled when he saw me squirming around in my cocoon and promptly offered to help release me. He insisted on checking me over, where my wounds were, my eyes, and my pulse before he prescribed exactly one much-needed hug from a doctor who could really use one. I had laughed at his antics and reached for him first, and somehow, that was better than when the guys had reached for me first. It gave me that added boost of control, which I didn't know I needed, but much appreciated. When we pulled back, he had smiled, but it didn't reach his dark green eyes. I was going to ask him what was wrong, but he stood to leave, cutting our time short.

Jace had come in with a couple of extra pillows for me and helped me prop myself up against the armrest. We had sat in awkward silence for a minute or two before I launched into an apology. I told him how sorry I was for not telling him that I forgave him well before any of this had happened. I told him how heartbreaking it was, thinking I'd never get to tell him that. I finally told him that I knew who the surprise gifts were from and how much I enjoyed them. I hung my head sheepishly as I explained why I named his giant bear Big Jace, but he just smirked at me and said that one day, I'd find out why I'd never call him Little Jace again. After a wink of his golden eye, I shoved him playfully and he got serious, not that I knew what he was talking about anyway. He thanked me for apologizing but said it was unnecessary, and he enjoyed having to earn my affection after what he did. He had promptly pulled me in for a hug, his strong hand stroking up and down my back in a comforting gesture before we pinky swore never to fight again. He then held out his other hand with his fingers crossed and shrugged with a smirk on his lips. "What can I say? I like fighting with you, Fun Size," he told me. I laughed and hit him lightly with a pillow. He had taken my hand in his and kissed the back of it before he excused himself. Ever the gentleman, that one.

Remy came in last, and he closed the door and stood in front of it. It hurt my heart that he wanted to keep so much distance from me. He asked how I was, and I told him I was fine. He turned to leave, but I stopped him with a question. "Are you mad at me Remy?" I asked in a small voice.

"What?" he asked, confused.

"I know I've caused a lot of trouble…" I started.

"No, Kitten. I'm not mad at you. Nothing of the sort. It's just…" He let out a frustrated breath. "I couldn't protect you. You were taken from me, and I was too weak to stop it," he said, defeated.

"Remy, don't think that way. Nothing was your fault, none of it," I said emphatically. "You are strong. I thought you were dead, but you survived. And not only that, but you then came for me. You're here now," I whispered.

"Of course I'm here. Did you really think I wouldn't come after you?" Remy asked as he came to crouch in front of me, lifting my chin with a thick finger, my eyes meeting his.

I sighed. "I don't know. I mean...it all just seems so strange. Ever since I met you all, it's felt as if I've known you far better than I should have. If that makes sense." I shake my head slightly, not even making sense to myself.

Remy just tapped me under my chin and smiled up at me. "I know exactly what you mean, love." My heart jumped crazily in my chest at the endearment, and I struggled to keep listening. "We may have some answers to why that is now, but they can wait. All you need to know is that things are more complicated than they seem, but my brothers and I would like you to stay with us if that's what you wish." He broke off at the end, like it was even a question anymore.

"Of course I want to stay with you and the others. I've missed you all so much, and I thought you and Tristan were dead, and I thought I was ready to die but... I just wanted more time with you," I blurt out.

His previous frown turns into an amused smirk, and he shakes his head as he stands to his impressive height. "That's all I needed to know, for now. It may be hard for you, but you're going to have to meet with your grandfather, the man you so kindly asked to leave." He chuckles deeply, that rumbly voice bringing a smile to my face. "He's not so bad; you'll see. Do you trust me, love?"

My heart melts, wondering if this is his new

nickname for me and really hoping that's the case. "I do. Always," I respond firmly.

I notice his shoulders relax a bit as he continues. "Then trust that I will never allow anyone to harm you again. You are part of my family now, and I promise to take better care of you," he promises, and I can feel the weight in his words.

I stood so that I could bury my face in his chest and wrap my arms around his waist as best I could. I felt the tears welling up, but I didn't want to cry. I didn't want to dwell on what happened these past weeks or be sad about what I couldn't change. I had them back now; that's all that mattered to me. These amazing boys had come for me, and I just wanted to be happy for once. Being with them was the only time I have ever been happy, and I wasn't going to waste a minute of any more time I was lucky enough to get with them.

"Okay, Remy," I sighed deeply, pulling back to look at him. "I'll meet him, but only if you guys are with me."

He leaned down to kiss the top of my head. "I wouldn't have it any other way."

CHAPTER SEVEN

I pull back from Remy and clear my throat. "When can we go home? I don't want to be here anymore," I tell him.

His handsome face transforms from stern leader to beautiful young man with just a grin. "We'll head home soon. First, there are some things we need to discuss with you, and I'd like for your grandfather and Albert to be here for that." He pauses until I nod my head. "Good girl. I'll go see if Logan got clothing for you so you can get dressed and have a bite to eat."

My stomach lurches at the thought of food, but wearing clothes again sounds nice. He leads me to the bathroom, and I wait for a few minutes before there's a knock on the door. Logan holds out some folded clothing to me, and I thank him before shutting the door. I smile to myself in the mirror behind the sink, my eyes widening as I take in my appearance. I don't know what I was expecting to see, maybe some sign of all that has happened to me, maybe a tattoo on my forehead that says 'crazy'. But I just see me, eyes too big for my face, small nose, light blonde hair. The only sign that anything has been done to me are the sunken cheeks and overall too-thin look I now have. I guess the blood can keep me alive, but it can't exactly keep me healthy.

As I'm dressing, I notice that my skin feels…off. Not torn or bruised, just tight to the point where it's a little uncomfortable to move around. I splash water over my arms, seeing if that will help, thinking my skin is just dry maybe. I search through the cabinet and find a bottle of lotion. I open the lid to apply some in my hand, and the smell hits me like a ton of bricks, overpowering and scented too strongly for my tastes. I toss it to the back of the cabinet and make a face. Hopefully no one ever finds it.

I take a little longer than I should, but soon enough I'm dressed in a pair of black leggings and a loosely-fitting white tank-top. When I step out of the bathroom the guys are all there, some sitting down in the living room, some moving about, and the two men from before are there as well. I swallow down the bile that rises in my throat as I look over the older man. He looks so much like Uncle, and I have to remind myself that he helped my guys find me.

Still feeling uncomfortable, I look at each of the guys until I spot what I'm looking for. Kellan has on a dark green zippered hoodie over his black shirt and I make my way over to him. As I reach his side, the older man, my grandfather, clears his throat to get the room's attention.

"I'm sorry to rush you, my dear, but there are

matters at hand that cannot wait," he tells me.

I sigh deeply, feeling tired already. "Okay, then let's deal with them." I pull on Kellan's sleeve, and he puts his arm around me, snuggling me into his side on the couch.

"We are holding Marcus and his accomplices in the room we found you in, but they will need to be dealt with as soon as possible," he says, his voice holding an undercurrent of anger.

I turn my head to blink at him a few times. "So deal with them." What does this guy want from me? I tug on the front of the jacket, and Kellan unzips it all the way down and places one side of it over my hands, probably thinking they're cold.

"You're the leader of the pack now, dear. Their fates now rest in your hands," my grandfather tells me.

"So you're asking me what I want to be done with them?" I ask. I pull on Kellen's other sleeve, and he brings his hand up to my cheek, turning my head to look at him.

"Is there a reason you're pulling at me, or is this just another nervous habit of yours?" he asks, his brow lifting and his mouth set in a look of amused annoyance.

I bite my lip and feel my cheeks heating. "I wanted your hoodie." I shrug. He laughs lightly as he pulls the jacket off and places it around my shoulders. I quickly put my arms through the sleeves and zip it up as far as it goes. It's huge for me, but it feels like armor to me.

Grandfather clears his throat again. I turn my body to him and make myself meet his eyes. Eyes that look like mine, I notice. "If it's really up to me, then I say they need to die."

Remy sits forward in his chair, clasping his hands together. "I know this must be hard for you, Kitten…"

"No, it's not hard at all. Besides what they did to me, they almost killed you and Tristan. I don't know about all this wolf stuff, or if there is a death penalty, but Uncle and Adam do not deserve to be in this world any longer. Uncle is cruel and unfeeling, and Adam wanted me as his mate and was willing to do whatever it took to make that happen, including working with Uncle. And there was another man in the room who was trying to steal my eggs from me, my future children," I explain, my tone leaving no room for argument.

"I agree that their punishment should be severe, but are you sure you want their blood on your hands?" Grandfather asks me.

I look down to my lap, picking at the seams of the jacket sleeve. I shrug my shoulders. "If I have to do it myself, then I will. And I want it done in front of the rest of your wolves, so they know not to go after my family again."

Kellan's hand closes over mine gently. "We'd never ask you to do that, Kitten. I'm sure Maksim can arrange for that to happen; you won't even have to watch."

"I want to watch. I need to," I whisper.

"Look at you! A great leader already. Ivaskov blood definitely runs through your veins. The treasonous assholes will serve as a warning not to mess with our new princess." Grandfather claps happily, a smile plastered on his face.

I frown at him, thinking he's a little too happy over the death of his own son. "I don't know if I could've forgiven them for what they did to me, but I think I would have tried. The message I want to be sent is never to go after the guys. That, I will never forgive."

Grandfather cuts his hand through the air. "Either way, it will be done. I'll arrange for the whole pack to meet at the pack house in Colorado within the week. Albert, start spreading the word immediately." He nods to the man sitting next to him.

My body stiffens as I recognize him. "You," I choke out.

"Yes, my Princess." The man bows deeply as he pauses on his exit from the house.

"You remember him from when you were in the basement?" Kellan asks me.

I nod my head, still staring at the man. "And from the dining room," I say.

"What dining room? What happened in the dining room?" Logan demands to know. I shake my head, refusing to answer and daring the man to answer as well. He's the man who told me to be quiet, the one who pointed out the knife on the table when I was struggling with Uncle and Adam. The only person who didn't turn away from me.

Albert continues on his way, and the room is left in silence after our weird exchange. To change the subject, I ask a different question. "Why is everyone calling me 'Princess' and why did you," I look to Grandfather, "say I was the leader of the pack?"

The subject change is welcomed, but I'm filled with nerves and agitation as Remy explains that I'm the lost princess of the Ivaskov pack. So I guess Grandfather helped them rescue me not because I'm his family, but because they needed me as a leader, or my mate I guess, whatever that means.

I let them tell me everything, starting with what they

did to find me, to when they met Grandfather, what happened after they got here, and what was said when I was recovering. I don't say a word. I stare at Maksim the whole time, wondering what was wrong with the people I came from that made them so cold-hearted and unloving. Was I like them? Would I toss my child into a dumpster and leave her to die? Would I abuse a niece because she was powerful? Would I kill my own brother or only admire a granddaughter because having her around benefited me?

"Can we go home now?" I ask Remy, interrupting whatever Grandfather was going on about,

The subject of my stare looks back at me, a frown in place. "Your home is with your people, your wolves, in Colorado," he tells me.

I shake my head slowly. "No. It's with the men who cared for me without asking anything in exchange. I already have a home, with them."

"Kitten…" Remy says my name softly. "We should probably talk about this before you dismiss them entirely. You've been through a lot and have learned a lot today. You don't have to decide now, but know that whatever you chose, wherever you go, we'll go, too."

I think his words over for a few moments before I decide that my head hurts, and I'm done with today. "Fine, we'll talk about it, but I want to go home, for a little while at least."

Grandfather splutters. "The pack will want to meet you…"

I cut him off. "And they will, maybe. I need some time to think things over, and I need to talk about this with my family." I emphasize the word 'family', looking for any reaction from Maksim, but there is none.

He frowns harder and crosses his arms over his chest. "That's something else we need to talk about. Your name. Kitten is not a proper name for a wolf princess, let alone an Ivaskov. Katerina would be better suited for you; it would explain the nickname and your grandmother was named Katerina."

"I already have a name and it's Kitten. It's a name I've earned, and I'm keeping it, suitable or not."

"You *earned* it? What does that even mean?" he scoffs.

I sigh and close my eyes, leaning my head back against the couch. "If you knew anything about me, you'd know that I was first raised as a cat by a mentally-challenged woman. You'd know that I was left alone my entire life up until I met Ash and Tristan and the others. I took care of myself, taught myself everything I know, and ignored the rest of the world. But you don't know that because you don't know me. You're just part of a family that decided I was trash."

"Well...I-I didn't..." he started.

"It doesn't matter. Now, if you'd excuse us, I want to leave. Unless you plan on making me a prisoner like your son had."

Maksim looks confused and angry, but he gets to his feet and brushes imaginary dirt off his pants. He meets Remy's eyes and jerks his head to the door. "A word?" he asks him between gritted teeth. He stalks off, slamming the door behind him.

"Well, that went smoothly. The rest of you get packed up and ready to go. Jace, make the arrangements, something private. I'll be back in a few," Remy instructs before following him outside.

I sit patiently as Logan tries to untangle my messy hair. Jace offered to start on my bangs while he did the back. I feel like a gross monster in front of these perfectly-styled boys. Tristan had brought in a platter of cheese and crackers for me to snack on while I was to be poked and prodded, but the sight of it alone had my tummy upset. Great wracking sobs came out of nowhere and took me by force. The guys instantly went on alert, and I tried to explain what had me so upset, but it's hard to manage through all of the never-ending crying. After my explanation of why the sight of food caused such a reaction in me, my boys wore expressions of horror, heartbreak, and sadness. Tristan's generally cheerful and soothing features transformed into something I can only describe as murderous rage and was enough to scare me into calming myself. He had closed his eyes and breathed deeply for what seemed like forever, and when he opened them again, the look was gone, replaced by a look of determination. He instructed Jace and Logan to move to either side of me while he sat in front of me on the bed and offered me a cube of the cheese from between his thumb and forefinger. I shook my head at first, Adam's voice ringing in my head, telling me if I eat, he gets to touch me. Tristan laid his forehead against mine and whispered so low I couldn't understand the words, but the soothing effect his voice had over me was there, as were the electric sparks from earlier. My eyes closed of their own accord and I just listened to him. Eventually, I felt the slide of the cheese over my lips, and my tongue flicked out to taste it on instinct. My mouth flooded with saliva, my body telling me I really wanted that bite of cheese, and Tristan's voice was convincing my mind that no harm would come to me if I ate it.

I opened my mouth, taking in the small bite of food, and chewed it slowly, moaning deeply as the delicious flavor washed over my taste buds. Then the tears came again.

"Oh, sweetie," Tristan sighed brokenly.

I shook my head quickly, offering him a smile as well. "It's not that, I promise. It's just so good." I hiccupped, giggling at my ridiculousness.

Tristan smiled, too, and offered me another bite with his lean fingers. Logan and Jace resumed their brushing, and we fell into companionable silence. I felt odd at first, knowing I was being fed like a baby, but accepted his offerings anyway. Somehow, him offering me the food instead of me reaching for it myself made it easier. I'd be embarrassed once my belly was full for the first time in months.

"There you go, Doll, pretty as ever," Jace states as he sits back and Logan fluffs my hair. I blush a little at his compliment but tell him thank you. He turns his cheek and leans closer, so I give him a quick kiss, blushing further. My emotions are all over the place, and it's hard to remain calm. Just this morning I was being stabbed to death, and now here I am, being taken care of again by the people I cherish most in the world. It feels unreal, and I'm still waiting to wake up any second, broken and bleeding on the cold concrete floor.

Remy steps back into the small house and scrubs a hand over his red hair. "So, we ready to go then?" Logan asks through a mouth full of crackers, getting a few crumbs on Tristan, who just brushes them off with a roll of his eyes.

Remy scratches at his eyebrow with a thick finger. "I suppose we are. Though, I'll be escorting the prisoners to the pack house before I return home, along with some of the soldiers we brought with us. If you don't mind, Kitten, I'd like to kill them as quickly as possible, and I'd like for you not to have to witness it."

"Okay," I answer him, even though it wasn't a question. I'm not sure if I really want to watch that anyway. I just want to be done with them.

"Okay." Remy nods. "I promise to do the job myself; they'll cause you no more harm. I'll only be a few days, but when I return, we'll uh, well, we'll have some guests," he states reluctantly.

"Guests," Ash repeats with a raise of his brow.

"Maksim agrees that Kitten needs some time to recuperate, but he's asked for himself and Albert to stay with us as guests so he can get to know his granddaughter and for Albert to tutor her, and us, on wolf policies and politics. Even if you choose to walk away from it all, Kitten, you can't control what others do, and the Ivaskov pack will still look to you to lead them. It's in their nature," Remy explains with a shrug.

"And you thought this a wise idea?" Finn asks warily.

"I do," Remy states confidently. "The rest of us either had to choose to leave our families or were chased away from them. Kitten has an opportunity that none of us had, and I think she should be given the chance to know her family. I won't force the issue, but he'll be around if she changes her mind."

"I understand," I tell him, meeting his eyes. I see no judgment in them; he really does just want me to have the option.

"Right then!," Logan jumps to his feet. "Let's blow this joint!"

CHAPTER EIGHT

KELLAN

The first few days back home were interesting, to say the least. To the ignorant eye, Kitten appeared to be just fine. She smiled when she was supposed to, laughed when she was supposed to, and was around people when she was supposed to. When she thought no one was looking, though, her gaze would drift away, and she'd shut down. She swayed between being too busy with lessons with Finn and yoga with Reed and car maintenance with Ash, to locking herself in her room for hours, lying in bed where sometimes we could hear muffled crying.

At a loss for what to do and how to help her, my brothers and I kept ourselves busy as well. There was a lot to be done after having been gone for so long. The entire house needed a good dusting, groceries needed to be thrown out and new ones purchased, mail needed to be sorted, things of that nature. There were also our professions to be dealt with, but no one wanted to leave the house for any length of time, so we left our businesses and practices in the capable hands our employees.

I sit up in bed with a sigh. It hurts my heart that someone I care about is suffering, and there's no medicine or medical procedure to cure her of her pain. I slip on a pair of my favorite faded jeans and a white undershirt, determined that today will be the day that I get through to Kitten. I pass Tristan on my way to the kitchen, looking forward to my first cup of coffee of the day.

"Is that for her?" I ask, indicating the plate of scrambled eggs and toast he's carrying.

"Yeah, she still won't reach for the food herself. I've tried leaving her alone with her meals, but she never touches it, and I usually find her crying afterward. Even with me feeding her, she's not eating enough. A few bites here and there aren't enough to keep her healthy," he says, frowning at the plate like it's the eggs' fault.

"I know," I sigh. "Maybe it's a good thing that Maksim is coming back with Remington today. She might end up needing more of his blood."

"Yeah, I don't know, man. Something tells me having him around isn't going to be good for her."

I shrug a shoulder, not knowing what to say when I don't have a clue what would be good for her.

"Hey, guys!" Kitten chirps from the end of the hall. We both turn towards her to see her waving happily as she approaches.

"Good morning, Kitten. Sleep well?" I ask, smiling back at her. Her smile falters momentarily, but she regains it quickly.

"Sure." She shrugs. "I was thinking that I'd go into

work today. I can have my lessons with Finn when I get back and do yoba with Reed this evening."

I share a look with Tristan. This seems like a bad idea. "I don't know, Kitten. Leaving the house might not be a good idea. You don't have to worry about money or anything." I trail off as her face falls. I don't like telling her no. Luckily for me, there's someone I know who won't mind it a bit.

"I'll tell you what. You convince Ash it's a good idea, and the three of us will go together, deal?"

KITTEN

"No," Ash grumbles before I even stop speaking.

"But I want to," I demand.

"No, not happening," he persists, throwing on his black long-sleeved T-shirt and getting ready like he's not in the middle of a discussion.

"Well, I'm going anyway. With or without you. I want to check in with Miss Annie, and Mikey should be there today." I turn on my heel and stomp from the room. Big moody man is not going to tell me what I can do.

"This is about the little boy?" Ash asks from right behind me. Apparently my angry strides are no challenge for his longer legs. Stupid tall people.

I huff in annoyance. "Yes, sort of. I just want to go back to being me, Ash. The me who went to work, the me who tried to help others, and the me who didn't want to cry all the time."

"So the you, you were before you met us?" He crosses

his arms, and his face darkens menacingly.

"Yes...no. I don't know." I shake my head and bite my lip. I really don't know. "I just feel like I need to get back to the real world for a moment."

His face softens, and he opens his arms to me for a hug. They've seemed to notice that I need it to be a choice. I walk into his waiting arms instantly, inhaling his distinct Ash smell gratefully. I rub my face against his chest, feeling instantly calm and protected, if only for a moment. "I'll take you there, but you're not working. We'll just hang around for a while."

"I can live with that," I tell him gratefully, with a smile up at his gorgeous face. All hard angles and dramatic swooshes of his eyebrows. My scary man and protective shadow is beautiful in his intensity. "Kellan wants to come, too," I tell him.

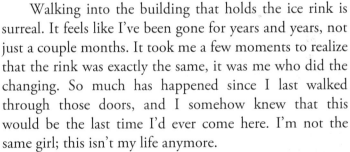

Walking into the building that holds the ice rink is surreal. It feels like I've been gone for years and years, not just a couple months. It took me a few moments to realize that the rink was exactly the same, it was me who did the changing. So much has happened since I last walked through those doors, and I somehow knew that this would be the last time I'd ever come here. I'm not the same girl; this isn't my life anymore.

"Well, look what the cat done drugged in." Miss Annie's southern drawl and too-loud voice were as welcoming as ever. She was simply one of the most interesting people I've ever known.

"Hi, Miss Annie," I tell her as she squeezes me in a

tight hug.

"Been ages since I seen yur purdy face 'round here. And I sees you gots yourself 'nother one of dem fellas. Though those other one were a might purdyer ta look at and weren't so…big," she tells me as she studies Ash up and down.

I giggle at her assessment and Ash's responding tilt of his head and frowning face. "She means Logan and Jace," I tell him. Ash rolls his eyes and nods his head. I know Ash isn't offended by Miss Annie's statement; he doesn't try to be a pretty boy like Jace and Logan do.

"So are the rec kids here today, then? I figured the days stayed the same," I ask the short round woman who I've thought as a grandmother ever since I met her.

"Those young'uns will be here shortly; they got the fundin' they needed for a 'nother hockey team, did ya hear?" she tells me happily.

I look to Ash, and he nods his head slightly. I beam at him, happy tears threatening to come to my eyes. So even with all that's gone on, Jace found the time to keep his word.

"Mikey must be thrilled," I say to Miss Annie.

She purses her lips and rocks her head back and forth. "Shame what happened ta that boy. His daddy done tore him up good this time. Put him in the hospital he did, and bless his no good heart, I hope he rot away in that cell for what he did ta that poor child."

"They let Mikey go back to his father? Why?" I ask no one in particular.

"They'd sure did," Miss Annie answers.

"What hospital is he at?" Kellan asks firmly, not too

happy about this news either.

"He over at St. Joseph's, last I heard. Those cute girls from the rec center had me sign a card to take to the poor thing." She shakes her head again.

"Thank you for telling us, Miss Annie," I tell her, offering another hug because she looks likes she needs it now. I glance at Ash and Kellan, silently telling them I need a minute alone. They step away from us, but I'm sure they can still hear me.

I take the older woman's hands in my own and meet her pretty brown eyes. "Miss Annie, I probably won't be coming back anymore, but I wanted to thank you for all you've done for me over the years. I don't know if I would've made it without you and this place. I don't know if I can ever express what it meant to me to come here."

"Awe, Sug, no need ta go thankin' me. I coulda done more for ya, and I shoulda, but I was afraid of runnin' ya off, and I liked having ya 'round here. 'Twon't be the same without ya, but I'm glad ta see ya findin' a place in this here world. Those boys treatin' ya good then?" she asks seriously.

I smile shyly at her. "They treat me very well, Miss Annie. They're my family and are very courteous and respectful to me. I wouldn't be here if it weren't for them," I tell her, glancing over my shoulder to look at the guys. At that moment, I realize that I've been unfair to them. They've given me so much, and all I do lately is pull away from them.

"You'll always be one of mines, far as I'm concerned. You go gettin' married ta one of dem boys, and I'll be 'spectin' an invitation in the post, ya hear?" she says as she cups my cheek in her warm hand.

"Of course, Miss Annie," I tell her with a giggle. Do wolves even get married? Do I want to marry just one of them?

We finish our goodbyes, and each of the guys gets pulled into one of Miss Annie's famous hugs before we exit the building and walk to the car. To our surprise and my delight, Remy is waiting for us when we make it there. He looks annoyed, or angry, but I smile at him anyway and start to run over to him. I slow as I recognize the two men standing next to him and my smile turns into a frown.

Maksim and Albert wear matching pleasant grins as they spot me, and Albert takes a step forward to bow in greeting. "Nice to see you again, my Princess."

I hold a hand up to wave at the both of them but quickly turn my attention back to Remy. "I missed you. What are you doing here?" I ask as I hug him around his waist.

"I believe the question is, what are *you* doing here?" he asks, but when I look up at him, I realize his question is directed at Ash and Kellan.

"Oh, I asked them to bring me. Demanded it really," I quickly defend the guys.

"Well, now I'm demanding that we return you home," he says stiffly.

I pull away from him and sigh deeply. "No can do, Rem. We have to go to the hospital now."

"What? What's wrong now? And why the hospital? I can heal you myself." Maksim speaks quickly, his lips pursed as he looks me over.

"It's not me; Mikey is there, and he got hurt really bad," I speak to Remy instead, owing no explanation to Maksim.

"The small child that you are fond of?" Remy asks, looking to the others for confirmation. I simply nod at him.

"If this concerns a human child, then he is fine with the doctors. I don't see why your presence is required," Maksim states.

I place my hands on my hips and stare him down. "He is my favorite *human child* and I *want* to go see him. You know…to make sure that he's okay and to offer any assistance that I can, even if it's just holding his hand and being there for him. Oh, right, you *wouldn't* know about that," I sneer at him before heading to the car and getting in the back seat.

I glare at the guys until they get in the car, too. The silence makes for a long and awkward ride to the hospital. Kellan takes my hand and places it in the crook of his arm as we approach the sliding doors. To my discomfort, it seems Maksim and Albert have decided to tag along, but they hang back behind the rest of us. The lady at the information desk is friendly and kindly asks us if she can help us. I tell her I'm here to see Mikey, and when she asks who I am, I tell her I'm his sister. She eyes me warily as she looks at her screen, but shows me the room number and says only I will be allowed in to see him. Ash grunts, but no one disagrees with her.

We take the elevator to the third floor and walk quietly to the children's wing. We stop at another desk, and the male nurse behind the counter tells us he was informed of my arrival and points out the room for me.

Everyone except Remy finds seats in the small waiting area, but he continues to follow me.

"You're not supposed to go in with me," I tell him quietly.

"I won't go in, but I'm standing at the door. It's not safe for you to be in public alone," he tells me, his expression daring me to argue with him. I don't, I'm just grateful he's not throwing a fit about being here in the first place.

Leaving Remy to his post at the door, I step into the dark room, only beeping machines making any noise. I leave the door cracked open and move the empty chair by the wall over to the side of the bed. Mikey's little body looks even smaller than usual on the wide bed, and with the big machines towering over him like they're ready to close in on him any minute now.

I carefully take his hand in mine, being mindful of the tube in his wrist and the contraption on his finger with the wire coming out of it. "Hey, Mikey, it's me," I whisper to him. "If anyone asks, I'm your sister. Sorry about lying but they wouldn't let me back here if I didn't."

I lean forward and brush his messy brown hair away from his face. "Sorry I wasn't around, buddy. I came as soon as I heard. I was a bit broken myself for a while, but I don't think that's a story I'll ever tell. Miss Annie told me the hockey program is up and running; that's good, right? You know, you're the reason it happened, so you should be proud of that." I smile sadly at the sleeping boy. His face looks peaceful in sleep, even if a machine is breathing for him, making his chest rise and fall rhythmically. His bruised skin has turned greenish-yellow, and I hate to think what he must have looked like when they were fresh and with all the swelling.

My chest aches seeing Mikey like this. He was always so full of energy and spunk, always saying exactly what was on his mind. For one so young, he sure has had a rough life, which is probably what bound us together from the start.

After a while of just sitting here quietly beside my buddy, I hear the door creak open further, and someone step inside.

"Just a few more minutes," I plead, thinking it's Remy telling me we should go home now.

"Take all the time you need. You're his first visitor who isn't a social worker," a cheerful voice replies, making me jump at the unexpected volume in the quiet room. It was an average volume, but I've been whispering.

"Sorry, I didn't mean to startle you. I'm just doing my rounds." The doctor smiles politely as he takes up position on the other side of the bed.

"It's okay," I respond automatically. I watch as he checks different machines, tapping at the screen of a tablet, which, thanks to Finn, I now know the name of.

"You know," the doctor starts as he flips the tablet case closed. "I didn't know Mike had a sister. In fact, I know he doesn't." He lifts a dirty blonde brow at me, hands going behind his back in that stance that doctors always do.

My heart pounds faster, as I sense I'm about to get into trouble, but his demeanor tells me that he's just playful and inquisitive. I don't think he'll rat me out to security.

"Okay, I'm not his sister, but I know him and care

about him. He used to come into my work, and we'd talk. He doesn't really talk to many people." I lift my lips in a sad smile.

"I know! He's been here a week and hasn't said one word to me," the doctor exclaims, *tsk*ing and shaking his head.

My eyes widen in shock, glancing from Mikey and the tube coming out of his mouth, back to the doctor, thinking he can't be serious. The doctor chuckles at me, and I realize he was joking around. I giggle nervously at his weird sense of humor.

"Sorry, long days around here. I have to keep myself entertained or else I'd just be depressed all the time. So, sister, do you have any questions for me?"

I shrug a shoulder and look back to Mikey. "I don't know medical things, but is he going to be alright?" I ask.

The doctor sighs. "I honestly don't know the answer to that question. His broken arm and ankle will heal, his bruising will fade, and the scar on his abdomen will turn into a scar he can be proud of on the playground, but the brain is a tricky thing. When he came in, he had trauma to the head, and there was some swelling in his brain. The swelling has gone down, but we've seen little improvement in his brain activity. That doesn't mean there won't be any; the question is always how long do we wait for it to happen."

I swallow thickly. "I understand."

"I've been at this for a while now; I've seen many a miracle, so don't give up hope just yet," he tells me as he starts for the door.

"Wait!" I call after him. He turns to look back at me questioningly. "I'll take over his medical bills. I'll cover all of it, pay in cash if I need to, just do everything you can, okay?"

He raises an eyebrow. "He's a ward of the state; they hold his power of attorney and I'm not supposed to go to any extraordinary measures."

"What they don't know won't hurt them. And I'm asking you to be extraordinary, Doctor." I meet his green eyes with my own, begging him to be on my side. He doesn't respond verbally, but his eyes spark, and I swear his head bows just the tiniest of bits. It's the most I can hope for.

With his exit, Remy enters. "We'll do everything we can for him, Love."

"I guess I'm going to need to work now after all," I tell him.

He shakes his head at me in wonder. "There's a few perks to being a princess, you know; an expansive bank account being one of them. You're the richest wolf in the world now, Kitten. Money isn't a problem for you."

"Oh," I say, tilting my head to the side. I guess I haven't thought about that. "Well, then, can you help me make sure his bills here are covered?"

"Of course. We'll make an anonymous donation, more than one if needed. And we can ask Kellan to look over him as well; he may have rights to work in this hospital. If not, he can obtain them."

"Thank you, Remy. I'll never be able to make up for all you guys do for me," I tell him sincerely.

"We're family. It's not tit for tat; we help when we can, and so do you," he tells me, placing a kiss on the crown of my head. "Now, let's allow the boy some rest. You can return tomorrow if you'd like."

"I would like." I beam at him. Before leaving, I give Mikey a quick kiss on his forehead and tell him I'll see him tomorrow and to hang in there.

The next week seems to pass by quickly. I keep busy with yoba, lessons, laundry, and visiting the hospital. Kellan was able to sign paperwork that allowed him to take over Mikey's care and between the two doctors and an off-the-books brain surgery, they've gotten him to where he's breathing on his own now. It's too soon to wake him up out of his medically-induced coma, according to Kellan, but his tests are coming back showing improvement. I'm told the real worry now is how functional he'll be once the new swelling goes away.

Lessons with Albert are excruciating, considering we spend most of the time with him explain exactly why things are the way they are. Pack rules make no sense to me whatsoever. The ranking system regarding dominance for instance. Apparently it pays to be bossy in the wolf world. The more people the bossy wolves have to boss around, the happier they are, and some people actually like to be bossed around and take no offense to this. I can't help but think this is the opinion of bossy people. His constant talk of mates has made being around the guys a bit uncomfortable. Since no one seems to know just what exactly I am, they can't tell me whether all eight of my guys are my mates, or if I'm just mated to Tristan and find comfort within his pack. I was beyond shocked to find out that I bit Tristan when they found me and that meant that I had marked him and bound him to me, and that's also the cause of the static-like electricity when we touch.

"I have some news for you, my Princess." Albert greets me with his usual bow before taking the seat across from me in the library.

"Maksim got bored and is leaving?" I answer hopefully.

Albert frowns at me and shakes his head, taking a leather-bound book out of his satchel. "You haven't spoken to him since the day we arrived; you should give him a chance. But no, he's not leaving and no, that's not my news."

He flips through the worn pages of the book before turning it to face me and sliding it in front of me. "What's this?" I ask, staring down at the words that are not words.

"Oh, right. I forgot you can't read Russian. This is Mikel's personal journal. Here, he talks about his success in impregnating a woman in the Australian changeable wolf colony. He mentions that the woman was actually half wolf, half human, but chose to go unchanged so she could stay with her family in the colony," Albert explains.

"So I was an experiment? My father didn't love my mother?" I ask, confused.

"I believe Mikel had a relationship with this woman, your mother, but his feeling toward her was not made clear in this journal. This is the last entry he made. The fact that this was found amongst Marcus' belongings when most of Mikel's personal things were destroyed makes me believe that this was stolen," he says with a thoughtful expression.

"And my conception may be the reason he was killed," I state more than ask.

"It's a possibility, Princess, but it wasn't the only reason Marcus would have wanted your father dead. It won't do you any good to think like that."

"I guess you're right. Are you sure that this is me he's talking about? That I'm the baby mentioned? Because it still doesn't make sense for me to be found in a dumpster here, when my mother was from Australia. And if there is a colony of changeable females, then why don't you change them to make more girl wolves?" I ask.

"How you got here is still a mystery, but as to why no one changes the females of the colony, well, put simply, they don't want to be changed. The more in-depth answer would be that the colony is protected by the Australian wolf pack, and even Marcus knew not to mess with them. We have greater numbers on our side, but an Australian wolf with home field advantage is one of the most dangerous fights you can be in. They offered the females sanctuary on their own pack lands and still honor the pact they made with them."

"So the Ivaskovs aren't the most feared and respected wolves in the world, the Australians are?" I say with a smirk, having read between the lines.

Albert seems to contemplate his answer. "Yes and no. The Australians have something worth fighting for, whereas we Ivaskovs have not had to defend our position in some time. Sometimes in war, it matters not how many soldiers you bring to the field, but the passion and righteousness of those soldiers. Victory tends to favor those who want it more."

"I see." So the answer is, he doesn't know.

"As for what this entry does tell us, it may put your mates' minds at ease to know that you are nineteen or twenty years old, depending on how long you were carried in your mother's womb.""Will I be able to speak with these Australians one day and see what they know of me, if anything?" I ask hopefully.

"Of course; the entirety of the wolf community is eager to meet you," he tells me. Okay, no pressure then.

And so began his lesson on the proper etiquette and procedures when dealing with other high-ranking wolves. Our lesson is cut short though, as an annoying, blunt pain takes up residence behind my eyes and I excuse myself to lie down.

I pass Reed in his studio working on a painting on my way to his room. "Hey, babe. What are you up to?" he calls to me as I pass by.

"My head hurts and I was craving some time in your cloud bed; mine isn't as comfy," I tell him, realizing I should have asked first."Oh." He blinks at me, surprise written on his face.

"Is that okay?" I ask, biting my lip.

"Always, it's just...you've been sleeping in your room since you got back, I thought...maybe things have changed," he says, sounding unsure of himself.

I look down at my toes, feeling ashamed. "I just needed to be alone sometimes." I shrug. In all honesty, I just didn't want them to know that I sometimes woke up crying. I've cried more since I've been back than I did while I was being abused.

"Hey, I completely understand. There's nothing to feel guilty over," Reed croons.

"Okay. Do you, I mean, if you're tired at all, want to take a nap with me?" I stutter out, sounding like an idiot.

Reed smiles brilliantly, tossing the paintbrush behind

him, not even watching where it landed. "Sounds delightful."

I crawl up the bed, sinking slightly into the soft mattress and blankets while Reed shucks his paint-splattered clothes. He folds the comforter down, and I slip beneath it, wiggling around in the luxurious softness.

"Can I hold you?" he asks as he moves in next to me. I nod my head and in moments, my face is cradled in Reed's shoulder as his arms wrap around me.

The pressure behind my eyes lessens slightly, and I sigh in relief. In doing so, I get a lungful of Reed and boy, does he smell good. I can't place what he smells like exactly, something sweet and wild. My blood feels warm as I feel it rushing through my body, my ears filled with the sound of it. My mouth waters, causing me to swallow constantly. I lick my lips, and by default, end up licking Reed's shoulder.

"Reed…" I start, my breath coming in short pants. "This might sound crazy but, I think I want to bite you."

I expect a laugh, or maybe for him to run away from the crazy person, but instead he answers me with a light rumbling sound that I can feel in his chest. Before my brain can wonder if that means go ahead or get away from me, there's a sharp but quick pain in my mouth and then a delicious flavor coats my tongue. My tongue darts out to lap at the honeyed goodness and Reed gasps, his hand going to the back of my head to draw me in closer.

Once I've had my fill, and I feel as if I'm floating, I release him and fall back onto the cloud, I mean bed. I feel Reed nuzzling my neck and I let my head fall to the side, giving him more room. A tiny prick of my skin and then lightning is coursing through my veins, and my hands are fisting the sheets. "Oh, my," I groan. Every inch of my body is acutely aware of every inch of Reed. It only takes a minute or two before the electricity dies down to a pleasant hum, much like what I feel when I touch Tristan. To test my theory, I run my fingertips down Reed's bare back. Yep, exactly the same.

Reed pulls back; then the next second Kellan is standing in front of me. When did he get here? My head swims as I try to remember him entering the room.

"Come here," I smile at him, or at least I think I do. He bends down, bringing his ear close to my lips like I'm going to tell him a secret. For some reason, that makes me laugh, and I laugh harder as Reed starts to laugh next to me.

"What?" Kellan starts to pull away, but I grab him quickly.

"No, wait. You have to try this." I tell him, pulling him closer to me. I kiss his neck lightly before I sink my teeth into his exposed neck. I feel euphoric as Kellan's clean taste washes over me, through me. I pull away and he blissfully returns the favor, the full force of the lightning returning. I feel Reed snuggle into my back, his hand resting on my hip and his breathing evening out to that of a sleeping person. Kellan collapses onto the bed on my other side, moaning out something, but I can't concentrate on the words. My eyes feel heavy, and my soul feels at peace, a deep, rich peace that I've never felt in my life. Kellan continues to nuzzle at my neck as I feel myself drifting away.

CHAPTER NINE

"And just what the fuck do we have here?" Logan thunders, waking me up with a start. "No, scratch that. The real question is why the hell wasn't I invited?" he asks, crossing his arms over his chest, one foot tapping impatiently, a cat-that-got-the-canary smirk in place.

Reed grumbles behind me, snuggling his face deeper into my shoulder. Kellan, on the other hand, reacts like he's just been shot, his body jumping off the bed a foot high before he falls off the side, smacking his head on the nightstand.

"It's not what it looks like!" he exclaims, his eyes wild and his hands up in front of him.

"That's what I would say, too," Logan *tsk*s playfully. "I expected this behavior from Tristan, or maybe me, but you, Kellan." He shakes his head, trying to hold back his grin.

"I...I..." Kellan struggles adorably.

I take pity on the poor man. "It's okay, Kel. You didn't do anything wrong, and he's just messing with you," I tell him through my giggling.

Logan pouts at me. "Aw, you never let me have any fun."

"Did you come in just to be nosey, or did you actually need something?" Reed asks, his voice muffled from talking into my skin.

"Oh, right." He claps his hands together. "It's Thanksgiving, you bunch of bums, so get your asses up and moving!"

"Thanksgiving is tomorrow," Reed informs him.

"Nope, you lazy mofos slept through the night. Tristan needs some help in the kitchen and you know I'm not fucking doing it," he tells us as he leaves, making a point of leaving the door open as far as it goes.

"Looks like that's you, bro. I'm taking Kitten with me to the gallery," Reed says to a still-sleepy-looking Kellan.

"Alright, I better get to it then. You know how Tristan can get... today is his diva day." Kellan rolls his eyes. He starts for the door before pausing and coming back to me. "May I?" he asks with his face in front of mine.

I nod my head, leaning up to make it easier for him. He gives me a lingering kiss with his soft, pouty lips. It's like kissing pillows.

"So this is your gallery?" I ask as Reed helps me out of Finn's orange truck.

"Yeah, it's one of the businesses that I own. They found a couple of new artists while I was gone, and want me to take a look at their work." Reed shrugs. "I figured today would be as good a day as any since we're closed for the holiday."

We walk along the sidewalk of a quaint-looking strip mall. The shop he leads me to has a wall made entirely of glass and through it I can see all kinds of things. Reed pulls out his keys and unlocks the glass door, allowing me to enter first.

On the ceiling are different light fixtures, none of them matching, including a hanging light made entirely of spoons. The walls are lined with every shape and size paintings, some of them heartbreaking, some silly ones, but each of them beautiful. In between each painting is a pedestal with a sculpture sitting atop it; they vary in material and color, and I hope I have time to study every detail of each one.

He takes my hand and leads me around a corner where there are smaller paintings, a few sketches, and lots of framed photos. A long counter sits in the back of the space, and I think that's where we're headed, but Reed leads me around the table and opens a door that matches the dark hardwood floors throughout the space.

We step around a few shelves, and Reed holds out a chair for me to sit in at a high table at the back of the room. I climb into the chair and watch him as he digs around on a shelf.

"Here we go," he says as he brings a big black folder with him to sit across from me at the table.

"So what are we doing?" I ask.

"We're going to look through this young man's portfolio and see if he's created anything we'd like to sell here in the shop. The manager I hired here said he saw some promising work, but I insist on having the final say." He flips through the first page and shakes his head. From where I'm sitting I can't see, and it's bugging me.

I slide from my chair and walk around to Reed. I kick off my shoes and scoot his chair back.

"What are you doing?" Reed smiles at me curiously.

I hop up on the bottom rung of the chair and climb into his lap, sliding the black book closer to me. "I couldn't see."

Reed laughs loudly at that and scoots us closer to the table, placing his head right next to mine so we can both look at the pictures.

We take our time going over each photo of different paintings. I wish we had the real things in front of us. I want to run my fingers over the painting and follow each brush stroke that this haunted young man created. I want to ask him what was behind each movement. Was it pain? Was it anger? Sadness or frustration?

Somehow I managed to take control over the page-turning and after the third time flipping through it, Reed lays his hand over my own. Stopping me.

"What do you think?" he asks me slowly.

I chew my lip, taking in the picture we stopped on before meeting his eyes. "These pictures make me curious about the artist, about his motivation behind them. I know why I draw, and I wonder if it's the same for other people," I tell him.

Reed chews on his bottom lip as he thinks about it.

"I've met a lot of artists in my time, some good, and some not so good. From my experience, the best ones are the ones who can channel emotion into their work. Not always, as some people just have a God-given talent and can create anything, but most of the time I have found this to be true."

I nod, letting him know I'm listening and encouraging him to continue.

"Some people can only channel certain emotions, such as anger or pain, doing their best works when they are feeling those emotions. For some, like me for instance, strong feelings of any emotion can be used as fuel for art."

"Like this guy," I say quietly as I trace the edge of the photo and look back to the book.

"I'd have to agree with you there, as his portfolio shows good range. I'm not as impressed with his 'happy' works as I am with the rest, but he's talented nonetheless."

I tilt my head at him before flipping through the book once more. When I reach the end, I stare at Reed a moment, wondering what he's talking about. "What happy pictures?"

Reed brushes my hand out of the way and flips to the front, stopping on a collection of three photos, the ones I like best.

"These aren't bad, but they're pretty generic scenes. Kids playing on a playground, a man and woman sharing an embrace, a father and son facing away, staring at a baseball field. These are probably just memories from the artist's childhood that he enjoyed and wanted to paint," Reed explains.

My head is shaking even before I speak. "But these

are sad pictures."

"Why do you say that? They seem like the quintessential picturesque scenes that litter the art world," he states, eyes combing the pictures for something he may have missed.

I point to the first picture. "If you'll notice, the sun is actually shining down on the kids playing, but the rest of the scene is painted in gray. The branches here on the side aren't from a tree; they're from a bush, and the angle is wrong for it to be someone in a tree. The onlooker is hiding. And the tall kid isn't playing with the short one, look at the short kid's feet and arms; he's preparing himself for a fall. My guess is the tall kid is a bully, and the onlooker was hiding from him."

Reed nods his head slowly but doesn't say anything, so I point to the second picture. "The man and woman *are* embracing, but it's a goodbye, not a hello. The painting is blurry; my guess is to signify tears, not rain, though the window pane does have raindrops on it, but if you look through the window of the black car in the background, the artist has painted a driver's cap on a man behind the wheel. The woman's hand is wrapped around the man's wrist. So, the onlooker's father is leaving and the woman, the onlooker's mother, is pleading with him not to."

"Right, right," Reed says more to himself than to me.

"The third picture isn't real, or well, not a real memory. Where some people might see the shading as a beautiful sunset behind the baseball field after a game well played, and the father and son are basking in the memory, what I see is the artist adding a dream-like quality to the picture. Notice that the father is painted wearing the same clothing as the goodbye picture? And since that man is clearly the same man used before and is standing with a child, and you can't see yourself, I have to imagine that this painting is a dream that the artist had about his father who abandoned him coming to one of his games."

Reed turns his head and smiles brightly at me. "Huh, I guess I forgot the first rule of art," he says and then chuckles deeply.

"And what's that?" I ask.

"That all art is subjective. I still see the happy side of these paintings, but now that you pointed out certain details, I can understand what you're saying, too. Is that why you kept flipping back to this page?" he asks.

"Yeah, I really like them. And I like that there are two sides to them. It's almost like he was trying to paint what people see and what they want to see," I try to explain. The truth is, I don't know why I like them, I just do.

Reed grips me around the waist and flips me around until I'm facing him with one leg on either side of his.

"I know you've been through a lot, and I promised myself I wouldn't rush you, but talking art with you is so damn hot. Can I kiss you, Kitten? Is that too much too fast?" Reed asks, his voice bordering on pleading.

I place my arms around his neck and move closer to him. "I love you, Reed. You never need to ask for kisses."

With my permission given, Reed loses all semblance of control as his warm lips press against mine. His tongue flicks out to lick at the seam of my mouth, and I open for him. My body goes warm all over as his taste invades my mouth, and his hands travel over my back and under my shirt.

I gasp for breath when we break apart, and stare up into his amazing eyes, fascinated as his irises change from blue to green to gold and mixtures in between.

"I love you, too, Kitten. I'm pretty sure I have since I first met you and positively sure since I first kissed you outside of the bathroom."

I blink at him. "Wait… you meant to do that?"

Reed huffs out a laugh. "Of course I did. Did you think it was an accident this whole time?"

I bite my lip and shrug. "I figured it was either an accident or a pity kiss," I answer.

"Well, then, let me show you just how un-accidentally I want to kiss you," he says before bringing his mouth to mine once more.

I allow myself to get lost in Reed. In his kiss, in his arms, in the passion I feel from him. Reed may be quiet; he may be my sad boy, but when he feels something, he feels it so strongly, so intensely that it's easy to get caught up with him.

He tugs my shirt up, his eyes seeking permission. I raise my arms in answer, and he sweeps it off of me in one fluid motion. His kisses move from my mouth down the side of my neck. The sensation makes me moan, and Reed bucks his hips up in answer. Every inch of my being suddenly becomes fixated on how good that felt between my legs.

I rock my hips forward and press back into him, and this time, he's the one moaning. His hands go my waist, and he helps guide me back and forth over him as he uses his teeth to move my bra strap out of the way and his skilled tongue works over the flesh of my exposed shoulder and collarbones.

I tug on the back of his shirt, wanting my own free rein of his skin. He leans forward and helps me get his shirt over his head. I toss it aside and run my hands over his smooth chest, taking pleasure in the rumble I extract from him. Reed is slim, but each one of his muscles is clearly defined. I take my time admiring his lean and cut body and find myself thanking any god who's listening for yoba.

"Kitten, please," Reed begs. "I need…" He releases a deep breath. "If it's not too much to ask."

I cut him off. "Ask anything, Reed," I say, dragging my eyes away from his chest and up to his eyes.

He keeps his eyes on mine but doesn't say anything. Instead, he shifts me back a little and unbuttons his jeans. My eyes fall to his hands, but he pauses to lift my chin up. He kisses me softly, hesitantly, like he's asking for permission through his lips. I meet his tongue with mine and feel his hand guiding one of mine from around his neck to place it between us. I feel something hard yet incredibly soft in my hand, like metal covered in velvet.

Reed gasps for air and we both vibrate with his deep moan. He guides my fingers to close around the object and moves it up and down. On an upstroke, I feel moisture, and it helps lessen the friction on the way back down. Reed moves his hand away from mine, and I continue on my own.

"Oh, yes, baby. Just like that. Keep doing that," he whispers hotly.

I feel his hands on my back for a mere moment before my bra drops from my chest. Reed's eyes darken as he takes me in and I use his moment of distraction to look at where my hand is. My eyes go wide for a moment in wonder as I see what I'm holding. I figured as much, but seeing is an entirely different matter. Knowing I am touching him so intimately excites me, and my hands reflexively squeeze. I hear his breath catch, and then he's on me.

His kiss starts at my lips but quickly moves downward. He flicks my nipple with this tongue and my whole body jolts in shock and pleasure. That climbing feeling that I've felt before starts and I bring my other hand around him as well, just to feel like I have something to hold onto.

With his hands now free, Reed takes my other breast in one hand while his mouth takes turns sucking and licking my hardened bud. His other hand snakes between us and presses on my core through my pants. The repeated movement of his hands and mouth pushes me higher and higher until I'm falling, going over that unseen edge and shouting out my pleasure. I feel Reed's body tense before warm liquid coats my stomach and my hands.

I remain in a dazed state of bliss until Reed places a hand over mine, stopping my stroking motion that I didn't realize I was still doing.

"Babe…" he coos, kissing my shoulder before resting his head there for a moment. He turns his head and licks at the heated flesh of my neck. "I love you, Kitten. I am yours, now and forever," he says passionately.

"I love you, too, Reed," I say with a smile before kissing his lips once more.

After we had spent lots more time kissing, he had dragged us to the floor so we could regain our wits and catch our breath. We cuddled and nuzzled, but words were not needed. My skin tingled wherever our skin met, and I explored this lazily, feeling content to lie here for the rest of the day.

"Mmm, this makes touching you even more fun," Reed says after an unmeasured amount of time has passed. "C'mon, Kitten, let's get cleaned up and head home."

He helps me wash off all the stickiness in the washroom, and I laugh as he shakes out his wet hair after a dip under the faucet, the long locks flicking water all over me.

"You ready to go?" he asks me.

I nod and take his hand in mine. As he's locking up the gallery behind us, I nudge his shoulder with mine to get his attention. "Hey, Reed?"

"Yes, Kitten?"

"We should talk art more often," I say with a sly grin worthy of Logan.

Reed beams a smile back at me. "Oh, I plan on talking art with you as much as possible from now on."

With a wink from him and a brief smack to my bottom, we climbed into Finn's truck and made our way home.

CHAPTER TEN

My mouth was watering long before we reached the door to the house. Whatever Tristan was making was filling the air with the most delicious smells. The local shelter always had really nice turkey dinners for the holiday, and even I didn't pass them up. I can only wonder how much better Tristan's dinner would be, if I could eat it.

I frown at the thought, wishing eating was as easy as it used to be.

"You're late," Tristan accused as he came toward us. I offer him a smile that says sorry, but not sorry.

"I don't mind that you went out, but you didn't leave any time for you to eat before we sat down all together," he tells me.

I pout, knowing I'm going to have to smell all of the yummy food for a while before I can have any. Oops.

Dinner is served at the kitchen island instead of the

dining room. I never told them the details about what happened with Uncle, but I suspect that's why they only eat in here now.

To my displeasure, Maksim and Albert are seated around the island as well.

"Glad you two could make it," Remy jokes, giving Reed a playful evil eye. I wave at him as I take my seat at a spot left open next to Jace and Logan.

A loud clattering makes me jump, and my eyes dart to Maksim. "She's carrying more than scent now?! When did this happen? Was it forced? Did they force you?" he asks the last of me, but I just look at him like the crazy person he's turned into.

"Uh…no?" I answer, looking to Remy to see his face turning a scary shade of red.

"This is not proper! One does not play around with the bonding of wolves, especially an Ivaskov!" he exclaims.

I rub at my forehead with the palm of my hand, my headache back in full force and now traveling down my spine to make my back hurt. "Can we just stop with all the Ivaskov stuff? Please?" I say tiredly.

"Excuse me?" Maksim huffs.

I turn my attention to him, meeting eyes so much like my own. "You know, the whole 'Ivaskovs are better than everyone else' thing? No one is better than anyone else, and with the little knowledge I have of your family, I'd have to say that you don't have much to brag about."

Maksim sits back in his chair slowly, just staring at me in horror. "*Our* family," he states.

"What?" I ask, not understanding.

"The Ivaskovs are our family; you're part of it. And

uniting the wolf packs, forming a government that brought peace to our kind and enabled us to thrive not only as wolves but in the human society as well is not something I should take pride in? Our family members were conquerors, peace-bringers, innovators, world-renowned scientists, and leaders; the hell if I won't be proud of that! You should as well, young lady," he chastises.

I sigh heavily, looking down at the empty plate in front of me. "Was," I say.

"What was that?" he asks, maybe not hearing me because I spoke so lowly.

"I said, was. As in, once upon a time, your family was all of those things. Now, though, it's just a name. Your family has turned into a bunch of bullies who experiment with the lives of children, abduct and humiliate and attempt to murder, who only come to the aid of family for what you can get out of them and what they can do for you. And by the way, my family is seated around this table, excluding two of you," I throw out as I push my chair back and stomp from the room.

I'm no mood to listen to him go on about how great and honorable his family is. To quote Finn, actions speak louder than words. And so far, his family's actions have done nothing but tear my world apart, time and time again.

I hear feet pounding on the floor behind me, but I don't bother to look who it is. I know the guys are following me and will probably try to comfort me. I don't want comfort right now though, so I hold my hand up, asking them to stay back. I head out the back door and down the steps of the deck, and out into the yard where

Reed and I do yoba.

The weather has turned colder since I was away, but right now, the chill in the air is a welcome balm to the fire I feel in my heart. The grass is crisp as I take a seat, preparing for the beautiful spectacle Mother Nature greets the world with each evening. The clouds have turned shades of pink, yellows, and blues, cast about like a lost painter. I feel eyes on me from behind, and somehow I just know that the entire dinner party has followed me out here. I sigh, plucking at the grass in front of me. They should have just stayed and had their meal, as waiting for me to eat is pretty pointless these days.

I sense his approach even before I see him take a seat next to me out of the corner of my eye.

"Your wolves have chosen a charming piece of land to call home," he starts.

"Yes," I reply shortly.

"Look, my dear, I had no idea you felt so strongly against our family," Maksim says resignedly.

"It's not like I've kept it a secret."

"Yes, but in my defense, you have chosen to ignore since my arrival here. I know you have a lot to deal with, but I had hoped that you would come around in your own time," he confides. "This isn't how I thought this would go."

I snort. Me neither. "You may have helped my family rescue me, but it came with conditions."

"Your release never had conditions, Kitten," he says after some time.

"It sure seems that way," I tell him honestly.

"I'll admit that the second thought that went through my head after learning about you, is what this means for our pack."

I debate whether or not I want to know the answer to the question I'm about to ask, but I can't help myself. "What was your first thought?"

Maksim doesn't answer straight away, finding the right words. "It was more a jumble of feelings than it was a thought. First was elation at having a granddaughter in the first place. Then, sadness at not having been able to be a proper grandfather. Anger, at whichever of my children kept you from me and raised you outside of the family. Disbelief, confusion, denial, you name it. Your wolves explained your previous situation. I still have mixed feelings about that." He shakes his head.

"I can see how I came as much of a shock to you as you did to me. I've made peace with my life, Maksim. I don't forget the past or push it into some dark corner of my mind. It's a part of me; it's what made me. It was all part of a path that led me here, to my family," I explain.

He chuckles lightly. "You're like your father in that, then. Mikel never dwelled on the past either; he used it as fuel for the future. When my wife and daughters died, it was I who leaned on him for emotional strength. He was an old soul even when was five." He laughs heartily at some long ago memory playing in his head.

"I don't see you as the enemy," I admit quietly. "I just wanted to come back to the guys; that's all I wanted. I see you, Albert, and nearly everyone as a threat to my new family and I'm having a hard time with it. I don't know how to be a princess; I'm just a street kid." I shrug.

Maksim shifts to face me and I turn my head to look at him. "You may have been a street kid, but you've always been a princess. I'll never be able to express the amount of regret I'll always have for not being able to help you, for not being there. The only upside I can give you is that you would have been raised under Marcus' care. From what he did to you recently, I can't imagine that would have been good. Though, had I known of you, you can bet that I would have been fighting for you."

The conversation lapses back into silence, and I give myself a few minutes to imagine what it would have been like if I had been raised by Maksim. Would I have worn cute, ruffled dresses like other little girls? Would kids have played with me on the playground? Would I have had friends? I dismiss the questions as quickly as they come, deeming them useless. None of it matters; I ended up right where I wanted to be all along. With people to love and love me back.

I sigh into the night. "Where do we go from here?" I ask tiredly. This day has been altogether overwhelming.

"We can start by not being enemies. I want to help you; it's what I'm here for. Our pack has been treated unjustly under Marcus' reign of terror, and I want better for them. Actually, I want the best for them. For all of us."

I meet his eyes, so much like my own. "My wolves are the best. Anything that any of us don't know, we'll learn. There's no personal agenda with any of us. We were happy living outside of any pack, until your pack came for us. I could tell them that I don't want this, you know."

"And yet you haven't. Dare I hope that you will embrace your heritage out of duty for the people of your pack?" he asks with hope-filled eyes.

I nod my head slowly. "I will, but I have my own

conditions. I'll let you know what they are once I've discussed them with the guys. My guys have been my pack from the very beginning. I haven't rejected my position outright, because of them. When Uncle's men came for me, they hurt them, too. And I find that unacceptable. With us in charge, that will never happen again. If we happen to help others along the way, then that's great. That will be our job. But my reasons are ultimately selfish; I want to keep my family safe."

"That's a start," Maksim smiles at me.

I smile back. Maybe this won't be so hard after all. We talk at length, asking questions of one another while skirting around the fact that we're related. Albert has taught me about pack laws and procedure, but I ask Maksim to tell me what it's really like to be a part of the pack. What the daily life of an Ivaskov is like. I'm disappointed with much of what he tells me. Especially how the pack does not live in the pack house, but in camps and trailers around the property. It wasn't always that way, but that was one of Uncle's first orders as Alpha. He wanted the grand house to himself.

I tell him how I would like to change certain things, how I would like to offer sanctuary to other changed wolves, and the benefits of doing so. Maksim doesn't agree to some of my suggestions, but it doesn't matter. By the end of the conversation, the dew has settled around us, and Albert has been brought over to take notes on things that could be done immediately before I've even gone there.

As the conversation dies down, Remy clears his throat behind us. I know they've listened to every word, but they kept their distance and let us work through it.

"Why don't we head back inside? Tristan and Kitten can take their meal in the living room and pick out a movie for us to watch, while the rest of us eat in the kitchen and clear up."

"Sounds good, Remy." I smile shyly at him, a tad embarrassed over my earlier fit and keeping them from their dinner.

CHAPTER ELEVEN

Moments later, I find myself seated in the red living room, facing Tristan as he sits next to me, a plate of warmed up food in hand. "I'm sorry I ruined your dinner, Tris. It smelled splendid when we came in earlier; it still does, actually."

"It's no biggie, sweetie. You and Maksim were bound to have it out eventually, and I'm just happy that we're past it now," he says as he holds up a bite of turkey covered in gravy for me.

We forgo conversation as he feeds both himself and me. His food is a yummy as always, each bite a savory combination of sweet, greasy, and salty, as every Thanksgiving dinner should be.

When I've had enough, I sit back and pat my tummy, thankful for this amazing boy who goes above and beyond to take care of me. "So you've been speaking to Maksim, then?" I ask out of curiosity.

"Yeah, him and Albert both, we all have. I understand where your anger stems from, and I don't disagree with you, but that's between you guys. We knew which path you'd take, if only because we knew you'd see it as an opportunity to help others. It's kind of your thing." Tristan winks before popping the last bite of gravy-smothered biscuit into his mouth. It's hard not to stare at his luscious lips as he chews.

When he starts to get up to take the plate to the kitchen, I place my hand on his arm, stopping him. "Wait, can we just…have a few moments to ourselves?" I ask, biting my lip.

Tristan smiles his magnificent Tristan smile and sets the dish aside on the coffee table. "I thought you'd never ask," he responds playfully.

I spend the next half hour or so wrapped up in Tristan's arms, cuddling and Kissing. Oh, the kissing. Kissing my sweet boy is like floating on a river of chocolate, marshmallow pillow included. His lips are plumped nicely, adding a luxurious quality to each peck and nibble. I really like to nibble on that bottom lip.

He pulls away reluctantly, brushing his thumb over my now- swollen lips. "The guys are getting restless; I can hear them. They're going to bring in their desserts, pie and whatnot, but would you like me to make us some popcorn?"

"I'd rather keep kissing you, but I'll settle for popcorn," I tell him with a smile.

He laughs, giving me one last parting kiss before leaving the room. A minute or two later, the rest of the guys filter into the room. Ash sits next to me, and I giggle at his dessert.

"What?" he asks defensively through a mouthful.

"Nothing," I giggle some more. When Tristan said the others were bringing treats in, I didn't expect Ash to bring in an entire pumpkin pie with at least half a carton of vanilla ice cream on top.

Finn takes over finding a movie for us to watch before taking a seat next to me. Jace brings in a few throw blankets for those who want them, and he decides to tuck the softest one around me before sitting at my feet so we can share it. I reach my hand out and play with his golden hair, scratching at his scalp with my fingernails. He seems to like that.

"Huh, I suppose you might be right, Albert," Maksim says curiously from across the room.

"About what?" I ask.

"Well, my dear, you have already claimed three mates, which is odd by itself, but Albert here was telling me that you might be mated with all eight of these wolves."

I blink at him a few times. "Well, yeah," I state slowly. Seemed fairly obvious to me.

"You really think so?" Finn asks, intrigued. Albert nods his head quickly. "She's shown no preference toward any of you, even after she mated with the others."

"And that proves something?" Logan chimes in. He takes a handful of popcorn from the bowl, dropping pieces as he brings it to his mouth.

Maksim sits back, stretching his legs out in front of him. "When I first met you, I had thought she was just your friend, someone you cared about. The big guy's stuffed wolf made me have doubts, though. Then, I thought maybe she was just Remington's intended mate and his pack was feeling the loss their Alpha felt. Since I've been in this room, several of you have touched her affectionately, and not one of you has tried to rip the head off of one of the others. It has been that way ever since we recovered her. I assure you, if you were not mates, that would not be the case."

"Is this a normal thing for born wolves, then? Having multiple mates?" Logan inquires. He's now claimed the bowl entirely and every time he digs in for more popcorn, some spills over and lands on Remy. Remy frowns deeply at him before standing and huffing away to sit in a safer seat.

Maksim makes a non-committal sound in his throat. "There's no way to be sure if this situation has ever arisen, or if there are any other females capable of taking on more than one mate. I've never seen it myself, but it's not an impossibility. However, due to our shortage of females and the competition for them, I can't imagine anyone would be willing to share, even if she were destined for more than one mate."

"So you're saying that she won't be forced to choose one of us as her mate, even for just the sake of naming an Alpha for the pack?" Finn questions, doubt filling his words.

"I would say that the idea of having eight Alphas would be an issue, but you boys have done well for yourselves for this long, and have been managing your own affairs just fine. As long as that continues, I don't foresee any complications within the pack," Albert tells us, looking to Maksim for confirmation.

"So all I have to do is bite the others, and they're all

mine? Forever? Jace didn't even like me when we met, so how is that possible?" I ask. From my understanding, mates are like soulmates, always searching for one another until they're found.

Maksim nods his head. "Mates can have different effects on each other depending on their dominance level. Some males might feel extremely protective over their mate if they're more dominant, or have an instantaneous friendship-like feeling, a sense of belonging. Some mates tend to be empathic toward their mate, feeling their pain, pleasure, and happiness, something that draws them together from first sight. On rare occasions, mates with equal levels of dominance can feel threatened by one another and are argumentative at the beginning of their relationship, testing each other while still not able to pull away from one another completely. What seals the deal as mates is if the female allows the male to touch them and be close. Female wolves tend only to want the touch of their mate, even from birth, except for members of her family and other females," Maksim explains.

Tristan moves to Remy's abandoned spot and steals some of Logan's popcorn. "That would explain how someone as beautiful as Kitten remained untouched for long," he says with a wink. His normally soothing voice is sultry and sends shivers all along my skin. Oh, how I love that voice of his.

"Well, that, and for a total shorty, she runs pretty fast," Logan pipes up, elbowing Tristan and spilling popcorn all over him. Tristan only shakes his head at Logan and brushes away the fallen snack.

Our attention turns back to the movie and after a while, Ash leans forward to place the empty pie pan on the table. "That was better than the last one you made. Thanks, man," he says to Tristan before patting his tummy with a sigh.

Logan snorts. "Did you get enough there, big guy? I'm surprised you didn't lick the pan clean."

"Your point?" Ash challenges.

Logan shrugs a slim shoulder. "Eh, just that your fat ass nearly killed me twice when you landed on me," he finishes with an evil smile.

I frown as I look Ash over carefully. Black-as-night hair to his shoulders, strong jaw, broad shoulders, arms that look like he could lift a mountain, his chest and stomach well defined even when sitting idly as he is. Even his thighs are massive mounds of corded muscle. "Ash isn't fat," I tell Logan when I'm finished with my assessment.

Remy groans. "Do me a favor and never look at Ash like that when I'm in the room again, Kitten," he says as he adjusts himself to a more comfortable position.

Ash throws a massive arm around my shoulders, and I lean into his chest, cuddling into him.

"Don't worry, baby girl; he's just jealous of all this muscle." And as if to prove a point, he tightens his whole body, flexing said muscles. I shiver in delight.

Logan snorts and tilts his chin up. "Uh, no, Fatty McFatpants, you can keep your gladiator physique, and I'll stick with my classically charming, model-like good looks, thanks."

I roll my eyes as those two continue their good-natured teasing and take in the sight of the three good-looking guys sitting across from me. Remy, Reed, and Kellan continue to watch the movie playing, and I try not to sigh at their handsomeness.

Sadly, Reed looks my way and catches me staring, cutting off my perusal of them. I look away quickly, trying not to let on that I've been staring at them all for a while now, but a quick glance at Reed lets me know I wasn't quick enough, if his slightly smug and satisfied smile is anything to go by.

"Want to know something cool, Kitten?" he asks.

I pretend that my face isn't on fire and nod my head, meeting his multi-colored eyes. I may be slightly embarrassed, but I'm not ashamed. It's not my fault they are so fun to look at; they should try to be less beautiful if they don't want people to stare.

"Finn, here, actually knows how to fly those beasts." Reed continues as he prods the man in question with an elbow to the ribs. Finn's handful of popcorn goes flying onto Remy, who shoots Finn a glare.

"W-what?" Finn looks between Reed and me.

"You really know how to fly airplanes?" I ask him.

"Oh. Yeah. I spent some time as a fighter pilot in WWII and flew commercially for a while after that. Now I just fly smaller aircraft for fun every now again." He shrugs like it's no big deal.

I can practically feel my eyes popping out of my head. "Wow, Finn! Really? That's so cool." I bounce slightly in excitement and Ash gives a squeeze to make me stay put.

Finn's cheeks blush slightly, and he smiles at me, holding out his box of popcorn in offering.

Before I can accept or decline, Reed's hands shoot out as he exclaims, "Duuuuude! Did you see that? That chick is really a robot. Totally makes sense now," sending the container flying, with most of the popcorn landing on Remy. Remy glares deeply at Finn before standing and moving away to sit at the end of the couch by himself. He eyes Albert, the closest person to him now, and looks approvingly at his popcorn-free hands.

I giggle uncontrollably at Finn's lost expression. He looks over at me and gives me a 'did you see all that' look. I nod my head in answer, and he shakes his head, smiling at me and sitting back in his seat, seeming defeated by his crazy family members. I snuggle back into Ash, my head on his chest, and drift in and out of sleep as the movie plays on.

***

Ash insists on taking me to bed while the rest of the guys smoked imported cigars or something, a gift Maksim had brought for the guys. My eyelids have been fighting to stay open for about a half hour now. Ash leads me to his room and sits me on the bed and now I watch him as he removes my socks.

"Would you like a shower, or a bath, baby girl?" he questions, looking up at me as he rubs his rough hand over my toes.

"Bath," I reply sleepily.

"Wait here then," he instructs before striding to the bathroom.

Moments later he returns, grasping my hand within his huge one. Ash has already started the bathwater running, and he even added bubbles.

"Come, Little One, I will wash you, if you'll let me," Ash's deep voice rumbles out as he guides me to the steaming room.

My lids try to close on their own, without my permission, and my sleepy brain barely registers what he's doing as he strips my clothes from me. I'm lifted by my hips and placed in soothing warm water. I bend my knees and lay my head on top of them, opening my eyes to see Ash kneeling beside the tub, his blackish eyes smoldering at me. He gently pushes my hair off my back, his fingers lightly brushing across my skin. I watch as he wets a washcloth in the water and lathers some body wash on it. His free hand cups some water and drizzles it over my skin and he washes my back in gentle circles; his eyes focused on his task. While he watches me, I look at him.

"I love how you take care of me," I tell him softly.

Ash leans forward and presses a hard kiss to my lips. "You take care of us, too, baby girl."

I smile goofily at him. "I love you, Ash."

"Love you, too," he rumbles back at me.

I let him clean every part of me, wondering if I'm not as shy or as embarrassed as I should be because I'm sleepy, or if nakedness just doesn't mean to me now what it used to, or because I know that Ash loves me and cares about me. I suppose it doesn't matter.

He takes his time towel-drying my hair gently once we're done, and wraps a different towel around me, carrying me to his room. Once we reach his bed, I release the towel and crawl under the covers on my own.

Ash flicks the light off, and I hear him shuffling around before the bed dips so much that I roll towards him. I giggle as I scoot back over so he has room. I shouldn't have bothered because as soon as he's under the blanket, his big hands reach out for me and I'm gathered against his rock-hard body. One hand moves to the back of my head and guides my face to his neck, placing me exactly where I like to be. His scent washes over me, and I melt into his hold.

"Where's AJ?" I whisper to him in the dark.

"I put him in the chair and covered him up," he replies.

I find that odd, but don't comment on it. Instead, I cuddle closer to Ash, stealing his body heat and soaking up the comfort that being around him always makes me feel. Ash grunts and moves his middle away from me. I scoot closer anyway.

"You're tired, baby," Ash sighs.

"The bath woke me up a little," I tell him, not understanding what being tired has to do with me snuggling up to him.

Ash rolls so that he's hovering over me, supporting his weight on his elbow. "Is that so?"

"Yes."

"Then you don't mind if I have some dessert, do you?" he asks hotly.

"No?" I answer, confused.

The bed shakes as Ash pushes up and rips the blankets away from the both of us, sitting back on his knees, gazing down at me in the moonlight streaming through the window. His face is cast in shadow, but I can hear his breathing slightly increase.

A hand comes up to cup my cheek for a moment before gliding over my shoulder, down my arm, grazing my thigh and calf until he cups my foot. He lifts my toes to his mouth and places gentle kisses over the tops of each one, repeating the process on my other foot. I feel his hands shake slightly as he slides them from my ankles up to my knees, parting them.

I inhale sharply when I feel his lips touch the sensitive skin on the inside of my knee. He flicks his tongue out for a taste, and his resulting purr sends shivers up my spine. I bring my hand to the back of his head, wanting to touch him back in any way I can. Now that I know where this is leading, I help him and spread my legs wider. Embarrassment rears its ugly head, and I blush, but I don't try to hide myself. I want to be intimate with Ash, in any way that he'll let me.

Ash takes a deep breath before relaxing his body down on the bed. His lips move to my inner thigh, and my hips jump upward of their own accord, wanting his mouth on my core desperately. The scruff on his face only adds to the intense feelings and excitement for what's about to come.

"I've wanted to do this for so long, Kitten. You have no idea." His breath falls over my skin, and I moan. Just a little higher, please.

My eyes go wide, and my mouth falls slack as I feel a jolt of pain, followed by pleasure, as he sinks his teeth into my thigh, so close to my core that the electric pulse shoots right to my button, and I explode, shouting out his name.

Ash pulls his teeth from me and laps at his bite with a few licks before moving his tongue right where I want it, and he laps hungrily at me. I feel his tongue prodding my entrance and my hands grip at his head, not knowing if I am pulling him closer or pushing him away, as it feels amazing, but also like too much at the same time.

My Shadow is relentless as he makes me explode for him over and over again. I beg, I plead that it's too much, and demand that he never stops. His groans at my pleasure only make me hotter, and I'm sure I'm going to melt into a puddle at any minute.

Ash's head comes up, and he kisses my belly lightly before crawling up my body, only stopping to take a quick pull at each of my breasts, then bringing his mouth to mine in a searing, hot kiss. His face is slick with my wetness, but under my own flavor, I taste Ash, and I feel an inexplicable need to show appreciation for the tongue that loved me so well. I try telling his tongue with mine that I absolutely adore it, and come to the conclusion that Ash has completely fried my brain.

We pant heavily at each other as he pulls his head back from our kissing. He shifts up, and I tilt my head back so I can still see his face. He aligns himself at my core, his eyes seeking permission, and I lick my lips hungrily, wrapping my legs around his waist in answer.

Ash moves in slowly, pushing in a little of himself at a time and backing out, just to push in more the next time. I try to regulate my breathing and concentrate on the stretching feeling inside of me. If Reed felt huge in my hands, then Ash is a monster, and as he keeps pushing I wonder how much more of him there is, and if all of it needs to go in.

Thankfully, I don't have to wonder for too much longer. With a deep thrust and a loud growl, he seats himself fully inside me, and my core spasms as his whole body vibrates on top of me and inside of me. I press a kiss to his chest in front of my face and Ash takes that as a sign to move. He sets a slow rhythm at first, building into a pounding thrusting that has my body shifting up the bed with each movement of his powerful hips. My nails rake over his wide back as my pleasure climbs higher, and this only makes him go harder. My name falls from his lips in heated whispers and grunts, and it's more than I can take. As stars dance in my vision, I bring my head up and bite down on his chest, eliciting a pleasing roar out of Ash as he slams into me hard one last time.

I feel him pulse and expand inside of me before a pleasant warmth fills me, flooding my insides, and Ash relaxes more of his weight on me. Normally, he'd be crushing me, but I revel in the feel of his weight on top of me right now. It's oddly comforting.

Ash presses a lingering kiss to my forehead and gently extracts himself from me, and I try not to wince. He gathers me close again, and I drape myself over him, relaxation and exhaustion settling in as the sun is peeking through the pink sky outside of the window. I hear Ash tell me he loves me, but I don't remember if I managed to say it back or not as sleep rushes in to claim me.

CHAPTER TWELVE

Kellan and I return from the hospital, where there was no change in Mikey's condition, and meet Finn for my lesson. Today, he promised to teach me how to use a cell phone. Instead of leaving us in the library like he usually does, Kellan decides to rest on Big Jace, picking up the second Harry Potter book that Finn and I take turns reading. It's one of my favorite stories, and because it's an entirely made-up world, it's fun to read it slowly like normal people do, and imagine myself there, even though imagining things I've seen is hard for me sometimes.

After Finn shows me how to place calls, send notes to people, and take pictures, he shows me how to use the internet, and we set up an electronic mailbox for me. I send notes to some of the guys, giggling at all the silly faces I add to them. Logan sends me back a moving picture of a cat jumping at the sight of a cucumber; it just replays and replays. After I watch it play for the fifth time, Finn places his hand over mine, chuckling at me.

"We haven't gotten to memes yet," he says playfully.

"Can I call Remy?" I ask, pulling up my phone book.

Kellan laughs from his spot by the window, his eyes closed as he rests on the bear. "You should ask him if his refrigerator is running."

"And you don't have to ask to make a call, Kitten. It's your phone; I told you that," Finn adds.

I push the green phone next to Remy's name and hold the silver phone up to my ear. "Hello, Love," he answers after two rings.

"Hi, Remy!" I chirp excitedly. I've known what phones are for a long time, and almost everyone has a small one like this now, but I've only used one once before, and the idea of having a conversation with someone a long distance away is still exciting to me.

"I see they've finally given you your phone, not that you really need one at the moment, but Jace has been on me ever since he bought it. Do you like it?" he chats.

"I do, this is fun. Where are you?" I ask as I kick off my shoes and swing my feet back and forth.

"I'm at the office downtown. Just boxing up some things and preparing to close it down," he tells me.

"Close it down?" I question.

"It would be pointless to keep the office here once we move, and I mostly work at home anyway," he says, and I hear papers shuffling in the background. So cool.

"Why would we move? And where do you work?" My back starts to hurt from sitting in the hard, wooden chair, so I get up and pace the floor, rubbing at my spine with my free hand.

"To the pack house in Colorado. You've decided to take on the role of Ivaskov princess, so it's inevitable. Maybe we can speak about this when I'm home; I'll be back in a few hours," Remy states.

"Okay," I sigh. "Oh! I forgot, is your refrigerator running? Kellan told me to ask, though I'm sure we could go see ourselves."

Remy's laugh rumbles through the phone. "It's meant to be a prank, though it seems they didn't explain it to you. Ask Finn about it. I'll see you soon, Love."

"Okay, I'll ask him," I say, but Remy doesn't say anything back. I sit for a minute, wondering what he's doing now. "Are you still holding the phone?" I ask.

He laughs again. "Yes, Kitten, I'm still here. When I said I'll see you soon, I meant I was getting off the phone, or hanging up," he explains.

"But you didn't get off the phone," I state slowly.

"Because something told me you didn't understand that I was saying goodbye, and I wasn't risking a kick to the shin later if you thought I hung up on you." He chuckles more now.

"Oh. Goodbye then, or see you soon," I tell him before hurrying to push the red button.

"I lover, I mean, I *really* love her," Kellan exclaims, speaking to Finn I presume.

Finn sighs. "I apologize. Maybe we should have gone over how to close out a conversation," he tells me.

I scratch at my itchy skin as I shake my head at him. "I know how to have a conversation, it's just easier to tell when it's over in person. I can manage on my own."

"What's the matter, Kitten? You've been squirmy since before we even left the hospital," Kellan says as he gets up, making his way over to me.

"I don't know." I shrug. "I just feel uncomfortable. I'm sore and itchy."

Kellan nods his head, looking over me critically. "Sounds about right. Have you experienced any soreness in your gums? Feeling like your bones are in pain? Skin feeling tight? Headaches?"

My eyes widen, and I nod my head. It's not all of the time, but I've felt each of these things. Kellan gives me a lopsided grin before continuing, "There are a few medications I can give you if you get to feeling too uncomfortable, but it's nothing to worry about. There's no way to tell if you'll be able to shift or not, but it sounds like your wolf is getting restless. If you experience anything else abnormal, come and tell me. You can always talk to me, Kitten. Whatever happens, we'll get through it together." I frown in confusion but nod at him anyway. He gives me a hug, then turns me so I can face Finn, who also hugs me.

I smile nervously. "But I'm fine, though, right?" I feel the need for clarification here.

Finn smiles down at me shyly. "Yes, you're fine. Forgive us if we're just a bit hopeful."

"Hopeful of what?" I ask as Finn tucks my hair behind my ear, his thumb lingering on my chin.

Kellan steps closer behind me, pressing a kiss to my head as his hands rest comfortably on my hips. "That you'll shift like us. That you'll be like us and live as long as we do," he explains

"Oh," I say, looking up at Finn's gorgeous green eyes, knowing that's the only difference between him and his twin behind me, appearance-wise. "I want to be a wolf like you guys are."

Finn smiles beautifully, and I have the sudden urge to kiss him. I place my hands on his shoulders and lean up on my toes. After a moment of just standing there awkwardly, I put my feet flat on the ground and deflate a little. He's too tall to kiss.

Kellan chuckles lowly behind me, his warm breath feathering over my ear. "She wants you to kiss her," he tells his brother.

Finn's eyes go wide. "Oh! I didn't...sorry," he says before bending down and giving me a peck on the lips.

I pout for a second before I grip his shoulders tightly and tug, letting him know I want him back down here. He complies, and I press my lips to his gently, enjoying the smooth, cushiony curves of his lips. I flick my tongue out to taste him, and he gasps a bit in shock, my tongue entering his mouth out of instinct. His hand comes up to hold the side of my face, and I sigh into the kiss in contentment.

I feel Kellan pulling away behind me, but I place a hand over his on my hip, wanting him to stay. I reach my free hand back, raising my arm to wrap my fingers in his silky black hair.

Finn takes a step forward, effectively pinning me between the two twins. My body heats, and I hum my approval. Turning my head, I meet grass-green eyes and lift my chin, hoping he'll kiss me, too. Kellan dives in, trapping my bottom lip between his teeth and tugging slightly. I hiss at the pleasure-pain it causes, though a second later his tongue sweeps in to take the small sting away.

Finn moves his mouth down the column of my neck,

sucking my skin into his mouth. I lose track of what he's doing as Kellan's hand snakes around to my front, one finger circling my belly button before starting a lazy journey up my ribcage.

I release Kellan's mouth as I gasp in shock. Finn's teeth pierce my neck, the heat and electricity of the mating mark flooding my body. My head rolls back to lean on Kellan's chest as Finn laps at me, drinking deeply. The constant rumble of his chest makes my breasts ache with need. As if reading my mind, Kellan's fingers finally reach my bra, tugging the cup down so he can tug playfully on my peaked nipple. I moan loudly, enjoying every sensation but needing more desperately.

Feeling bold, I release Kellan's hair and move my hand to Finn's neck. I tug him away gently, then bring him in close, pressing a small kiss to his throat, before working my way around to his neck. I bite him harder than I meant to, but he moans out his pleasure anyway. I smooth my hands down to his waist, unbuttoning his pants and reach inside, finding the soft but rock-hard object I was looking for. Finn hisses through his teeth, his head now resting on my shoulder.

"Arms up," Kellan whispers hotly in my ear.

I only pout for a moment, as I have to let go of Finn to accomplish this. Kellan strips me of my shirt, my bra following shortly after. Both of his hands come up to cup me, and I reach for Finn again. I slide my hand the way I had with Reed, and to my delight, beads of moisture appear at the end as it had before. Kellan's mouth works its way up the other side of my neck until he captures my lips again. Finn holds onto my waist like it's a lifeline.

"Mmm...I need you..." Finn groans before cutting

off with a gasp of pleasure.

"What do you need?" I manage between kisses with Kellan.

Finn drags his teeth over my bare shoulder before responding. "Your mouth, Kitten. I want your mouth."

"Oh." I blink for a second after pulling away from Kellan. Have I been kissing his brother too long?

Kellan nips at my ear, reading my mind again. "That's not what he means. Come lie down on the pillows," he says before tugging me over to the pile of pillows where Big Jace sits.

I move to lie down, but Kellan holds my waist, stopping me. Instead, Finn sinks to his knees in front of Kellan and me and I follow. In an instant, Finn's lips are on mine in a heated kiss, his hands palming my breasts before smoothing down my sides to my yoga pants. His fingers dip inside before I feel them sliding down. Kellan helps me get them over my knees and all the way off, my kiss with Finn never breaking.

I chase his pouty lips as he repositions himself to sitting, then to lying on his back. Kellan's hands smooth up and down my exposed back, from shoulder to hip, then back again. The next pass taking his hands down my bottom, one hand staying on my hip, the other using a finger to slick through my wetness.

"Oh God, you're so wet, Kitten," he whispers hotly behind me. I push my hips back at him, wanting more, but not being able to voice it. His fingers continue to tease at me until I feel like punching him. Finally, he places his long, deft fingers at my entrance and plunges them into me, twisting on the way back out. I have to pull away from Finn to shout my approval of his twin's actions. Kellan uses his thumb to play with my button as his fingers continue their maddening stroking.

"Kitten," Finn gets my attention. "Please, can I have your mouth?" His question is boarding on a plea.

Some of the hazy lust leaves my body as I start to wonder if I'm doing something wrong. Does he mean kiss? Because Kellan said that's not what he meant. Seemingly out of nowhere, images of some of the guys from the ice rink come to mind, leaning against lockers with their pants down and girls' heads bobbing back and forth. Is this what he means? Oddly, the thought excites me. I slowly crawl back towards Kellan, keeping my eyes on Finn for signs of disapproval, but what I see are his eyes darkening before his head drops back with a prayer.

I tilt my head to the side as my face reaches between his legs, wondering exactly how this all works. I bring both hands to it and slide them back and forth, watching as more wet stuff comes out of the tip. I lose my concentration momentarily as Kellan uses his knees to part my legs wider and presses down on the middle of my back, firmly but gently.

"Use your tongue, then take as much of him as you can into your mouth," he says distractedly from behind me, his fingers parting me below. The slow slide of his tongue on my core almost causes me to collapse on top of Finn. He reaches out to my face, pushing his hand through my hair as I stare blankly, unseeing for several moments as his brother works his mouth over me, stealing my wits from me.

I remember that I'm supposed to be doing something and take the task in hand. Literally. I tentatively lick at the beads of moisture on Finn's manhood, much like I would an ice cream cone. He seems to like it, as he brings his head up to look at me, eyelids at half-mast, pillowy lips parted, his hand fisting in my hair.

I place my lips over him, relaxing my jaw so I won't bite him. I bring my head forward, taking as much as I can before cutting off my airway.

"Jesus, Kitten!" Finn whispers. I pull back and lick him again. It's kind of fun actually. I push down, sucking as I come back up and lick at the gooey stuff at the tip my action caused. It's almost like a reward for doing the action. I decide I like this game. I nod my head faster, keeping my hand at the base to keep his still and because that part won't fit in my mouth.

After a while, and two explosions later, one from me, one from Finn, Kellan insists that they switch places. Kellan is more verbal than Finn was, telling me new, fun things to do with my tongue in between his panting and praising of me. Turns out that if you lick around the mushroom top, you can make a guy go speechless.

Behind me, though, Finn had stopped licking at me, and I feel his hardness gliding between my legs, slowly. As if asking a question. I press my hips back at him, saying yes to whatever it is because that feels amazing on my button. He then lines himself up and slowly pushes into me. I nearly swallow Kellan whole as I attempt to moan and suck on him at the same time. He seems to like that, though, as his hips buck up off the pillows and he shouts a curse word.

After a moment or two, I decided that this was fun as well, as Finn would pound into me from behind, pressing me forward and onto Kellan. I didn't even have to move my head that much. I was just starting to see stars when

Finn froze behind me, flooding me with his warmth and whispering he loves me. He pulls away from me, gently, collapsing on the pillows beside me. I get one last lick in with Kellan before he quickly pulls me up, flipping us around until I'm the one lying down. He adjusts himself between us and starts a furious pace that leaves me breathless and clawing at his back in moments. It only takes minutes for me to reach my peak, still half worked up from Finn, and we're both shouting our pleasure out into the room. I feel Kellan coating my core with his warmth, and he leans down to kiss my forehead before collapsing on my other side. He pulls toward me and lays an arm over my sweaty and exhausted body. Finn rolls over to us, and once again I'm sandwiched between the gorgeous twins. My heart rate slows and I lift a tired arm to drape it over Finn before my heavy eyelids close. I just need a moment or two to rest.

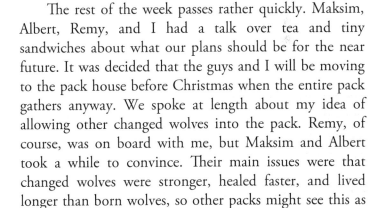

The rest of the week passes rather quickly. Maksim, Albert, Remy, and I had a talk over tea and tiny sandwiches about what our plans should be for the near future. It was decided that the guys and I will be moving to the pack house before Christmas when the entire pack gathers anyway. We spoke at length about my idea of allowing other changed wolves into the pack. Remy, of course, was on board with me, but Maksim and Albert took a while to convince. Their main issues were that changed wolves were stronger, healed faster, and lived longer than born wolves, so other packs might see this as us gathering forces and put them on edge. Remy's and my argument was that all of the above was true, so we'd win that fight hands down if it came to it. Another point was that being as resilient as my guys were made them dangerous. Albert had mentioned that we could make rules as to how many we accept, or they had to meet certain criteria, but I shot that down, getting the others to agree to make the decision on a person by person basis.

Logan pretended to have a hissy fit over news of the move. Not that he minded the change of scenery, just that he hardly had any time to prepare for it. He and Albert had moved quickly onto a long conversation about room sizes, en-suite bathrooms, and closet space. Albert was able to answer most of the questions quickly and was able to get a hold of some of the household staff for Logan to speak to at the pack house. I had helped him a bit with his design ideas and insisted that Reed's cloud bed from here be taken with us on our move. I also came up with an idea for his room, since he has such a hard time with it. Most of the things we bought online or had specially made were going to be shipped or created in Colorado and Logan will deal with it all when we arrive, putting it all together. It was actually a lot of fun.

Reed took me with him to the gallery a couple more times as well. Once just to pick out a few pieces we'd like for our new home, and another to meet the manager he hired to take over the place when we left. He explained how he actually had a few galleries and student art studios all over the place, so this was nothing for him, and if he felt like it, he'd open a new one in Colorado, but he hasn't decided yet. He mentioned maybe focusing on his own art for a while. I love the idea of hanging out with him, watching him as he paints.

I also learned so much about the guys. Like how Jace

works in real estate and owns properties all over the world. How Tristan is a two-star chef, and he continually goes through cooking schools to work his way from the bottom, all the way to the top again. Speaking of which, Finn also continues to go to school from time to time, though he tends to stick to traditional colleges, and sometimes even teaches. The more I learn about them, the more amazing I know they are, and the luckier I feel to have them in my life.

I wake up and yawn, stopping midway through as pain radiates from my gums. I wince and close my mouth quickly. Someone is drumming loudly, and it's a wonder that I've slept through it this long. There's a constant rhythm, but it doesn't sound like music, more like thudding.

"Ash," I whisper. My eyes go wide, and I scream in fear, or at least I think I do, as my whisper sounds like I shouted at the top of my lungs right into my own ears. The thudding gets louder and with shock, I realize that it's my heartbeat. The other drumming noise is coming from Ash, who is curled around me in his oversized bed.

I shake him roughly, waking him. "Ash," I try again, quieter this time. I whine in frustration when even that hurts my ears.

He stirs, taking one look at me and shoots up from the bed, alert and looking for the threat that has me so terrified. He takes in a lungful of air, his eyes checking every inch of the room before his shoulders unbunch themselves, and he looks to me with worry framing his dark features. I wave my hands frantically at my ears, picking up the sound of displaced air as I do so.

"Wha-" he starts, but I shake my head quickly at him, putting my hands up as if to block his words from reaching me. His brows come together in confusion, and he tilts his head to the side.

I wish I could fawn over his powerful, naked body right now, but I'm freaking out, and I can't even tell him why! What is happening to me? Other sounds reach my ears, the clattering of pans, Logan singing a fast song about telling him what you really, really want, footsteps thudding down the stairs, Remy coughing to clear his throat. It's all too much and tears stream down my face, as I'm sure my ears are bleeding now. I grab two pillows from the bed and shove them at my ears; it doesn't help.

Ash stands at the end of the bed, watching me. His eyes are wide, and his mouth is parted. He looks like he's about to shout for someone, but notices me tensing up. He thinks better of that, thankfully. Instead, he shoots me a brief, sympathetic look, uncovers AJ, and hands him to me before grabbing a pair of jeans and leaving the room. I can tell he tried to close it gently, but the *snick* sound it made sounded like a gunshot at close range.

I follow his thundering footsteps through the house, wondering if he's going to go tell them all that I've gone crazy. I hug AJ to my chest tightly, biting my lip in worry before I remember, too late, that my mouth feels like all my teeth have been ripped out. I focus on the teddy-wolf, stroking its fake fur to calm myself. The more I freak out, the louder I hear my heartbeat.

I focus on Ash as he very quietly gathers everyone else in the house and they walk to the back door together, sounding like a herd of elephants. They go outside, and I run to the window to see them. They walk all the way out to the tree line before anyone speaks.

Kellan waves to me as he turns around. "Can you hear me, Kitten?" he asks, and it sounds like a whisper. I sag in relief and nod my head.

"And you can see us clearly?" he continues. I nod again. "Anything else strange going on?"

I nod once more waving a hand in front of my mouth. Kellan looks at the other guys with a happy smile on his face. Logan bounces excitedly, but Jace slaps a hand over his mouth before he can shout anything.

"Don't be afraid, Kitten. We thought you may not be able to shift after you were changed and nothing happened for so long, except for your scent being different, but it seems that it just took you a while," Kellan explains with a shrug.

Shift? As in change into a wolf like they do? I don't know if I'm more scared or excited. I mean, I want to run around and play with them as a wolf, but it probably hurts, right? Bones cracking and shifting into different forms. I shudder at the thought. Sounds like torture, although the guys have never complained about it. I shift from foot to foot, wishing I could ask all the questions building inside of me.

"It shouldn't last for more than a few days, Love," Remy tells me from across the yard. "We'll remain mostly outside of the house for your comfort, though a couple of us will stay close to keep an eye on you. Hang in there."

Remy talks to Reed and Finn, telling them to shift because wolves are quieter, and Kellan tells me if I get desperate, to swish salt water around in my mouth to help with the ache. He warned me that the running faucet might hurt my ears, though. I pouted at them before slinking back to the bed. I don't want to be by myself; I want to be around them.

I buried myself under the pillows and blankets and eventually drifted off and on for who knows how long. My muscles began to ache, and it was hard to find a comfortable position to lay in. Rolling my eyes, because I couldn't even sigh, I got out of bed to stretch, my spine feeling tight and itchy. I sniff the air and my tummy growls at whatever Tristan must be cooking in the kitchen.

To pass the time, I look out the window. The guys are outside in their wolf forms, Logan trying to pounce on a butterfly, Reed rolling around on his back, and the others lazing about in the sunny yard. I sniff the air again, and my mouth waters like crazy. With the window partially open, I notice that the wonderful smell is coming from outside. The pain in my gums intensifies and my attention shifts to the trees behind the boys. My eyes track several small movements, and a growl rises from my throat. Something was out there, and it smelled delicious. I want it. No, I need it.

Before I knew what I was doing, I was running through the house, out the back door, and down the steps of the porch. I paid no attention to anything around me as the smell of whatever was in the woods lured me straight to it. My ears, gums, and sore muscles fled my mind as I got closer to my target. My viewpoint seemed off, and I was closer to the ground than I normally was, but I couldn't stop until I found whatever was out here.

A twig snapping gets my attention, and I chase after it. Ahead of appeared a spotted deer with pointy antlers, running full speed away from me. Adrenaline shoots through me, and all thought leaves my head except one word. Mine.

It seemed like in a blink, I was running, then I was face first in a bloody carcass. It should have disgusted me, but it was the tastiest thing I have ever eaten. I chew happily, making high-pitched sounds of glee. Something nudges my leg, and I growl before turning and snapping my teeth at it. I stop instantly when I realize it's Tristan's sand-colored wolf. My ears go back in shame for being so harsh, and I move over to let him eat beside me. It felt natural, and I didn't allow myself to question it.

Something occurs to me, though; eating a deer, low to the ground, growling, ears back...oh my God! I'm a wolf! I twist my head to look around at my body, moving in a circle as I tried to see more of myself. I yelp and stumbled awkwardly around, not knowing what to do with myself now that I realize I'm an animal.

A huffing sound gets me to sit still, and I look over to Remington's big red wolf. His silver eyes regard me with amusement, and he takes a step forward, towering over me. I sit down and lift my head to see him, keeping him in my sights through the corner of my eye. He hums in approval, licking at my nose. I bark happily at him and weave my way through his tall legs, my back and tail brushing up against his chest and belly. Ash sits off to the side, his tail thumping loudly on the fallen leaves on the ground. I make my way over to him and brush my side against his, feeling him pressing back into me.

I feel restless, full of way too much energy. Remy watches me, his light eyes shining with pride, mixed with something unreadable. I walk back over to him, rubbing my side against his, delighting in the electricity that sparks wherever I touch my mates. An idea forms and I nip at his rear leg when I reach it. He growls playfully at me, and I shoot off through the woods, running back towards the house, their scents guiding my path.

Eight wolves give chase, and I bark in excitement. Logan catches up to me first and nudges my side with his head. I stop running to turn and pounce on him, knocking him over. He tries to nip at me, but I hop out of his reach. He manages to tackle me, and I huff in defeat once he pins my squirmy body, caging me in with his paws on either side of me. The rest of them have caught up to us, pouncing and playing with each other, sometimes giving bites or growls of affection.

Remy takes the lead through the woods, guiding us around the massive property. We stride together as a pack, brushing up against one another, the sparks at an all-time high. I don't know what the others are thinking, but for me, I reflect on how awesome this all is, how I feel such a deep sense of belonging, and how I have never felt such security and solace until now.

We stop at a sunny spot in the yard and form a pile of sorts. Tristan licks at my muzzle, cleaning up my fur after our meal. Finn nuzzles his face against my side, and Remy's head lays over my paws, so I instinctively clean around his mouth with licks and kisses, occasionally nipping his ears for fun. Ash had gone back for the rest of the deer and dragged it back, so now he and a few of the others lay spread out around it, snacking on it every now and again We stay like this for a time, just soaking up the rays of the sun and hanging out.

A few of the guys must have decided nap, but Finn

was still awake, pawing at a yellow dandelion. His shiny black fur glistens in the midday sun, making flashes of blue shine through. Jace lays beside him in all his golden glory, flat on his back, upright paws twitching in his sleep.

The back door to the house opens, and I watch as my grandfather and Albert step out, both taking positions on the railing, leaning on their arms. They're both dressed smartly in tailored suits, and I wonder where they've been.

I untangle myself from the guys surrounding me and make my way over to them. Remy lifts his head to see where I'm going, bowing his head in a nod after a glance to Maksim. When I'm close enough, I lay on the porch next to him and scoot closer until I can lean against his leg.

Grandfather laughs lightly. "Well, hello to you, too, my dear. You have a lovely coat. It's been ages since I've seen a pure white wolf."

I bark my thanks at the compliment, and he reaches down to pat my head. In the back of my mind, I feel odd about wanting to be so close to Maksim. But the part of me in control now says that it's right, that this is my blood, my family, and he would give his life to protect mine.

He continues to scratch at the top of my head, between my ears, and I lower my eyes in contentment. Not the same kind I feel around my mates, but a different kind, one all its own. However, when Albert reaches out, I snap my teeth at him, trying to bite his hand. He's lucky he's fast.

Grandfather gives him a puzzled look. "You should

know better, Albert. And you should be extra careful with all of her mates nearby, and all shifted," he chastises. I narrow my eyes at the man, in an 'I told you so' manner. Even if I didn't say anything.

"Forgive me, Princess." He bows to me, then to Maksim. "And, sir. I have never actually seen a white wolf, and she just looks so…fluffy."

I huff at him, completely offended. Isn't fluffy another word for fat? Do I look like a fat wolf? I totally shared that deer!

Grandfather laughs harder. "Don't be offended, Kitten. You *are* fluffy for a wolf. Your coat seems to defy gravity itself, but that is a compliment. You are small like most females, but your fluffiness gives you just a bit of added bulk, so you don't appear as starved as you truly are," he says carefully. "Did you have some of the deer?" he questions. Have some? I *caught* the deer! I nod my head, knowing I will have to wait until later to correct him.

Remy lets out a short howl and instinct takes over once again, my wolf somehow knowing that he wants me back over with them. I don't hesitate to comply, more than happy to rejoin my mates. I trot back over, seeing that Jace has woken up from his nap. He holds himself low to the ground, tail held high and waving behind him. As soon as I get close enough, he jumps on me, and I roll to throw him off. We wrestle around for a while, each of us getting the other pinned. He won more than me and now I watch as he struts about in the yard. Even as a wolf, he struts around like he owns the place. Figures. As he passes me, I bite at his fluffy tail, making him yip in surprise, and I snort as he checks it over for damage.

His golden eyes narrow at me, and his growl is low, challenging me. My excitement builds, anticipating his next move. His lean muscles bunch together as he prepares to pounce, but I manage to leap out of the way, accidentally landing on Tristan, before I take off into the trees. I sense him behind me, and I run faster, pushing myself to see how fast I can go. I tire myself out quickly and pant through my mouth as I look behind me, confused when I notice Jace is nowhere around. Where did he go? He was right behind me a minute ago.

I'm just starting to get worried when I'm tackled from behind. Jace's rich musk fills my nose, and I chew on his ear for worrying me. He nuzzles my neck in apology, and I feel like something is missing. He licks under my chin, and I raise my head to give him better access, my eyes closing. It doesn't feel like kissing exactly, but my mind provides me with one word: affection. Jace stands after a while and jerks his head in the direction of the house. I stand up with him, and we walk side by side, taking a leisurely stroll around a small clearing, beams of sunlight pouring through the tall trees, giving it a magical quality. I stroll out into the middle, jumping from one spot of light to the next. I look back to Jace, silently asking him if he wants to play my new game.

The air seems to shift as my eyes meet his. They've gone darker, showing an emotion that I now know the name of: love. And mixed in with the love I see there, is wanting. I'm sure my own eyes reflect the same back at him as he slowly strides forward to circle me, brushing his long body along the length of mine. He pauses to lick and nuzzle some more, before he circles behind me again. I lower my head, stretching my front paws out in front of me. Jace mounts me from behind, his paws digging into my fur at my hips, holding onto me.

The whole experience is entirely different from what I've felt before. It's not about feeling beautiful or riding a high to the point of falling over an unseen cliff. It was more a feeling of rightness, of nature. Jace made me feel loved, cared for, but most of all he made me feel wanted. My wolf recognized him as one of the most beautiful of my wolves, and we were both pleased to be wanted by such a visually stimulating male. We found him worthy of being our mate.

As we finished our lovemaking, he collapsed his body over mine and began licking my face in earnest. I purred my appreciation back at him. Twisting my head around, I gave him a short lick before piercing his neck with my teeth. He growled in pleasure and quickly returned the favor. Immediately, the tiny pinpricks of lightning started up, communicating our bond.

We laid in the shade for a little while longer, but Remy's howl started up once more, this time, the other guys, and even Grandfather and Albert chimed in as well. There was no order in it, just a call to bring everyone home. Jace howled back and after a brief hesitation, I followed suit. The act was the definition of pure freedom. We ran side by side this time, and my happiness was ready to bubble out of me. I howled, long and deep and full of all the emotions I was feeling right this moment. A chorus of responding happiness and joy met my ears, and if I could have smiled right then, it may have split my face in two. Another lone howl followed, this one I recognized as my grandfather's. My wolf took his to mean one of welcome home. And I knew that he didn't mean it as a welcome back to the house, or the family, but as a welcome to myself, of becoming what I was always intended to be: a wolf.

When we made it back to the yard, the sun had moved and was beginning to sit low in the sky. Rem gave a swift bark that got all of our attention. He moved toward the house and we naturally followed behind him. I had thought that the guys deferred to Remy because he was bossy and was good at handling situations, but now I knew differently. Power radiated out from Remington, and something inside of me felt pulled toward him, something more than just the respect I had for him. It urged me to obey and pleased me to do so. It was more than that, but I can't process how Remy's power makes me feel and put it into words, or categorize it.

I watch as he shifts back into a man to open the door and strides inside. I'm not sure how to change back, so I don't, I just walk in still in my wolf form, enjoying the clicking sound my paws make on the hardwood flooring. Remy heads to his room, but I follow Logan to the big living room. I jump up on the couch, pawing at a throw pillow until I get it where I want it, and bark at Kellan to join me. Finn, who had shifted to human form, laughs.

"Bad girl! Down!" he shouts playfully, snapping his fingers at me. I snort at him, remembering when I had mistaken him for a dog and had done the exact same thing to him. Ash, who has no idea it's a joke, snaps his teeth at Finn and jumps on the couch, too, laying his big body over mine protectively. Finn rolls his eyes and strokes my head once before leaving to change. Ash takes advantage of being left alone with me and licks down my nose, cuddling with me.

CHAPTER THIRTEEN

TRISTAN

Watching Kitten as she comes into her wolf has to be one of the most beautiful things I've ever witnessed. Not only because her snowy coat is beauty personified, but because she's so damn good at it. Her wolf form is like second nature to her, genetics obviously playing a role here. When I was first turned, it took me almost a week to control my shifts and learn to even walk as a wolf.

The best part of it all is that she eats plenty now, on her own. She's gotten better at eating the meals the other guys and I make for her, but most of her meals now come from her own hunting. After her yoga, lessons, and evening activities, I take her out in the woods and we hunt for her meals. Sometimes we bring back some leftovers for the guys, sometimes they come with us, but we always let Kitten get the catch. She's very skilled, surprisingly so. It's actually quite a turn-on to watch her stalk her prey. It's also worth noting that she has no trouble sharing her kills, but she still hoards chocolate like they'll never make any again, a fact I find hilarious. Especially when one of my brothers forgets and gets kicked in the shin for his candy theft. I, too, have a sweet spot for sweet treats, but I'm smart enough not to tell her they're hers; that way she shares them with me freely.

"Can we get these?" Kitten asks, carrying a jar of pickles big enough to feed an army…or an Ash.

I double over in laughter at the sight, the grocery cart bumping into the canned goods by accident. "Oh my God, I have to ask, is that the first jar you saw or did you hunt for the economy size aisle?"

She pouts her plump bottom lip out at me. "So that's a yes?" she asks as she adjusts the giant jar in her arms.

"You can get that if you want it, but we're moving soon, so I don't think you'll have enough time to eat all of those."

"Yes!" she mutters under her breath and bangs the jar down in the cart as she practically drops it. "Oh, and we have to get Logan some Lucky Charms; he made me promise before we left."

I roll my eyes and push the cart toward the dairy section. Kitten had said she would push it, but she kept wandering off, leaving the cart to walk around and grab things, her arms overflowing, then bringing them back to the cart. It was painful to watch.

"No, that bastard isn't getting any more Lucky Charms. He doesn't even eat cereal; he just picks the marshmallows out. There's a shelf in the pantry dedicated to his discarded boxes of marshmallow-less cereal."

"Really? Hmm, then let's get a bunch of boxes," she

says excitedly, nearly bouncing.

"Why?" I ask in amusement.

"So I can make him a whole box of just marshmallows," she states like that's entirely rational and the only conclusion to such a question.

I sigh, wondering if I should have gotten another cart. "Fine, but only because you're cute, not that he deserves them. And I'll get some real marshmallows so I can turn all this unused cereal into some breakfast bars."

"Yay! Ooh, and if we get some honey and granola, we can make bars for Reed as well," Kitten chirps, disappearing around the corner to the cereal aisle. She comes back with her arms full again. I hope one of these days she learns that's what the cart is for.

"Look at you, making more work for me," I tease.

"I'll help you," she offers. "I love watching you cook and move around the kitchen." Her cheeks turn a light shade of pink, but she holds my eyes. Damn, she's sexy.

I grab a couple gallons of milk and look over the cart, checking if I've forgotten anything. Damn, I passed Maksim's Nutella earlier, and now I have to go back for it. Who knew the old Russian would be completely obsessed with the stuff.

In the kitchen, Kitten helps put away groceries with me, though I mostly hand her frozen or refrigerated items due to her choice of making the giant pickle jar a centerpiece on the island table. I have a feeling that thing will be the bane of my existence until the move. Not that I would ever deprive her of easy access to the food she wants to eat. That girl is still too thin, in my opinion. She'll always be gorgeous, but I'll feel better after she puts on a few pounds and gets a little rounder. She's eating healthier now, but it's been slow to show on her thin frame.

"Hey, Tristan, do we have any more of those brownies you made last night?" Jace asks as he walks in. A grin forms on my face. Yes, those brownies were a hit last night; even Reed the carb-counter had a handful of them.

"If we do they'll be in the fridge, or maybe Remy froze one for his ice cream." I shrug.

"This brownie?" Kitten asks, swinging her short legs as she perches on the counter.

"Yes, those. Are they in the freezer or the refrigerator?" he asks.

"This is the last one," she tells him with an evil smile.

Jace's eyes widen. "No, the last one?" he says, disappointed. "Can I have half?"

"No," Kitten replies, taking a bite of the brownie.

Jace tilts his chin up, affronted. "Now that's not very fair of you."

"Who said I was fair?" Kitten mumbles through her bite.

"I could take that from you if I wanted to, you do realize this," he responds haughtily.

I lean back against the stove, groceries forgotten, to watch the show. These two are always going at it. If Jace wasn't so easy to rile up, I don't think Kitten would be so combative with him. As it is, he makes it too much fun for her, and she can't resist. If I didn't know any better, I'd blame it on sexual tension, but I know for a fact that they go at it often enough that it shouldn't be a factor.

"You want it, come get it…Little Jace." Shit, she just threw down the gauntlet.

Jace splutters for a comeback as he leaps after her,

but she's quick to hop off the counter and make a run for it. Too bad for him that she's a quick learner and realized early on in their shenanigans that she can't outrun any of us, but her small body can outmaneuver with the best of them. Her best move is leading him around in a circle like she does now around my kitchen island.

I laugh at the two of them, silently putting my money on Kitten for the win, but outwardly encouraging my brother, showing solidarity.

Kitten pauses in her giggling to taunt at him. "I guess you don't want it badly enough," she calls, sticking her tongue out before bursting into laughter again.

Jace hops over the counter, taking a surprised Kitten down with him to the floor. She shoves the last of the brownie in her mouth whole, choking it down as he tickles her mercilessly.

"Why you little brat!" he shouts in humor.

She is barely breathing as he relentlessly goes for the ribs, her ultimate weakness. "Do you give?" He pauses as he waits for an answer.

"Never!"

He continues to tickle her as Logan walks in, opening a new box of his cereal and leaning next to me. "What was it over this time?" he asks idly as he munches away, dropping more food than gets in his mouth.

"The brownies from last night," I tell him. Kitten lets out a snort-giggle combo, and Jace pauses to laugh at her. She reaches up quickly and messes up his perfectly styled hair, resulting in more tickling.

"Oh man, those were awesome!" Logan tells me. "Did you get milk?" I nod, and he steps around the two crazy people to get to the fridge. "You mean these brownies?" he says as he holds up the Saran-wrapped plate with at least a half-dozen brownies left on it.

"Yep," I chuckle. Damn, my sweet girl can be devilish when she wants to be.

"What! Oh, now you're really going to get it," Jace warns the hysterical girl.

Ash saunters into the room, picking an apple out of the fruit bowl before plucking Jace off the floor with his free hand. "No, she's not. The brownies are over there, and she needs oxygen to live." He gives him a light shove toward Logan, who stands in front of the open refrigerator door even though he has his cereal in one hand a brownie in the other.

"You were looking for milk," I call out helpfully.

"Oh, right." Logan tucks the box under his arm before reaching for the milk. He has to bend over, so naturally, the open box spillsall over the place on his trip down. He doesn't even notice.

Ash reaches down and helps Kitten to her feet. "Why do you always have to pick at him?" he asks her.

She smiles up at the big guy, her face flushed and her hair wild. "Because it's fun, and because I always win."

"You do not!" Jace huffs indignantly.

"Don't even start this again." Ash sighs at Jace.

"Me? I didn't start it; she started it," he points out.

Logan laughs as he starts putting Lucky Charm marshmallows on top of the brownie. "Oh my God! What are you, five?" he teases.

"The things I deal with," Jace mutters, finally getting one of the brownies he came in here for in the first place.

Remy pauses at the doorway. "And just what the hell is going on in here?" he questions with a raised brow at the room.

"Nothing!" they chorus, the four of them suddenly finding better places to be.

He steps over to the coffee machine, making himself a fresh pot to refill his mug. "So who won?" he asks with a smirk.

I shake my head in amusement as I go back to the task of putting away food items. "Definitely not whoever is on cleaning duty today," I joke.

Each of us takes a look around the messy kitchen, our eyes meet, and we share an evil grin before shouting at the same time.

"Reed!"

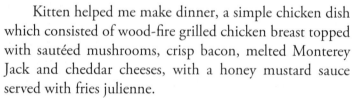

Kitten helped me make dinner, a simple chicken dish which consisted of wood-fire grilled chicken breast topped with sautéed mushrooms, crisp bacon, melted Monterey Jack and cheddar cheeses, with a honey mustard sauce served with fries julienne.

She has no cooking skills to speak of, but she seemed eager to learn, and she helped with what she could. Every now and again I'd catch her staring at me, watching what I was doing, and I have to admit that helped the ego quite a bit. She was especially interested in learning how to make the cheesecake with a strawberry glaze and topped with fresh strawberries.

I may, or may not have fudged a few pieces of information on that topic when she wasn't paying attention. Don't judge me; keep a woman coming to you for baked goods and you've got her for life.

Dinner was a fun affair, with good conversation and

laughter and a dash of wine, just as it should be. Throughout dessert, I took a moment to sit back and notice how much things have changed since Kitten came into our lives. Not only do two new people sit at our table, people I'd be proud to call friends, but the light of my life, my reason to breathe, sits near the middle, engaging with each of my brothers, making them laugh, telling them stories, giving them looks that make their eyes ignite with life. I don't share a table with perfect people, because none of us are, but I share my table with my family and to me, right now, this is perfection. And it's all thanks to one tiny woman, who has stolen my heart and given me back so much more.

As the guys drift off to do their thing, and Maksim retires for the night, I take Kitten's hand in mine, bringing our joined hands up for a kiss. "Will you join me for bed tonight, sweetie?" I ask her.

She smiles at me, nodding her head in that way she does. I scoot her chair back for her and leave the dishes to Reed tonight. I need some Kitten time, and I couldn't care less if he leaves the mess for tomorrow.

I let Kitten get showered in my bathroom and take my own in the shared one in the hall. Drying my hair with a fluffy white towel, I peruse the closet in search of something to wear for bed. I choose a pair of silky basketball shorts, knowing Kitten likes the feel of them. I take a seat on the bed as I wait for the slowpoke. The bathroom door opens, and I'm ready to greet her with a smile. However, she opens the door so hard it slams against the wall behind it. I stand and take a few steps toward her, thinking something is wrong.

Kitten steps out of the bathroom, her face on fire in

embarrassment, looking as sexy as ever. She's too innocent to realize that a white tank top and a wet body produces a lovely see-through effect. And I'm never going to point it out to her, either. Her matching white short-shorts are cute, but she's paired them with red panties, and the sight makes my own shorts a little tighter.

"Sorry, I tripped," she explains.

I don't believe her for a second, but I let her get away with it, now more curious than ever why she slammed the door open. The incident is quickly forgotten though as my roaming eyes finally make their way to hers and my smile turns into a knowing smirk at the heat I see there. Kitten inhales deeply, and I swear her eyes light up like Christmas lights. "Come here, sweetie."

Her sexy bare feet shuffle forward until she's standing right in front of me. If I didn't know any better, I'd swear she was checking me out. Her pink tongue flicks out, licking her upper lip, and I hold in a moan.

"You smell *so* good," she says breathlessly. Thank the lord I showered. Her chest heaves and my eyes focus on the swell of her breasts. Her warm breath fans my chest, and it's a struggle not to think very naughty thoughts.

"I want you…" she trails off as she lifts her hand to my chest. Using the pad of one of her fingers, she reaches out and lightly traces my pec. Damn, that feels good. The rest of her fingers and her palm join in and before I realize what's happening, my head is tilted back, and her soft hands are running insistently all over my exposed chest and abs.

"Fuck…Kitten…" I pant. "You have no idea what you're doing to me."

"No," she says sweetly with a smile in her voice, only

serving to make me harder. Playful Kitten is a sexy Kitten. She takes another step forward and my brain stalls out at the feel of her chest pressed to mine, then I'm falling backward as she gives me a light shove, catching me off guard.

I bounce on the bed once before Kitten bounces herself up next to me, her hands never leaving my skin. I close my eyes and let her explore.

Her fingers drift over my shoulders, over my collarbones, tracing every line of my ribs and abs. She finds a spot just under my ribs that she seems to like and circles it with a dainty finger. I fist my hands in the comforter when everything in me is screaming for me to grab her hands and put them where I really want them.

"Kitten. Seriously. I'm not complaining or anything, but is this something you really want to do? I'm not just a man, Kitten; I'm a wolf as well, and right now both parts of me are begging me to flip your beautiful ass over and take you."

"Don't you feel it?" she asks me. I open my eyes and look into her pale green orbs, the gold streaks looking brighter than usual.

"Feel what?" I ask her, slightly dazed by the hunger I see in her.

"The tingles. Every time I touch you, they jump and dance along my skin, like there's electricity in me and it wants to touch you, too."

"Our mating bond? Of course I feel it; it's amazing," I tell her.

I groan as she leans over my body, hovering her lips over my sternum. Her lips barely graze my skin as her hot little mouth moves up between my pecs and traces the column of my neck. Her tiny nose nuzzles behind my ear, and my chest vibrates with a low growl.

Kitten inhales deeply again, and I feel her body tremble on the bed next to me. I hear a low growl that is more a purr before her soft lips part, and she takes an unhurried lick at my neck.

"Holy fuck!" I shout out. My hands reach for her waist, and I roughly pull her body down over mine. I just hold her there, pressed tightly to me, not trusting myself to move. A pulling sensation starts at my neck, and I realize she's sucking on my skin, probably giving me a lovely hickey. I feel the sensation all the way to my cock and I almost cum right then and there. I'm turned on, shocked, and just downright hot and bothered, and I swear I can feel Kitten singing through my veins. But I never want it to stop. I do, however, want to make love to her, not just fuck her into next week like my smaller brain is begging me to do.

I fist my hand in her long wet hair and yank her head out of my neck. I need to see her. Wild green eyes, flushed cheeks, and rosy red lips, swollen from her ministrations. Damn, she's hot. I pull her head forward and crash my lips to hers. My tongue swipes her lips, and she gamely opens up for me. I taste the tang of toothpaste mixed with Kitten, and my wolf instincts go into overdrive.

I pull roughly at her shirt and tear it away from her body. I flip us over, and she lands with her blonde hair fanned out beneath her, draping over my red pillows. I watch unabashedly as her beautiful tits heave up and down as she pants with excitement. Excitement for me. I test out these new tingles and watch her face as I gently tease her nipples, rolling them between my fingertips. Her swollen lips part and she gasps, arching her back up for more. Gorgeous.

I slip my fingers under the waistband of her shorts, leaving the panties. I can't wait to see her in nothing but her little red panties. If I weren't so impatient, I'd get my phone out to snap a pic to hold onto the memory forever. As soon as her shorts slip past her feet, I move to my knees and look down on her for a better view.

"Part your legs for me, sweetie," I tell her in a hoarse voice. Kitten spreads those gorgeous legs apart, and I nearly die. I run my hands down her smooth legs, stopping just before touching her where I need to most, or she needs me to, or something like that, I can't think straight. "If you want to stop and just cuddle, now's the time to say so, because I don't know if I'll be able to once I tear these off you," I warn her.

"I don't want you to stop. Please, Tristan. I need… something," she begs me.

I moan at her words and breathless voice, gently tracing a finger over her satin-covered clit. "You are so wet, baby," I whisper. Fuck, she is so hot, so wet, so ready. My hands shake with eagerness as I peel the panties off her and spread her legs wider for me. Such a pretty little pussy. I lick my bottom lip as I use my thumbs to spread her perfect pink lips. My cock jerks painfully at the sight.

Shifting myself on the bed, I position my shoulders below her knees and nip at her thigh as I slide a finger through her slickness. She gasps as I circle her clit, and her hips rock up off the bed. I suck at her thigh hard enough to leave a mark as I slip my index finger into her womanly heat.

"Tristan!" Kitten shouts. I smirk up at her as I lower my head and flick her clit with the tip of my tongue. I keep my eyes trained on hers as I flatten my tongue and lap up her juices. My eyes close unwillingly, and I growl as her flavor flows over my taste buds.

"Sweeter than honey," I murmur hungrily before diving back in, pushing my finger in and twisting it out of her as her legs shake on either side of my head. I could do this all damn day. All. Damn. Day. Her sweet flavor fills my mouth as her intoxicating scent swirls around me. I feel her pussy tighten around my finger, and male pride swells in my chest. I want to make my sweet girl see stars. Her hips match my finger's thrusting as she nears her orgasm.

I get on my knees and push my shorts down my legs, not letting up on her for a second. My free hand fists my swollen cock, having plenty of pre-cum to make it nice and slick. Damn, I'm not going to last.

In a last-ditch effort to make her cum before I do, I bend down to graze her clit with my teeth. Kitten screams my name as she shatters in my hand and I position the head of my cock at her entrance just before I blow. I don't think I've ever shot so much cum in all my life.

Her breathing evens out and her eyes close as I lean back on my heels. Seeing her pretty pussy coated in my cum is the most beautiful thing I have ever seen. *Her* coated in *me*. The possessiveness I feel right now is new, but not unwelcome. I swirl my finger around in her folds, pushing as much of me into her as I can, still feeling her body's aftershocks. If she wasn't still in her blissful state, I'd see if she liked the taste of us mixed together. Oh well, there's always next time. And the next.

Before I can make myself hard again with thoughts of all the things I want to do to her in the future, I crawl up the bed, bringing the covers with me. I tuck Kitten close to my body and tuck the blankets around us. I still feel the warm tingles that come with touching her. I brush the damp hair away from her face and kiss her forehead reverently. A satisfied smile graces my lips as I drift off with the best girl in the world in my arms.

Several times that night I awoke, needing her, and several times her love and lust rose to match my own. We were both exhausted by the time we gave into sleep for good. And just in case anyone is curious, my sweet girl loved the taste of our mutual release, as did I.

CHAPTER FOURTEEN

KITTEN

Kellan shakes me awake, but before I tell him how rude that is, I notice the panic in his eyes. "What's wrong?" I ask, immediately sitting up and looking for my clothes.

"I just got a call from the hospital; we need to go," he responds as he pulls on his pants. "Damn it, where's my shirt?" he mutters.

"Need me to come with you?" Finn asks, pulling a shirt over his head on the other side of me.

"It's up to you," Kellan answers shortly.

My hair is a mess as we rush through the hospital hallways, and I wonder if everyone can tell that I've been having sex lately. The car ride was silent on the way over, Kellan not giving Finn and me any more information, just telling him to park the car after he dropped us off at the sliding doors.

"You made it," the doctor sighs in relief when we

enter the small room where Mikey is.

"We came as soon as we could," Kellan replies stiffly as he grabs the tablet at the end of Mikey's bed, what he calls his chart.

"What's going on here? Why is he back on the breathing machine? I thought he was improving," I ask rapidly as I take in the sight of the giant plastic tube that's been reattached to the boy's mouth.

"He was having some complications, seizures to be more precise. We ran some tests, and it appears we missed a brain bleed when we were in there; it's been leaking this whole time. I'm sorry, Kitten, there's nothing we can do now except to make him comfortable as he goes. We did what we could, but this time it wasn't enough," he says sadly before heading to the door.

"He's wrong, right, Kellan?" I whisper shakily.

"I'm so sorry, Kitten," he replies, putting the tablet back and coming to wrap me up in a hard hug.

"No, I don't accept this. There's always something, there's all this equipment and all these people here, there has to be something!" I cry hysterically. He's just a kid. Just a little boy who wants to play hockey who had a terrible father. It's not Mikey's fault that he's here, he didn't deserve to be here, doesn't deserve to die over someone else's mistakes.

I sob into Kellan's shirt, feeling useless and heartbroken. Then I get angry with him and pull away, moving to Mikey's side, and take his hand in mine. I shouldn't be mad at Kellan, but I am; I'm angry with everyone, with the world. Why does life have to be so hard and complicated? Why did I have to know such loneliness before I met the guys? Why did I have to know such pain before I could keep them? Why does this little boy have to die before he even has a chance?

"I'll give you some time," Kellan tells me. "I'll be right outside the door if you need me." I hate the defeated tone in his voice, but there's nothing I can do for it. I feel pretty defeated myself.

I'm not sure how much time passes as I sit there. I look at the boy in the bed, the silly picture of puppies on the wall, the sink and anti-bacterial soap, and the machines and equipment surrounding the bed. The tall stand with a hook and a bag hanging from it hold my attention. There's a steady *drip, drip* noise that it adds to the beeping of the other machines. Following the thin tube that comes out of the bag, I see that it leads to Mikey's wrist.

A nurse coming in startles me out of my thoughts. "Sorry, dear," she says with a tight smile. "I'm just here to turn the monitors off and remove the breathing tube."

"What? He needs that!" I say, outraged.

She sighs. "It's what I've been ordered to do. He's been declared braindead, and the state doesn't want to keep him on as he is, now that there's no hope."

No hope. She said no hope. People often say 'I hope he will be okay,' 'I hope it works out', but no one is hoping for Mikey anymore, not even the nurses and doctors. She said he's braindead, but I have to wonder…is there a part of Mikey left in there, hoping that he won't die? Does he know I'm here, hoping that there's something that I can do?

I look away as the nurse does what she has to. My earlier anger at the world fades away to understanding. People do what they can; people do what they have to do.

When she's gone, I notice that she left the dripping tube in his arm. Why am I so fascinated with it? Obviously, the liquid in the bag passes through the tube and into him.

I blink a few times, an idea forming roughly in my head. If my family members can give me blood to heal me, then can I do the same? But no, I'm not like them; my mother was different, so my blood is probably different, too. And I can't heal myself. Or, well, I guess I can, just slower.

I chew my lip as I watch the fluid slowly drain from the bag. Should I try? What happens if it works? What happens if he doesn't get the fluid that's in the bag? He needs that, right? Would I be killing him faster? I look back to his face, now uninterrupted by the giant tube. He's just a boy; he deserved to have at least one person in this world fight for him.

I yank the needle out of the bag, looking to the door as if someone heard it and they're going to come in and try to stop me. But there was no sound. I look at my arms, at the blue veins that show through my pale skin. I just have to put the needle in one of those, right? Then my blood will go to Mikey, or so I think. I wonder what pushes the liquid through the tube. Gravity, or something else? This would be a good question for Kellan, but I'm not sure if I want him to know what I'm doing. I have to have hope that everything will be alright. I have to have hope for Mikey.

I stick the needle in my arm and watch as two drops of my blood slowly make their way down the tube. Then a third. This is taking forever. Following the tube again with my eyes, I see the small plastic thing on it that I noticed before. I don't know what it's for, but surely it has a purpose. To my delight, there's a moving circle, and when I turn it one way, the tube clears of all liquid, the other way…there we go. My blood starts to fill the entire tube and make its way into Mikey.

After a few minutes, I slump back in my seat, disappointed. Maybe my blood actually won't work. Or maybe I'm just doing it wrong. I guess I could try to bite him, but I don't think I can turn others into wolves, and the thought of biting a dying boy makes me shudder, not to mention I don't know if I would be claiming him as a mate, which makes me want to punch myself in the face. Besides, I don't need his blood; he needs mine.

"What the hell are you doing, Kitten?" Kellan yells in a hushed whisper, his face panicky.

"Trying to help. I have hope," I tell him with a frown. Isn't it obvious?

"You can't just…" He cuts off, waving his hand wildly at my arm and to Mikey.

"Uncle and my grandfather could fix me with blood; I had to see if mine could fix Mikey," I explain. "It isn't working," I add, shaking my head sadly.

"Kitten, honey…I know you liked this kid, and I understand the need to help, but do you realize what you're doing?" he coos.

I nod my head, albeit a little unsurely now. Kellan continues. "Even if your blood did heal him, he'd wake up changed; he wouldn't be human anymore. Do you feel like you can make this kind of call for him? This choice? And then we'd have to take him with us, because he couldn't be left on his own, especially in a hospital with a miracle cure. The government would take him and experiment on him. Are you ready to be an adoptive mom, to care for this boy just because you liked having him around at the ice rink?"

I shrug a shoulder. "I didn't really think about it. He's my friend; if I can help him, I want to do that," I tell him.

"And the rest of what I said?" he asks impatiently.

"I don't know how to be a mom, but I think he would have a better life with me than he did before, and he likes dogs, so he would probably like wolves," I say.

Kellan scrubs at his face with both hands. "We will have to talk about all the things wrong with that statement later." He sighs deeply. "For now, I have to do damage control. Your friend is waking up. Your blood worked after all."

I turn my head quickly and look to Mikey, his eyes just fluttering open. He blinks at me before going into a coughing fit. Kellan had anticipated this, I guess, because he already has a cup of water with a straw for him. "Stay quiet for now, okay?" he instructs.

Mikey smiles nervously at me, and I smile back at him, kissing his forehead to hold back the happy squeal that wants to come out.

Kellan stands by the door, speaking into his cell phone. "Hey, Rem, it's me. Look, we have a problem. To keep it short, Mikey was dying, and Kitten healed him with her blood...No, I didn't allow it, I wasn't in the room... Yes, it worked. Okay. Okay. Sounds like a plan. I get it!" He hangs up and rolls his eyes, pushing at the phone again.

"What did say? Who are you calling now?" I ask him.

"I'll explain later; we need to move quickly here. I'm

getting Finn to erase all footage of any of us from security tapes, but I need to find Mikey something to wear out of here. Get him up and see if he's able to walk. I'll be right back."

I have a sinking feeling that I did something wrong, but that thought changes as soon as I look back to Mikey. I help him sit up and shift the blankets around to keep him covered.

"Uh, hey, Mikey," I say awkwardly.

"Hey, Kitten," he rasps back.

I sigh heavily. "I know you've been through a lot, and you have no clue what's going on, but would you like to come and stay with Jace and me and the rest of the guys?" I ask, hoping he'll say he wants to because I'm pretty sure it's the only option now.

"My dad?" he chokes out. I hand him the water glass for another sip.

"He's in jail now. He'll never hurt you again. I won't let anyone hurt you again. Ever," I vow, and I mean it.

"Did you really save me, like the guy said?" Mikey asks shyly.

I nod my head. "Yeah, I had to try; you're my little buddy," I say playfully and ruffle his already-messy hair.

"So you're gonna adopt me? Like, you're gonna be my mom now?"

I shrug. "I can if that's what you want. I'll warn you, though, I'm probably bad at it. I didn't have a mom either, but I promise to do my best to care for you and make you a part of my family. The thing is, Mikey, my family is...well, we're different. There are things about the others that you might think would be scary, but they're not scary at all. They will never cause you harm, and they will help you in any way they can, I just know it."

"Okay," he says with a smile.

"Okay? You want to come with us?" I ask, just to make sure.

"Yeah. You've always been really nice, and Jace is cool, and you said there would be food." He laughs cheekily.

I laugh, too. "Tristan is going to love you."

Kellan comes in with a set of scrubs that are way too big for the small boy, but he holds the pants up as best as he can as we walk behind Kellan to the elevators and through the hospital to the truck outside. He tells us to get in and wait for Finn, while he goes back and cleans up the room of all evidence of my being there and erases Mikey's record.

Finn jumps in behind the wheel and shakes his head at me. "Remy is going to kill us; you know that, right?" He turns to Mikey next to me. "Hey there, kiddo, welcome to the family. Happy to see you up and moving again."

I smack Finn's shoulder lightly. "How come he gets the welcome back greeting while I get the impending death one?"

Finn laughs. "Because you're the one who turned us all into kidnappers."

"I'm not a kid!" Mikey exclaims with a huff.

"The only thing we kidnapped him from was death. Children's Services are the ones who thought giving him back to his father was a good idea; they shouldn't be trusted with his care anymore," I state, crossing my arms over my chest. "Besides, Mikey said he wanted to come with us."

"Yeah!" Mikey pipes up, defending me.

Finn puts his hands up. "I don't disagree with what you did. I just wish you would have let us in on the plan so we could prepare is all. Now we have to go wipe Kellan's office completely, and the three of you will need to get out of Dodge quickly."

"Oh," I say, deflating and now feeling terrible. I'm not sorry for helping Mikey, and I'm even happy that he's coming with us now. I won't have to worry about how he is anymore; I'll know he's being taken care of. But I did bring the guys into all of this without even asking, and I've brought a child into their lives that they might not have wanted.

Kellan comes out shortly, and the three of us remain quiet on our way back to the house as Mikey plays with the radio, listening to ten seconds of a song before changing the station and doing it all over again. He seems happy enough; I just worry how the rest of the guys are going to react.

CHAPTER FIFTEEN

Mikey and I rush out of the truck as we pull up to the house. Reed jogs over to us, placing a quick smacking kiss on my lips, telling me he's proud of me before he jumps in the truck in with Kellan and Finn, heading for the clinic.

I stare at the open front door nervously, rocking back on my heels. I guess the rest of them know already. "I guess we should go in," I propose.

As we're climbing the steps of the porch, Maksim appears with a broad grin on his face. "I suppose this is the newest Ivaskov!" he greets happily.

Mikey looks up at me with a puzzled expression. "What's an I-vash-cough?" He pronounces the name so funnily that it's hard not to laugh.

"Well, apparently that's what we are now. It's a name."

"Oh. So is Mr. Jace around?" He walks to the door and peeks his head around.

"We can go find him in a minute, Mikey. First, I want you to meet my grandfather, Maksim," I introduce.

Mikey waves and Maksim takes that as an invitation. He steps up to him and places his hand on his shoulder. "Come on, boy, how about we get a bite to eat before we seek out the duke's son, hmm? And you can call me 'Grandfather'... most people do."

The two of them walk off without me, and I glare at the back of Maksim's head. He had to know I was planning on using Mikey as a shield from Remy, and he stole him from me. I stick my tongue out at him, even though they've disappeared into the house. I roll my eyes at myself before deciding to act like an adult and find Remy before he finds me.

I know if Remy is actually home, he'll be in his office at this time of day, so I head there first.

REMY

Kitten knocks lightly on the open door, and I throw her a look that tells her she knows better. She shrugs her slim shoulders unapologetically, her smile forced, but beautiful all the same.

"Don't be mad," she says, looking around at all the empty shelves in my office.

"I'm not angry with you, Love. Just worried that you didn't think this through, and worried how the boy will react when he learns what we are," I tell her softly.

"Oh." Her shoulders relax, and I can tell she was

worried about my reaction.

"Come here, Love. Let's have a chat." I slide my chair back, giving her room to sit in my lap. I brush her luscious platinum hair away from her shoulder and run my hand soothingly over her back before continuing, "I want you to understand that even if I do become angry with you, I will never raise a hand to you in anger. I also will never turn you away or make you feel ashamed for your mistakes or if we disagree on a matter. There's never a reason to fear me, Kitten."

"Okay. I understand." She smiles shyly at me, giving me a kiss on the cheek.

"Now, about young Michael. I assume you thought it was the only way to keep him alive, and if that's the case, then I feel you should be proud of your choice," I tell her firmly.

"Really? You mean that, Rem? I know bringing a child home is kind of a big deal, but I'll take care of him myself; he won't get in your way," she promises.

"Stop!" I bark, harsher than I intended, but I don't like where that was headed. I embrace her tightly in a hug to soothe the sting of my order. "You won't be caring for the boy on your own. You'll have us; that's what family is for. You forget that every other man in this house was brought home by me and cared for, welcomed into the family if you will. You don't have to do anything alone anymore, Love. We'll support you and the decisions you make. All I ask is to be included in making those choices."

Kitten smiles even though I can tell she feels like crying, the rims of her eyes turning red and heavy with unshed tears. "Thank you, Remington. I'll do better in the future. I was worried Kellan might try to stop me if I asked," she admits.

I snort in amusement. "You really think Kellan, the doctor, the man sworn to save lives by any measures needed and to the best of his abilities, would have told you to let the boy die?" I ask.

Kitten lowers her head, looking to her lap. "I guess not." She shrugs. "I just panicked."

"That's understandable." I nod. "Just keep in mind that sometimes having a partner in crime can help lessen the burden, and can be the rock in a storm for you. The men and I have faced many challenges together, our different skill sets allowing each of us to take turns being the rock. No one is great at everything, but sometimes letting others step in and take the lead is what's necessary for success."

She wipes away a stray tear from her cheek, giggling as she meets my eyes. "You let others take the lead?"

I raise an eyebrow in surprise at the question. "I have, I do, and I will. I do what's best for the family, even if that means stepping out of the way."

She searches my eyes for the truth in my words, and I allow her to take her time. "I love you," she says eventually. "I know I've thanked you before, but the words don't seem like enough. Thank you for taking me in, for loving me, for rescuing me. Thank you for taking the guys in so that they have a family, too, and so that I could meet them. Mostly, Rem, thank you for being you and caring about the rest of us."

I slide my hand to the back of her neck and bring her to me for a long, hard kiss. I keep her there until she needs air. "Thank you for being you, too, Love. I wouldn't want you any other way. Now, stand up."

She blinks at me a few times but does as I ask. "Face me," I order.

Kitten turns, looking down at me with a million questions in her lovely eyes. She doesn't voice them, which both surprises and pleases me. She trusts me with whatever is about to happen.

"Know that I am in love with you, Kitten. I would never do anything that you do not wish for me to do," I tell her, meaning every word of it.

"I know that, Remington. I love you. I trust you," she whispers back, curiosity now shining through her gaze. I see a hint of fear in her, but not fear of me; just fear of knowing something is going to happen, and she doesn't know what.

"There are certain things I enjoy, Kitten. Sexual things. They may seem intense, or sound scary if I was to sit here and describe them. But the things I enjoy are not designed to harm you. They are designed to give me control of you. Not just your body, but your focus, your attention. It is up to you to give me these things; I will not take them from you. I'd like to try the things I enjoy with you if you'll allow me. If you don't like them, then tell me so, and I will stop. Immediately, no questions asked, no pressure to continue. Do you agree to try?" I inquire of her. I keep my voice intentionally low, allowing her to hear how serious I am.

I let her take her time to respond, knowing that she needs time to process my meaning and intentions.

"Okay, Remy. We can try them," she responds. Her voice is unsure, but her body is already reacting to whatever thoughts are swimming around in her head.

I stand from the chair slowly, sliding it out of the

way. I hook my index finger under the hem of her thin sleep shirt, raising it a few inches to reveal her belly button. I circle it with a feather-light touch, pleased when her breath hitches at the contact. Now that she's suitably distracted, I bring my other hand up quickly, grabbing a fist-full of the material in my hand, and give it a quick yank.

The shirt falls uselessly to the floor, and Kitten's eyes go wide in shock. I let my own eyes linger on her exposed skin. Her pert breasts rise and fall with her increased breathing and her pink nipples pucker under my gaze. The sight is mouthwatering, but there's no rush.

Fighting my instincts not to dive my face into her delightful breasts, I slide my hands slowly up her sides, coming up to cup the heavy, rounded globes, testing the weight of her womanly curves. I avoid her nipples, releasing a satisfied hum when I glide my hands back down her sides, and she whimpers in disappointment. I dip the tips of my fingers into the waistband of her bottoms and caress the smooth skin of her hips. As I start to slide them down, I look up to make sure she's still okay with this. I want her desperately and want her to be desperate herself, but I won't continue if she doesn't wish to.

Kitten's pupils are blown wide with want, so I push them down further. The little minx is sans panties as well. I let the pants fall to the floor before taking her hand so she can safely step out of them.

I raise an eyebrow at her. "Is this how you always walk about the house?"

She blushes again, and this time I watch as it extends all the way down her neck and chest to her stiff nipples.

Pink is such a lovely color on her.

"I was in Finn's room. He didn't...I mean I...He doesn't wear panties," she struggles to explain. I wouldn't put it past the fucker, honestly.

I take a step closer to her, brushing up against Kitten's naked form. She arches beautifully towards me, but I back away quickly. The resulting pout almost breaks my will. "Stay!" I bark at her, using more force than is necessary. I move around the desk, striding to close the door to give us some semblance of privacy. Kitten stands straight as a rod and doesn't try to look over her shoulder at me, even though I'm sure to take my time. Her quick compliance arouses me further.

I take my time unbuttoning my shirt, unlacing my boots and taking both them and my socks off. I unbutton my pants and unzip them, letting her see how turned-on she has made me, but leave them on for now. I stroll to stand in front of Kitten, positioning myself mere inches from her. With me now in sight, she squirms as she takes in my bare chest and arms. Her eyes roam down to my undone pants and my hardened cock and she leans so far forward that I think she might fall. My amused chuckle brings her eyes back up to mine.

"Turn around," I instruct.

She moves slowly and unsurely, but once again, she complies without protest. I move in closer to her, pressing my hardened length into the small of her back. Kitten shivers and presses her ass back at me, seeking more contact than I'm giving her. I let my fingertips trail up her arms, taking note of the goosebumps they leave in their wake, and continue up to her shoulders. As they reach her neck, her head falls back, a stilted sigh escaping her. I growl deeply at her show of natural submission.

I leave one hand at her throat, resting lightly, as my other hand gathers her hair at the nape of her neck, wrapping it up in a good hold. Using my body to shift her forward, I press her until her hips meet my desk. The hand on her throat moves down, sliding between her breasts and around her waist to push at the middle of her back.

Kitten bends forward, gasping as the cool of the desk comes into contact with her flushed body. "Move your hands up to rest above your head. Good girl," I praise her when she does so readily. "Now keep them there, do you understand? Do not move them, no matter what," I instruct her.

"Yes, Remy," she answers throatily.

I use her hair in my hand to position her head the way I want it. Her face lies to the side, allowing her to see me. I smirk down at her, pressing my hips into her lush ass, and she moans, her eyes closing in pleasure.

"Eyes open," I tell her softly but with power in my voice.

Now that she's spread out the way I want her, I let my free hand caress her smooth back a few times, each time moving my hand down lower, closer to the prize between her legs. She whimpers as my hand ghosts over her cheek and down her thigh. On the return trip, instead of a caress, I give her a good slap. Kitten shouts out in surprise, but I'm quick to soothe over the sting on her now-pink skin. Her breathing increases but her eyes stay wild. She enjoyed it. I deliver a harsher blow to her other cheek, and her fingernails dig into my desk. Another five slaps to each cheek and my girl is panting hard, sweat beading on her skin, her ass a fine rosy shade. I figure I've tortured myself enough for now. I kiss the middle of her back lightly, then allow my tongue to trail down her spine and over her left cheek to where her ass meets her thigh, in that lovely little place all females have that forms a natural handle, made for gripping.

Now on my knees, I sit back and take a look at the gorgeous sight in front of me. "Spread your legs," I growl at her. "Further," I tell her, as the first time wasn't enough. I slide my index finger through her silky lips, feeling her slick juices on my fingers. The sheer amount is shocking and pleasing. She liked her spanking. Thank fuck for small miracles, because I enjoyed it as well. Without warning her, I press my face into her heated core and seek out her pleasure button with my tongue. Kitten's body jerks and goes taut until I begin to suckle at her, then her entire body melts, her legs giving out. I chuckle to myself and bring my hands up to spread her lovely ass wider for me, using those sexy handles. Her untouched rosebud begs me for attention, but that will come in time. We'll work up to that.

She cums hard on my tongue quickly, but I allow her no rest. Her pussy is better than the finest of wines, and I have no intention of depriving myself of it any longer.

I taste of my girl until her shouts of pleasure drift away to an ongoing moan, and her quivering thighs are the only part of her body still stirring. I stand fully and drape myself over her back. I nuzzle at her exposed neck, tasting the light sheen of sweat that has formed on her smooth skin. I press my hips up against her, my cock needing some desperate attention. I feel my canines lengthening and position my teeth on the back of her shoulder. I slide a finger into her tightness, feeling a rumble from Kitten as she groans deeply. My other hand aligns my cock at her entrance. As my teeth sink into her flesh, so does my cock.

Kitten inhales sharply, her body coming alive for me once more. Her hand slaps at the desk, and her growl is almost feral as she shifts her body back at me, needing more of me inside of her. I don't release her neck until I'm balls-deep in the most maddeningly tight pussy I've ever been in. I pause inside of her, luxuriating in the feel of her around me, the pulsing heat temporarily sending my mind to drift into orbit.

Kitten scrambles for my hand that's pressed next to her head and tries to pull it towards her mouth. It would be confusing if my mind weren't in such a state of pure lust, love, and sheer bliss right now, and I'd be dissatisfied at her disobedience. I let her have my hand, and moments later I feel tiny teeth at my wrist. The firestorm that emanates from her bite is like nothing I've ever felt before. Tiny pinpricks cover my skin everywhere that my body covers hers. My dick is now being massaged not only by her tight walls but by the delicious mating bond as well.

I can remain still no longer; a man can only take so much. I weave my fingers through her tiny ones and press our joined hands to the desk. My hips move back until the head of my cock is at her entrance. A deep thrust forward has us both growling in pleasure. I wait just a moment before doing it again.

"Remy...please," Kitten begs. God damn, does this girl want me to cum this soon? Her begging, in that voice...damn. Think of something else, anything else. To cut her off from speaking any further, and to eliminate the chance of me finishing too early, I begin thrusting in and out her quickly. She moans loudly, her hips thrusting back to meet mine. I pound into her, feeling my balls slapping at her clit before they draw up tight, ready to explode into my mate, my lover, my life.

I reach over and grip her hair tightly, bringing my mouth to her ear. "I. Fucking. Love. You," I tell her, each word accentuated with a hard thrust of my cock. If there was ever any doubt in her mind that she belonged to me, I'm sure I've fucked it out of her by now. Kitten pants that she loves me, too, and that's all that I can take. My head goes back and I howl as my seed leaves my body and enters hers. I collapse on top of her, not yet ready to move and wanting to keep my cum from spilling out of her just yet. The primal beast inside of me rejoices in claiming our woman this way.

'Remy," Kitten pants, sounding a little dazed. That's a nice stroke to my ego.

"Yes, Love?"

"I want to hold you," she says, shocking me, though I don't know why. She's not one of the women I've used in the past; she's Kitten. Lovable, adorable Kitten, who wants more from me than just sex and a thank you. She wants me, all of me. With anyone else, I'd never allow cuddling, but with her I'd more than enjoy it.

I pry myself off her, my softening dick reluctantly leaving her warmth. I pick her up gently, wrapping her legs around my waist when it seems she can't get them to respond just yet, and sit with her in my chair. Kitten moves her face to my neck and her fingers stroke through my hair. I close my eyes, loving the attention she's giving me now. It's sweet, just like her, and it soothes my wolf in a way I've never experienced.

· — ● ● — ·

After a while, Kitten gets squirmy, and I open my eyes to look down at her. "Were you working in here? Did I interrupt you?" she asks, biting her lip.

I chuckle at her. "Yes, I was just finalizing a few things before the move in a few days, but you're welcome to interrupt like that any time you wish," I tell her with a satisfied smirk.

She blushes and giggles. "Okay, I'll remember you said that. Can I help you with anything, Remy? It looks like you've got a lot of stuff here," Kitten says as she turns to look around the room.

"Hmm… Maybe. If you don't mind a bit of writing, you could copy this letter of rejection to these people here," I tell her as I reach back to the shelf behind us and slide a small stack of papers in front of her. "I don't mind if they are exactly the same or not. It could be done by email, but I've always preferred the more personal form of communication, such as letters."

"Yay!" Kitten squeals as she bounces up and down on my lap. A growl starts low in my throat, my cock finding new strength.

Kitten turns her head to look back at me. "Remy?" she questions softly.

"It's nothing, Love. You're just giving a certain part of me a beautiful ride." I smirk at her innocent blushing. I'll never tire of her reactions to me.

I pat her thigh, telling her that I'd love to have her help after she's showered and redressed, although I do momentarily entertain the thought of keeping her in here naked with me. Ultimately it's a selfish thought, and someone is bound to come looking for her at some point.

It turns out Kitten is quite nice to have around in the office. She had written out the rejection letters, sealed them in envelopes, and stacked them neatly in a pile for me. Her eyes had quickly sought out praise from me, and it took a decent amount of my control not to growl excitedly at yet another show of her submission.

She seemed eager to be put to task, so after I had rewarded her with a searing kiss that left us both wanting more, I set her about loading files into pre-marked boxes to get ready for the move. Now, almost two hours later, I'm putting finishing notes on the blueprints for a contractor in Florida. I glance at Kitten and notice she's waning in energy now. I observe her for a few more moments and note that she's pausing every few seconds to catch her breath.

"Come to me, Love," I call to her, holding a hand out to help her up. She places her small hand in mine and allows me to help her to her feet. I press a kiss to the top of her head, her arms going around me in a hug. "You've done an excellent job; thank you for helping me today. I think it's time for you to go check on the boy, yeah?"

She rests her head on my chest and speaks through a yawn. "Yeah, probably." She yawns again, giving me one last squeeze before pulling back. "I don't know what's wrong with me today; I feel so sleepy," she says before smiling up at me.

I grin back at her. "Well, you have been quite the busy woman as of late, and I'm certain the late nights aren't helping any."

She smacks my arm playfully. "Maybe I should stop with certain activities altogether then?" she asks in a mock-innocent tone.

I growl at her in answer, making her laugh. I send her on her way, returning to my work, though it proves a bit difficult when all I can picture is Kitten laid out on my desk. I'll probably always think of her in that moment every time I look at the piece of furniture. Maybe I didn't think that one through. Then again, it's not as if I would take it back.

CHAPTER SIXTEEN

KITTEN

Mikey settled in quite nicely. It was like he had always been there after a few days. He mostly liked to hang out with Jace, having made him his role model from the start a while ago. Ash had gone to Wolly's on his own the first day and returned with a brand new bike for him, complete with helmet, knee and elbow pads, and a reflective vest, in case he wanted to ride it at night I guess. Earning hero status in the young boy's eyes. Remy offered to help teach him to ride it, seeing as he'd never had one before and if Ash saw him crash on it, he probably would have ripped it apart and banned them from the house.

Logan had taken him clothes shopping yesterday, and the poor guy returned home looking exhausted and maybe even a little horrified, which the other guys found hilarious. Tristan was quick to cheer him up with chocolate ice cream cones, though, and I think the intense shopping trip was easily forgotten after that.

Grandfather and Albert left for the pack house this morning with goodbyes and see you soons from all of us and a hug from Mikey. The older man seems to have hit it off with him and Mikey even calls him Grampa, stating that saying Grandfather makes him sound like one of those spoiled rich kids on the television shows he watches. Maksim was okay with the new term, and Uncle Albert followed shortly. Albert was a little wary of allowing him to call him that, telling Mikey that he has no blood ties to the royal family, but Mikey had just made a face and asked how you would go about tying blood, so we had shrugged the episode off entirely. In my opinion, if Mikey wants to go around and start claiming family members, then he can have as many as he wants.

━━━━━ ◆ ⬤ ◆ ━━━━━

I collapse to the ground, panting in the early morning air after my yoba session with Reed. He breaks his pose to laugh at me, falling gracefully into a push-up position.

"You're done already? That was only your second pose, babe," he points out.

I shrug my shoulders. "Oh well, my favorite part is watching you anyway."

"I thought you liked doing yoga with me. You don't have to do it if you don't want to," he tells me before pushing up into a handstand. "It was supposed to help you clear your mind and deal with your panic attacks."

"It does, and I do like it most of the time. There's no clearing my head today anyway; there's too much going on."

Reed sighs, giving up his exercising to wrap me up in his arms. We watch the sunrise instead. "I know, babe. The moving guys will be out of here soon, though. We're not taking too many big things with us."

"It's not really the moving guys; it's about what happens when we step off the plane tomorrow. How much will things have to change with me being a princess and you guys some form of kings there?" I ask worriedly.

"Nothing between the nine of us has to change at all, and that's what's most important. In front of others, well, I guess we'll have to sometimes be different versions of ourselves. Not different people entirely, or fake, but a little more closed off is all," he explains.

I lean back against him, now squinting at the bright sunlight as I look to the sky. "What if they don't like me?"

Reed laughs happily behind me. "Kitten, you have one of those personalities where people either worship you or dislike you entirely. The people who worship you will go to battle for you in a heartbeat, and the ones who dislike you will on the opposite side of that battle. You never need to worry about the latter; those in your corner won't let them get near you. And I have a feeling that most, if not all, of our new pack will love you to the moon and back."

I smile up at the sky, feeling relieved and happy. "You're an artist even with your words, you know that?" I turn my head to kiss him, his dazzling hazel eyes taking my breath away.

I shower quickly, mostly because Logan stayed in the bathroom and rushed me, before he starts on my hair. He twists it up tightly and pins it to my head before adding a light spritz of hairspray. After applying what he called eyeliner to make my eyes stand out, he urges me into the bedroom where a beautiful light blue dress hangs on the back of the door. My mouth falls open, and I slowly step towards it.

"Nope! Not yet. It's yoga pants and a baggy t-shirt for you, girly. At least until we're ready to touch down, then you can wear the dress," Logan chirps.

I shake my head at him, and take the clothes I'm allowed to wear, slipping them on easily.

Outside waits a long car that Remy ordered so we could all ride together to the airport. I slide in next to Kellan, and his arm automatically goes around my shoulders. I smile up at him, and he smiles back. Everyone finds a seat on the long bench seat, and even though I feel like I'm not ready, the car starts driving away from the only home I have ever known.

"Wait!" I tell them, thinking over my mental checklist again.

"Baby girl, I promise that we got everything we'll need. If we missed something, we could always come back to get it," Ash assures me.

"Right," I huff. "Are you sure you got AJ, Noah, and the rest of the stuffed pack? And Big Jace, too?"

"Yes," he replies gently.

"And Mikey's things were packed away, too? And his bike?"

"I'm sure of it," he confirms.

"And Reed sent all of the paintings and my flag,

and…"

"Kitten, love, we got everything, did everything; you're worrying over nothing." Remy takes my shoulders in his hands and looks directly down at me.

"Okay," I agree.

"I can't believe I'm going to fly in a plane!" Mikey bounces in his seat next to me.

"Yeah, it should be a lot of fun. And Finn got us a movie to watch on it, too; I think it's called "Home". One of those Disney Pixar movies. I watched one before and it was really good, they're funny," I tell him.

"Yeah, I know. I've seen lots of them. I really wanna see "The Good Dinosaur" next."

"Well, Christmas is only a day away, so we'll see," I tell him, feeling better about my gift for him now.

The guys talk amongst themselves and with Mikey, but I choose to stay out of it. My heart hurts at leaving behind so many great memories, or at least the place where they happened.

"Try not to look so sad, Kitten. We'll make our new house our home in no time." Kellan tries to cheer me up.

I bite my lip and give him a nod. "Right. I know."

"I've been meaning to speak with you about something, but you don't have to if you don't want to," he starts.

"About what?" I ask curiously.

Kellan takes a deep breath and shifts around so he can face me. "I realize that you are all about letting the past go and looking to the future, but you've changed a lot since you've been back and I have to wonder if what happened to you affects you more than you let on to the rest of us."

I glance around at the others, knowing they can hear everything we're saying, but they're pretending not to. "Of course it affects me," I mutter. "How could it not? I don't want to be sad or angry about it, but sometimes I am anyway. The point is, I'm trying to be happy with where I am now."

Kellan nods slowly. "I understand that, I do. You can talk to me, to any of us, about anything at any time, though. We like to see you happy, but we are here for you no matter what you may be feeling, and sometimes talking about what doesn't make you happy can actually make you feel better."

"I will keep that in mind; thanks, Kellan," I smile brightly at him. "But I want you all, no, need you all, to understand something. Being locked in that basement, at the mercy of the merciless, changed something in me. I can't explain it, not really, but I don't want to be weak anymore. I don't want to ignore the world because it ignored me. I want...more than that. Does that make sense?"

"It does," Finn answers from the other side of Kellan. My eyes flash to his. "You've found something worth fighting for. You were worth it all along, but you never realized that. Now, you have a family, and you are willing to do things to keep it that you would never have considered before."

I blink at him a few times in disbelief. I've wondered a few times if Finn could actually be a mind-reader, but how is it possible that he understands my feelings more clearly than I do? I swallow thickly at the surge of overwhelming emotion that courses through me and nod my head.

A hand on my chin brings my focus back to Kellan. "It's okay, Kitten. We've all been there, one way or another. We feel the same way about you, and about each other. It's not a wolf thing; it's a family thing." He bends his head to lightly kiss my lips, and I sigh at the much-needed contact.

"But why am I only feeling it now?" I ask.

To my surprise, it's Ash who answers me. "Because we came for you. You're unsure of your place with us, but actions speak more to you than words. We came for you and now you know we always will. That's what family means."

Logan lets out a shocked gasp that has me frantically looking out every window, waiting for the truck to hit us. "Oh, my God! It has feelings!" he draws out dramatically, hand clutching his chest over his heart. A swift punch from Ash to his stomach has him gasping for air and trying to laugh at the same time. I raise a brow at Ash, questioning the sudden violence, and he just shrugs a shoulder in response.

"Way to ruin a moment, bro." Reed rolls his eyes at Logan before turning and winking at me. My increased heart rate from my near panic slows, and I relax back into Kellan's side.

The plane is one of the smaller ones I've seen flying overhead in the sky, the kind that makes lots of noise. Finn called it a jet. It has plenty of room to move around in, though, and even a bathroom and a small bedroom in the back of the plane. The seats are cream- colored leather and the long couch near the rear is, too. A flat screen TV gets Mikey's attention quickly, and Remy tells him that we have to sit in the seats with buckles for the takeoff.

I take a moment to wonder what it must have been like for people when these huge pieces of machinery first took to the sky, and what the sky must have looked like without planes dotting the view. As the guys find seats, I realize that there are people who would know those answers. The thought makes me giddy with excitement.

"Kitten?" Remy says my name like he's said it more than once already. My cheeks heat when I look over at him, but he continues like he doesn't notice. "Finn wants to talk to you about a few things; then I'm going to go over the itinerary Albert sent over so we're all on the same page about the next few days."

"Okay, Rem." I wave my fingers at him before pouncing on the seat next to Finn. The one without his computer.

"You want to talk to me?" I say with a grin.

He smiles back. "I always want to talk to you, Beautiful. But I thought we could use this time to talk about Mike's education. He was enrolled in public school before, but with being bounced around, he was falling a bit behind."

I look over to the little guy, smiling sadly at him as Remy give the go ahead to watch his movie. He's such a special kid, and it makes me sad to know he was slipping through the cracks.

"Now, I'm sure there's a public school available to him in Colorado, maybe even some private ones, but I'd like you to think about possibly homeschooling him, in light of our, well, lifestyle I guess. I could teach him myself, and it might be the better option if only so we don't have to make him a new identity."

"If you're sure that's what is best for him, then let's

do that. I know you're more than capable." I kiss his cheek for being so thoughtful.

"Thank you," he replies, finding my lips with his own for a quick peck. "After things get settled at the new place, I'll begin my lessons with him."

"Sounds good," I tell him.

I shoo Logan's hand away from my hair as he tries in vain to tuck a flyaway strand of hair into the up-do he has created. He meticulously braided the hair on either side of my face and pinned them in a circle around my head, while making an almost too tight bun with the hair in the back. I sense his nervousness and in turn, it's making me nervous.

"Stop picking at your dress; there's no lint there, not even the imaginary kind," Jace says as he saunters up behind me, placing a light kiss behind my ear. I shiver in delight.

"I'm not picking. I just like the feel of it," I tell him, though my voice sounds strange.

He takes one of my hands and has me do a slow twirl for him. My skirts flare out, but not so much so that it would be indecent. "Yes, silk does have that effect," he whispers lowly. "You, my love, are a vision to behold."

My face heats in a blush, but I can't help the smile that comes over my face. I feel pretty, and knowing Logan made this dress just for me makes me feel special. The bodice is snug against my chest and waist and has a lace overlay that shimmers. My shoulders are bare because there are no straps, but Logan assured me that it would stay in place. The silky skirt that hangs to my knees is my favorite part. It feels like air brushing over my skin as I walk. Logan called the color a nude-blush, but it looks like light pink to me. I was supposed to wear the uncomfortable high-heels, but I managed to get Ash on my side by pointing out that I could run better in the slipper shoes if we were in danger. Once Ash sets his mind to something, it's almost impossible to change.

I must have taken longer getting ready than I realized because the guys are all dressed and ready when Logan, Jace, and I step out of the bedroom on the back of the plane. Mikey is in a white dress shirt with a black vest over it, pulling on his red tie. Oh, he looks so adorable.

Remy is in a nice black suit with a black button-down under his jacket, and it both manages to hide his bulk and accentuate his muscles. Kellan and Finn have both chosen light gray suits, with Kellan wearing a silky-looking dress shirt and Finn wearing a white one under their jackets. Reed decided not to wear a jacket, but just a white dress shirt with the sleeves rolled up his forearms and the top button undone. Jace is dressed in a suit of white with a piece of fabric in gold in his pocket sticking out and his shiny gold watch on his wrist. Ash and Tristan must not have cared to dress up because Ash is wearing his signature black T-shirt that shows off his massive arms and pair of black dress pants with his scuffed up boots, while Tristan is wearing a red T-shirt under a leather jacket and dark washed jeans with white sneakers.

I take my time looking over my mates, and the pit of my tummy is filled with fluttering. Tristan takes a step forward and uses a long finger to close my mouth. I let out a squeak of mortification, not knowing that I was gaping at them, and briefly wonder if I was drooling, too.

"That's how we feel about you in that dress, sweet girl," he tells me before taking my lips in a searing kiss. I grip the sides of his jacket to bring him closer. Will I ever get enough of these amazing men?

A throat clearing loudly breaks me away from Tristan. "You haven't even seen the best yet. I saved myself for last," Logan says with a wink. I blink a few times at him, completely mesmerized. He, too, is in a suit. Black pinstripes make, him seem even taller, the blue shirt matching his eyes perfectly, but it's the way the suit fits him that has me drooling all over again. It's unexplainable, but Logan looks like he was born to wear that suit. His new hairstyle, with the sides and back cut short, and the top left long enough to comb back, as it is now, makes him appear as if he walked right out of an ad for pricey clothing. Only, no model could ever hold a candle to the man in front of me.

"Oh, I love making you look at me like this, Kitten. I wish we had time to act out every dirty thought going through your mind, but sadly, we do not," Logan says playfully with another wink. I shake my head at him, somewhat for his antics but mostly to try to clear my thoughts, so I don't pounce and attack any of the gorgeous males. Because that's exactly what I feel like doing right now.

The door lowers and people outside work to get the steps lined up correctly. The fluttering in my tummy ceases and is replaced with a feeling of dread. Grandfather climbs the steps and greets the guys before turning to me. A flash of emotion lights up his eyes as he takes me in. He clears his throat and approaches me with a fond smile on his lips.

"I have something for you, Kitten. Your mates will be crowned publicly, but this was yours all along." With that, he carefully unlatches the wooden case he carries in his hands. He motions for Remy to hold the case while he lifts the lid.

I suck in a breath as a silver tiara comes into view. With its stones of jade, sapphire, and rubies, it's the most beautiful piece of jewelry I have ever seen. I watch as Grandfather lifts it from its velvet home and steps closer to me.

My eyes go wide in panic. "What?! No, you can't mean…It can't be mine. I'll lose it, or drop it, or break it," I protest.

Grandfather chuckles deeply, along with a few of my mates. "It is already yours. Yours to lose, break, and drop. It can always be repaired, dear girl. You should wear it today, so as to leave no doubt as to who you truly are."

I swallow thickly, shooting a glance at Ash. He nods his head once, with a grave expression on his face. I allow Grandfather to place it on my head and take a deep breath once it's in place, and he steps back to look me over once more. A look of pride that I recognize from Remy shines through him, and my emotions go haywire. From Grandfather, my only family, the look seems to mean something different to me than when it comes from the guys. It's not more or less, just different.

I don't know how to react to this new knowledge, so I quickly turn to Logan, pleading with my eyes for something, but even I don't know what. His blue eyes search mine for a moment before he pulls me with him back to the bedroom, telling the others that he wants to secure the tiara better. Once he closes the door, his arms come around me, and he pulls me to him. We don't speak, just hold onto one another like we're caught in a windstorm, and it's trying to break us apart. It may be an hour or mere minutes, but eventually, I'm able to rein in my emotions, and we meet everyone else back in the seating area.

Mikey and I must have the same thought because we both pause at the exit and share a look.

"Can we come in to the out now?" we chorus, before laughing hysterically. That was such a great movie. Grandfather looks confused, but the guys chuckle at us, and the mood lightens up a bit.

Stepping from the plane was scary. I was expecting a crowd of angry wolves or a mob of villagers carrying lit torches. In actuality, it was just Albert and two drivers waiting by more long cars. Talk about getting worked up for nothing. When they see us coming, all three of them bow deeply at the waist and stay that way, as if they are stuck.

Finn elbows me lightly before leaning down to speak in my ear. "You're the highest ranking royalty right now; you must acknowledge them or dismiss them," he informs me.

"Oh!" Why didn't anyone tell me? "Hello, Albert, hello...sir and sir," I greet them all quickly. It would help to know their names.

"Princess Ivaskov," they chime in together.

I move closer to Remy, slightly hiding behind his shoulder. I already messed up once; maybe if I stick with him, he'll know what to do. We pile into the cars, me safely tucked between Remy and Ash, and the uncomfortable silence is nearly unbearable. With some of my mates in the other car and with Grandfather with us in ours, it seems no one has anything to say. Even Mikey is quiet.

Thankfully there are plenty of new things to take in outside of the windows. There's snow covering the ground everywhere, the sun is high in the sky, casting down rays of light through the clouds, making this new world glitter prettily. Holiday decorations fill the shop windows and skyscrapers stand tall as if they are fingers stretched out and begging the sun to shine on them

It's not long before the city falls behind us, along with the suburban areas, small towns, and occasional rural houses. The cars keep on going, though, reaching the base of a mountain and steadily climbing around it. The road is a constant gentle curve, and the higher we go, the more isolated everything feels.

Out of the corner of my eye, I spot movement in the woods. Taking a closer look, I realize that it's wolves matching the car's pace up the hill. It looks like they are having fun, racing one another. I smile and lift my hand to wave at them. The one in the front stops in its tracks and gets plowed into by the wolves chasing it. I giggle at the show, watching as they fix themselves and begin the chase once more. The one that caused the collision throws its head back and howls, causing the others to join in. Excitement, joy, and yearning rise up in me.

"Excited much?" Logan snorts, leaning over me to get a closer look. I realize that he's talking about them and not me.

"What are they doing out here?" I ask no one in particular.

"The whole pack is eagerly awaiting your arrival, Princess," the driver kindly explains. "Marcus' methods were not...I mean, We are very happy to have new leadership. Your father was a brilliant man, and we have heard the stories of your strength and kindness. Your mates may be feared by most, but the lower wolves already adore you, if you don't mind my saying so, your Highness. Those wolves out there just wanted the first glimpse of you is all, and they are bragging about it to the others."

Lower wolves? What exactly could they have heard about me? I've only been in this state for maybe an hour, and all I've done is ride in a car. The driver slows as we reach a set of tall metal gates, set into a stone wall. Two men in uniform, who I take to be guards, open them wide enough for us to pull through. They bow as the car passes, and I wonder if they will be stuck like that since I didn't have time to tell them hello.

An enormous building comes into view after several minutes of continuing up the driveway, and I frown in confusion. "I thought we were going to a house?"

"This *is* our new house, Love," Remy tells me.

"No way! It's even bigger than the one we came from!" Mikey says in disbelief, nearly crawling in my lap to get a closer look.

I look to Remy, then back at the house for a moment, then finally back to Remy. "I don't think you could call this a house," I tell him. The sheer size of it is intimidating. The thick, gray stone with ivy climbing up the sides doesn't give off a welcoming vibe at all. There aren't even any windows on the bottom few floors, just a set of wide double doors with a set of stone steps leading to the circular driveway. Cypress trees and square shrubbery form a line on both sides of the doors, while an ancient looking willow tree is the only decoration in the circle of snowy grass on the other end of the driveway.

"It's a pack house, my love. It is intended for the entire pack to use. For shared meals, celebrations, and to house those who do not fight in battle," Remy answers.

"Oh, so like a community center, just for wolves." I nod my head in approval.

Jace snorts in laughter. "Something like that."

The driver opens the door for us, and I step out into the chilly air. It's much colder here than it was at home. I catch sight of the wolves that followed us in the distance, making their way to the back of the house. Huh, I had thought they'd want to say hello. Then again, it's not as if they could, being in wolf form and all.

As the guys who rode in the other car meet up with us, Grandfather takes my arm in his, escorting me to the house. "Come, dear, there are several pack members that I would like for you to meet. They've prepared a feast for your arrival in the ballroom."

"Um, okay," I tell him, not knowing what else to say. I look over my shoulder at Tristan and Ash behind me. Tristan smiles slightly, shaking his head, knowing I won't eat the food he or the guys don't cook. Maybe no one will notice. Ash misses the silent conversation, as Mikey has taken to swinging from one of his arms as they trail after us.

As we walk through the entrance and down the hallways, I can't help but feel like this place isn't actually lived in. The old paintings hanging on the walls and the hand-carved trimming and other wooden pieces tell a story of people who cared greatly for this home. On the other hand, walls painted in different shades of the same color in spots and tattered rugs that I'm sure were ornate and priceless at one time, speak a different story. To my dismay, it seems like most of the home is nothing but a shell or a storage area for things they couldn't find a use for. Empty ballrooms, bedrooms, and common areas are everywhere. The place is clean, spotless in fact, but the love from times past is indeed missing now. I wonder if maybe Logan, Jace and I can come up with a way to make it feel more lively.

"Here we are!" Grandfather chirps happily as we come upon two more men in suits, much like the servants wore in Uncle's house, standing in front of closed doors. They bow quickly, and I am sure to tell them hello so that they can stand. They keep their eyes cast down and don't greet anyone but me, with what is becoming the standard, "Princess Ivaskov."

Grandfather lets me go to take Mikey's hand in his, explaining that they'll be announced first, then the guys, then me. Albert won't get an announcement I guess. We shift around, lining up as Grandfather tells the doormen which guy is which.

I can hear lots of people talking all at once behind the doors, but can't make out anything in particular. With a nod from Grandfather, the doormen open both doors with a practiced flourish. My guys stand straighter as Grandfather, then Mikey, is introduced to the crowd. A few whispers can be heard, but that's it.

Each of my guys is introduced as 'The Princess Ivaskov's Mate', and then their first name. I try to see around Remy, but he makes a better wall than a window. I narrow my eyes at his back, but of course, he doesn't notice. There is more mumbling when Ash is introduced, but no one speaks a word when it's time for Remy to enter. As he steps inside the doors, I get my first glimpse of the people inside. All eyes are fixed on Remy. Some individuals look frightened, some shocked, and a few look downright angry. I had put it out of my mind that Remy has already been here before. And his reason for his previous visit had been to kill their former Alpha in front of them.

The man announcing us cleared his throat, and my mouth went dry as everyone's attention was drawn to me. "Allow me to introduce to you, the granddaughter of Alpha Maksim, the daughter and direct descendant of The Fair Prince, Alpha Mikel, and bearer of the future Alpha of our pack, your Sovereign, Princess Kitten Ivaskov," he says formally, turning toward me and going to one knee, his head bowed. The rest of the room does the same, moving as one.

My heart was beating erratically, and I was sure I was going to faint at any moment now. I drew in a quick breath and stood as tall as I could. Taking a few steps forward, placing myself between, but in front of, Remy and Ash, who stood to either side of the door, I managed to get one word out. "Rise." To my relief, it came out strong and carried throughout the room. For the first time ever, I was grateful for Albert's lessons.

My guys stepped closer to me, each of them placing a hand on my back. In a 'V' pattern, we made our way through the crowd to a table that sat on a raised platform, overlooking the rest of the room. To my surprise, all of my guys took seats on the right of me, while Grandfather, Mikey, and Albert took seats to my left. It was uncomfortable not to be in the middle of my mates.

A procession of people came by our table,

introducing themselves and welcoming us. Many of them got caught up talking to Grandfather and Albert, probably people they've known for a while. Very few choose to say hello or introduce themselves to the guys, but all made a point to greet me and sometimes Mikey.

More servant-dressed men had brought out several trays of food to line our table, and I had dutifully piled a few items onto my plate and pushed it around with my fork. I wanted to appear to be eating it, so as not to hurt anyone's feelings. I know Tristan is very sensitive to that, so others might be as well.

"Bleh! What is *that*?" Mikey asks while trying to wipe his tongue off with the cloth napkin.

Grandfather chuckles and leans over to hand the kid his water glass. "It's escargot. Is it not to your liking?"

"More like S-car-no way. It tasted like poop. Who eats poop for dinner?" He makes a face as he chugs half of his glass. "Do you think they have any hotdogs? Hotdogs are good."

I giggle at the scene he's making, Albert looking way more embarrassed than he should be. I eye the black-ish looking stuff on Mikey's plate and have to give the credit for even trying it. It really does look like bird poop.

Grandfather eventually tells me that I should mingle with the people, and I reluctantly leave the guys at the table. Within two minutes, I'm already tired of being called Princess, but everyone just laughs and tells me how funny I am when I ask them to call me Kitten. Most of the men I meet are friendly, though no amount of social lessons with Finn can make having conversations with people I don't know any easier. Especially when they bring up people I've never met, places I've never been, and events that I never attended. I let Grandfather do most of the speaking, just nodding along and smiling when I'm supposed to.

It's during one of these conversations when my attention drifts to a boisterous man not too far away from us. He speaks louder than is really appropriate and his hands gesture wildly as he tells a story to a cluster of men gathered in front of and beside him. If I had to guess, he's had a little too much alcohol. None of this really concerns me until the man in question turns my way, sees me looking, and chortles in laughter.

"Oh no! It seems as if the Princess has her eyes set on me now as well. Should I just go claim my seat at the head table now, or do I have to fuck her first?" He roars with laughter at his own joke. The men surrounding him choke on their drinks and their eyes widen in fear as they look to me.

From across the room, I see Albert standing to remove Mikey from the room and my guys making their way to me, Ash shoving people out of his way carelessly, taking the lead through the crowd. My blood boils with a rage I didn't know I possessed. Without thought, my feet move of their own accord, heading straight for the loud-mouthed man.

When I reach him, he only stares at me with a frown on his face. His eyes are clearer than I'd thought they'd be, telling me it's not just the alcohol speaking through him.

"Is there something you'd like to say to me?" I ask with narrowed eyes, my voice calm despite the anger coursing through me.

Instead of bowing like every other person here has

today, the man stands to his full height, having at least a foot on me, and looks down with disdain. "Maybe I do. Maybe I want to tell you that it's disgusting to learn that my new Princess is a whore who thinks it's okay to lay with filthy changed wolves and dares to name an unblooded human child as my Prince," he spits out, his eyes and word issuing a challenge.

I tilt my head and study the man. His booming voice has carried throughout the room, and all conversations around us have come to a screeching halt. I sense, more than see, my mates taking up positions behind me. I hear Grandfather's request to let me handle it and can practically feel the guys' barely concealed restraint. But none of that matters to me right now. I can feel this man wanting to look past me, sensing the guys are the bigger threat to him, but I command him with my eyes to hold my gaze, not letting him look away from me.

A slow smile spreads over my face as I watch a bead of sweat form at his temple. "Is that all you *maybe* want to say?" I ask sweetly.

His mouth opens to speak, but words never make out. I reach out quickly, my hand going to his throat in an instant. I growl slightly as I feel my claws shift out from my fingertips. I'm holding him tightly enough to cut off his airflow, but not to draw blood. Not yet.

"No? Nothing more? Then I guess it's my turn. I *definitely* didn't ask your opinion on my mates. I *definitely* don't care what you have to say. I *definitely* want you gone from my pack. And I will *definitely* kill you if you insult my mates or my son again. If you had taken the time to get to know me, you would have learned that I dare to do a lot of things," I tell him coolly, pausing for a moment to take in his bloodshot eyes and purpling face before releasing him with a shove to the floor. Oops, looks like my nails dug in after all. He'll have a hard time getting blood out of his white shirt.

The only sounds in the room are the ones he makes as he wheezes for air and scrambles to his feet, fleeing the room. I make eye contact with each man who was gathered around the loud mouth, before addressing the room in as a loud a voice as I can without going high-pitched.

"Anyone else have anything to say about my mates or my child? If so, the door is right over there," I say as I point it out. "I won't beg for your membership in this pack. I won't beg for your friendship or loyalty; I won't beg at all. I won't keep anyone here who doesn't want to be here. This is your chance to go; I won't stop you. But if you stay, know that I expect your respect for my family, and I won't tolerate anything less. If you stay, you become a part of that family; you become people I will care for and about. You will be respected, acknowledged, and cherished members of our pack. I will offer you the same amount of loyalty that you offer us. So choose wisely, but it is your choice."

There's a shuffling in the room as at least three people make their way to the door, but the rest of the room falls to their knees, placing their hands over their chests and bowing their heads. My anger flies out the door with the realization that not every person in this room is against me.

I turn to face the guys, seeing that they are the only ones still on their feet; even Grandfather has taken to his knee. I look to Remy for a bit of help, not knowing what to do now that I'm not angry and my wolf is no longer in charge of me. He cups the side of my face, before placing a chaste kiss, full of unspoken emotion to my lips. He takes a deep pull of air before addressing the room.

"When you rise, you will stand as members of the new Ivaskov pack. A pack that looks out for each other, a pack that shares in both triumphs and pain, in glory and defeat. A pack that works as a team for the enlightenment and benefit of each and every member. Your Princess calls on you to act with honor and kindness in every action that you make. Now, will you rise to that challenge? Will you rise as better men, the best men that you can be?" Remy's voice raises as his speech progresses; by the end, he's nearly shouting, and the crowd stands to their feet, cheering loudly and clapping their hands.

I nearly have tears in my eyes after such a moving and motivational speech. I watch the now-eager crowd talk excitedly to each other, back-slapping and overall camaraderie all around me. Now this seems more like my kind of people. A thought occurs to me, though, and I turn to Grandfather for the answer.

"Is this everyone? The whole pack? I thought there were more of you." I remember reading that the Ivaskov army is the largest wolf army in the world, striking terror in the hearts of its enemies. Even if everyone here were soldiers, I'm not sure I would fear them, even if they were wolves.

"*Our* pack. And no, this isn't everyone," he corrects me.

"Then where are the rest of us? It's Christmas Eve… shouldn't everyone be at the party?" I ask.

He shifts on his feet uncomfortably. "Well, you see,

it's not common for the lower wolves to mix with the upper-class wolves. Most of the men here tonight are in charge of our off-site properties or in charge of other things here at the house," he explains.

"That doesn't answer my question. Where are the others?" I narrow my eyes at him, already knowing I won't like the answer.

He rubs at the back of his neck nervously. "The foot soldiers are in their housing units, and the lower wolves are still in their camps around the property," he admits.

I stomp my foot in exasperation and frustration. "Why? We talked about this! I told you to bring them in. What's the point of having a house this large and leaving my people out in the cold to fend for themselves?" I throw my hands up and stomp around him, heading for the door.

"Whoa, slow down. Where are we headed, Warrior Princess?" Tristan asks as he walks up beside me.

"We're going to go get the rest of the pack," I state, stopping my tracks as something else occurs to me.

"Albert!" I call.

He rushes over to me quickly, having already returned without Mikey. "Yes, Princess?" He bows. I wave that away, not having the time or patience for it.

"Please inform the men here that we'll be going for a run on New Year's Eve, so if they want to stick around for that, then they are more than welcome. And see if there is enough food prepared for the *entire* pack, please. If not, have them make more. I want every belly on this property stuffed full tonight."

Albert nods his head deeply and smiles at me. "Of course, right away Prin...Kitten," he quickly corrects himself before jogging off to the kitchen.

I continue to stomp around until I have to admit that I have no idea where I'm going. I finally give in and turn to Grandfather. "Can you show us where we need to go? I'd like to get Mikey then go to the camps."

"Of course, dear. Albert most likely took him to the only sitting room with a working TV. I'll lead the way if you'd like."

I nod at him and drop back to take Kellan's hand in mine, needing one of those rocks in the storm of my current emotions.

We find Mikey easily enough, and I'm happy to see that he hasn't been left alone in a new place that he doesn't know. A man in servant's clothing sits in a chair reading a well-worn book as we enter the room, but he quickly drops it as he stands to bow to us.

"No, no, don't do that. Now you've lost your place," I'm quick to say, feeling bad about interrupting him.

"It is of no importance, my Princess, just a bit of light reading," he tells me.

"Well, my first rule is that bowing and greeting me comes second to reading. I'll always allow you to find a good stopping point and carefully mark your place," I state firmly.

The man smiles. "Ah, I see you are fond of literature yourself then?' he asks.

"Who isn't," I say with a shrug.

Mikey looks over from his spot on the couch, his discarded tie and vest tossed next to him. Well, that didn't take him long. "Come with us, Mikey. We have more people to meet," I tell him, holding out my free hand for him to take.

"Aw, man. Do I have to put the tie back on?" he complains.

I shrug my shoulders. "I don't see why you can't go without them," I agree.

"Ok, cool," he says, taking the offered hand.

"You may be pleased to learn that there are a few other boys around your age where we're headed. Maybe you can make a few friends," Grandfather tells him.

My eyes nearly pop out of my head as I jerk around to look at him in horror. "What!" I ask through gritted teeth.

Kellan rubs my back. "Easy there, Kitten. You have a young audience," He reminds me. Right, Mikey.

Grandfather frowns at me. "I hate to point out that the wolves being out there is not only my fault. If them being out there bothers you so much, you should have come sooner. It's not as if they mind it; they've been out there for quite some time now. Some of the younger ones have lived there since they were born. Even if I had asked them to come in, I cannot issue orders, and it is not my house any longer," he defends himself.

I'm still irritated with him, seeing as I thought this issue was handled some time ago, and no one had told me differently. But he makes a good point. I should have followed up on it and made sure they were granted entry into the house. I'm to blame as well. The thought of leaving anyone out in the cold and snow breaks my heart, but I unknowingly left children to the same fate, and that feels like a stab to the chest. And I would know what that feel like.

"Do not blame yourself for this, Love. You did not actually put them out there, and you had no way of knowing. There's no point in placing blame in the first place. All we can do is move forward and offer them better now," Remy directs me.

"Right," I sigh. "Lead the way then, Grandfather."

I follow along behind him and Ash, the rest of the guys keeping close behind me. Mikey asks questions about this room or that as we pass them, and Grandfather is quick to answer him, telling him what they were once used for and what they are used for now. I take note of the room he points out as my father's former office, which is now boarded over with a chain and lock. I'll have to come back to that some other time.

CHAPTER SEVENTEEN

"What. The. Actual. Fuck." Logan says dramatically as he steps outside. Curious, I hurry to see what he's seeing.

I blink my eyes several times, sure that I've gone mad because in no way could this image be correct. The front of the house speaks of intimidation and wealth, the inside speaks of carelessness, and the backside, well, it's just a mess.

There's no grass to speak of or even a blanket of snow-covered ground. Just a muddy pit with rows and rows of dilapidated metal trailers. Tall white buildings are caging the trailers in on both sides. They almost look like run-down motels with their shabby railings and chipping paint. Both the trailers and the white buildings sit so tightly together, they appear to be nearly sitting on top of one another. The only break in them is a straight footpath right through the center, big enough for a car to drive on and enough space to walk between the trailers and the buildings themselves.

Those who were outside of the trailers quickly hurry inside when they see us. Almost all of them are wearing some form of gray, though I don't notice any real pattern other than that. Some wear sweatpants, some T-shirts, some sweaters, and others long coats; all of it in different shades and levels of shabbiness. Ash grunts behind me, and I turn to see him shaking his head. We pause on the path momentarily for the big guy to pluck an unsuspecting soldier away from his group. Ash and his new friend fall to the back of the group, and I imagine my Shadow has many questions he'd like the answers to.

Maksim leads us down the main muddy trail, and Reed offers me his back for a ride. I throw my arms around his neck and hug my body as close to him as possible. I'd hate to ruin the dress Logan made for me. I kiss his neck in gratitude.

We walk at a brisk pace, finally leaving the trailers and apartments behind and into the snow-covered fields that I imagine will be planted in the spring. After the fields are the orchards, and finally the wooded areas. The path continues on straight for a while before curving around and turning into a wooden bridge over a frozen stream. The woods are the best thing I've seen yet. Plenty of room and paths to run around on but dense enough for some cover and for tasty animals to try to make their homes.

Once on the other side of the bridge, I notice fewer boot prints in the mud and more paw prints.

"Is this where the pack runs? I thought you were

showing us where the lower class lives," I say to Grandfather. I think back on the trail, and I'm sure it didn't split off anywhere. Do we really have to wait to shift until we get all the way out here?

Grandfather sighs in front of me. "Yes and no. The pack does run here, but we run all over the property as well. And this is the way to the camps."

Well, I guess that answers that. A few seconds more and I can sense other people in the woods ahead of us. A few more feet and I see it. My blood boils at the same time my heart drops into my stomach. I only see a few of them, but as Kellan keeps walking, I see more and more of them.

"No," I grate out.

"Kitten? Are you okay?" Kellan asks.

I shake my head slowly, dropping my arms from around his shoulders and sliding off his back. I work my way around the guys in front of me, walk briskly to the plywood and blue tarp-covered box, closest to us and take a peek inside. Two wolves stare back at me with curiosity, laying side by side in the too small shelter. I stomp further down the path, the others following as I pass more and more shacks and tented dwellings. After a few minutes, the path opens up to a gathering area where handmade benches are placed around a smoky fire, and a few wolves and men are milling about. I've never understood the term heartache until this very moment. My chest actually hurts at seeing this. I've seen hobo villages before, and I've seen countless people in need. But knowing my own family has done this, to our own people no less. People they were supposed to care about. People who pledged themselves to them. The people who made me and gave me a last name have done this.

"Why?" I choke out, staring at the flames of the fire. I realize I'm crying, but I don't care who sees. "Why are people like this? Why does everyone have to be so cruel? I thought meeting wolves and knowing a whole different set of people would change things. It didn't, people are always going to be people, putting each other into classes and finding ways to hurt one another. Why?" I ask again.

Remy comes up behind me, wrapping me in his arms and placing his head on top of mine. He sighs deeply. "I wish I could tell you that there was a time when everyone got along and everyone was equal, but I can't. In any society, there will be some who have more than others."

"It's not about having, Remington. It's about not caring for each other. Everyone has been trying to explain what having a pack means, what being a part of one means, and now I'm convinced that they were all lying or just don't know themselves. I don't want this. I don't want to wear elaborate gowns and drink expensive wine while members of my pack...of my family, are out here in the cold. I don't want to live in an empty house when these people, my people, are living in boxes." I trail off as either sorrow or anger lodges in my throat.

"Don't upset yourself, dear. You knew you were coming here, so why the waterworks now?" Maksim asks, clearly not understanding my distress.

"I wasn't expecting *this*!" I shout at him, no longer caring that Mikey is here to hear me. He should hear me; he should know that treating people this way is wrong and that I'm passionate about it. "I thought maybe there were cabins or smaller homes of some sort. Not a full-blown hobo camp where people are forced to live literally like animals in order to survive. I'm allowed to be upset by this, so don't you dare try to tell me when I'm allowed to cry!" I point a finger at him.

Maksim gets that lost, panicky expression that all men get in the face of an emotional female. My guys hide it better, but even they do it. I huff one last time at him, deciding to ignore him, as I know everything I say now will be chalked up to me being an irrational woman in his eyes.

As I turn away from him, I realize that my shouting has caused quite a scene, and quite a few wolves and men have turned to watch what's going on. My cheeks heat in embarrassment, but I just brush away the tears on my face and hold my head high as I find the nearest bench and stand on it.

"Forgive me, I'm sure I haven't made the best first impression. As you get to know me, you'll come to realize that I'm not that great with people," I joke, trying to lighten the mood. It seems to work, as some of the men chuckle lightly, and more wolves and men step from their dwellings to crowd around me and the guys, who have moved to stand in front of me.

"I wanted to invite all of you personally to join us at the pack house. Bring your belongings as well, as you no longer live here. Y,ou live with us. I haven't figured everything out yet, and I don't know how it will work or where everyone will sleep, but please bear with me and we'll figure it out together. For tonight, though, there's plenty of food, and the house is warm. Thank you," I finish.

I step down from my perch and begin the long journey back to the house. I hear people talking and moving around and sense my guys behind me, but I ignore it all, just like I used to do. I figure that the men and wolves in the camp will follow along if they want to, and those who don't I can come back for another time. I made the offer for all, and it's all I can do right now. I've had enough. Enough talking, enough doing, enough messed up family legacies, enough peopling in general for one day.

No one tries to touch me or speak to me as we make our way back to the house. I'm grateful for it, even as I hate myself for being this way. I'm too upset to voice my thoughts, too angry to even think clearly. I walk away from the others once we're in the house, and they let me wander off alone, though I suspect they are just following at a distance. Anger is not new to me, but this time there's not a single person to be angry with. It's an entire system. It's everyone and no one, everything and nothing.

ASH

I watch as my brothers debate over who should go in after Kitten. She went silent on us and walked away. She's never done that before, and it's got us all worried, even me. Usually, Kitten speaks every thought in her head without shame; something I love about her. I knew as soon as we stepped through the doors of this place, that we had our work cut for us. I've never been inside a pack house before, but even I know that the fucking pack should be inside it. The people we passed had all had a gleam in their eye as they saw their new Princess, but underneath that was pain and longing for something more. In all honesty, I was just waiting for Kitten to clap her hands together and start throwing out ways to fix everything. When her eyes blazed with fury after Maksim asked why she was crying, I thought, this is it, this is where she demands her Kitten justice. Now, even I'm a little afraid of the ticking time-bomb this situation has created in her.

"I'll go," I sigh deeply, cutting off whatever Logan was going on about. I know he wants to have fun and cheer her up, but now is not the time. Besides, last time they did that, she just ended up finding things to rescue anyway. That gives me an idea. "One of you run up to our stuff and bring me Noah and AJ."

"You think her stuffed animals are going to make her feel better?" Jace snorts. I ignore him and call a thanks after Tristan as he runs to do what I asked.

"Shouldn't we all go in? I mean, there's safety in numbers, right?" Reed forces a nervous chuckle.

"Careful now; she can probably hear us," Finn tells him.

"Nah, she never listens in on purpose; she still thinks like a human and doesn't use her senses," Logan says as he slicks his hair back, his new haircut already getting on his nerves.

Tristan comes back quickly with the toys and hands them over. He pats my shoulder and stands aside for me, the others doing the same. I'm getting more looks of sympathy and good luck than I did when I used to go off to war. And here we men think women are dramatic, I think as I roll my eyes and move toward the door.

Kitten doesn't move as I enter the room and close the door behind me. She's found a cleared out room and is sitting Indian-style in front of a massive marble fireplace that is even taller than me. It's unlit, so I have to wonder if she's still seeing the flames she was staring at back at the camp. She's slumped forward, as if she's got the weight of the world on her shoulders.

I take a seat next to her and lean back on my hands, my legs stretched out in front of me. I keep the bear and AJ behind me for now and just stare in front of me like she's doing. I'll give her time and let her speak when she wants to.

I don't know how much time passes, but she finally talks. "You didn't have to come in here," she says in a whisper.

"I wanted to," I reply.

It's a few minutes before she speaks again. "I don't know what to do. Maybe we should just go home."

"Don't give up now, little one. We only just got here," I tell her.

Kitten turns her head to face me; to my relief, she isn't crying. "And so far I have choked a man and sobbed in front of people who have it worse than me."

Where did the ever-optimistic Kitten go? "You've defended your mates and showed those people out there that you care. You could've done worse." I shrug a shoulder.

"Yeah." She sighs, staring at the empty fireplace again. Okay, time to bring out the big guns.

I reach back and bring out her ugly-ass bear, sitting it in front of her. She looks down at Noah and then to me with questioning eyes. "Tell me why you wanted that bear," I demand, my voice intentionally going hard.

Her small fingers trace over the stitches Kellan gave

him. "Because he was forgotten. No one else would have picked him and taken him home," she tells me.

"Right. Those people out there, and even the ones you met at the party, are just like Noah. They need someone to remember them, someone to care about them, someone to give them a home and a purpose," I explain.

Kitten shakes her head. "It's not as simple this time. I can't just pick them up and carry them home. None of these people see what's wrong with this situation. Not the ones in the woods or the ones at the party. Why try to change things when they all just want to go on living the way they are? Maybe I'm the problem, not them."

I wince at the defeated tone in her voice. "Those people out there aren't happy, Kitten. Neither were the ones at the party. They live the way they do because it's what they know. It's the way it's always been done; they don't know any different."

I pull AJ out from behind my back and sit him next to Noah. "Ever since you picked him up off that shelf, AJ has represented my future, in a way. I don't know if kids are possible for us or not, and if we'll ever have any. But…he's my future with you. A promise of something more in this life. That's why, Kitten."

"Why what?" she asks, her green eyes now focused on me and sparkling with an intelligence that tells me she knows, but she wants to hear it.

"You keep trying because the future deserves better," I tell her and lean down to kiss the top of her head. I get to my feet and head for the door, giving her space with that thought. I look back at her as I'm leaving the room and smile as she picks up AJ and brings him to her chest, petting his furry head. I can't help but think that the fate of so many people landing on the shoulders of that tiny woman was the best thing that could have happened to us all. Here I was, going through life trying not to care about anyone other than my brothers, and this woman, this amazing woman, cares so deeply for those around her that she can hardly bear it. Yes, our future could not be in better hands.

The men openly stare at me as I close the door behind me, letting me know they heard every word of our conversation. I don't mind; it's better that they did so I don't have to repeat it. Saying those things to Kitten is one thing; to a bunch of men, well, that's another.

"You didn't convince her to come out," Logan states the obvious.

I shake my head. "No, she'll be fine once she steps from that room. I won't force her to do it before she's ready."

"She does like time to process." Finn nods in approval.

"I'll go see what I can make for Kitten in the kitchen. I don't know what the rest of us are having, but I want her to eat, and she'll only eat my food," Tristan says with a smirk. He loves that fact way too much. I never claimed my brothers weren't a bunch of crazy fuckers.

KITTEN

I tuck AJ and Noah under my arm and head for the door. I owe the guys an apology for walking off, and a thank you to Ash for saying just the right thing.

"Sorry guys," I say with a sheepish smile as I soon as I see them sitting and standing outside in the hallway.

"There's nothing to apologize for. You just needed a minute and maybe a pep talk. Which by the way, is probably Ash's first ever, so you should feel honored," Tristan jokes, his soothing voice just the balm I needed.

"Well, I don't know about you guys, but I think we've dealt with enough shit for one day. What do you say we go up and check out our rooms, find somewhere to just chill for the night?" Logan throws out.

"That might be a good idea. I'll go down and see how everyone is settling in and make sure everyone has eaten. I'll bring us back some food while I'm at it," Remy agrees.

"It's Christmas Eve; we can probably find a good holiday movie to watch," Finn suggests.

"In that case, I'll go get the food, and hunt around for some movie snacks, too. I need to make something Kitten will eat anyway," Tristan chimes in.

"Alright, here's the plan," Remy starts. "I'll go check on everyone and tell Albert to handle anything that comes up tonight and tomorrow. Kellan, you go and bring Michael up to our rooms. Tristan, figure out the food for us tonight and make sure the house has enough for everyone tomorrow, if not, send someone. Logan, find us a place to enjoy a film where we'll all be comfortable. We might want to look into the sleeping arrangements for later. Everyone else head on up to our floor; I'll be back."

There's a chorus of mock 'yes, sirs' and non-mocking okays as the guys who need to follow after Remy head toward the stairs. The rest of us follow after Logan, who seems to know where he's headed. Which makes sense since he's been in contact with people here to get the rooms organized for us.

I'm not surprised at all to learn that the entire top floor was reserved for the royal family only, but I was surprised to learn that there were guards stationed on the landing between the floor below it and our floor. Their orders are to kill anyone who attempts to enter who is not part of the royal family. Even Albert isn't allowed up here. The only exception is for house staff, and they are picked very carefully, I'm told. I feel like maybe someone should have told me this way before now. What if I had invited someone up there? Well, I guess I can see their point in not mentioning it; who would I invite?

Logan opens one door after the other, peeking inside to see which is which. I peek, too, and see that each room is painted, and the bigger furniture like dressers and beds has delivered, and clothes are hanging neatly in some closets, but nothing has been put together yet. Boxes are neatly stacked, and nothing stands out as messy, but there's still a lot to be done before bedtime.

The guys continue down the hall with a tall archway at the end of it, while I fall behind, being nosey. I close the last door before the open arch and frown. I still don't know which room is mine, or Mikey's for that matter. I don't really care about mine, as I'll probably sleep with one of the guys, but Mikey will need to get to bed before we do.

"Hey, Logan!" I call into the large room, impressed with the sheer size of it. The big red couch seems to have made it from the old house, and even that looks small in here. The only other piece of furniture is a flat screen TV mounted on the wall, though it looks as if there are built-in bookcases at the other end. The room is painted a deep purple, which goes well with the gold features throughout the room, like the big chandelier with crystals and a golden 'I' hanging from the ceiling.

"What's up, girl?" he calls back.

"I couldn't tell which room was Mikey's. He'll be needing to get to bed soon, so we should probably get it situated enough for him to sleep there."

I follow after him as work our way back down the hall. There are more rooms than we could ever need on this floor, but it looks like Logan has some of them set up as hobby rooms for some of the guys. Like a studio for Reed, and a room full of fabrics for himself. There's also bathrooms and another big open room at the other end of the hall.

"Huh, I wonder why they put his room as far away from ours as they could," Logan questions as he opens the last door on the right.

"Because the spare rooms are for the Alpha's own children, so they stuck him on the end like he's not important," I say with a disappointed sigh. The gesture is evident, even if I don't approve and think it's mean.

"Yeah," Logan says with a shake of his head. "You're most likely right. Don't worry; I'll move his room as soon as I can. Maybe we can crash in the family room down there for tonight."

"That sounds nice; I'd like that. Although I don't know if Mikey will agree once he sees you got him a racecar bed," I tell him, smiling at the red and blue plastic shaped like a car leaning against the wall.

Logan shrugs, smiling at it, too. "It's kind of tacky, but it was too fun to pass up. If he doesn't like it, I can get him a new one."

I walk over and hug him tightly. "I'm sure he'll love it. Thank you for being so thoughtful." He kisses me lightly on my lips, which quickly turns into a heated make-out session. Even Logan's tongue is fun.

"Child eyes are present," Remy coughs as he and the rest of the guys make it up the stairs with Mikey in tow.

I pull away from Logan and wipe at my now-swollen lips. He just winks at me before going to help Tristan with the bags and plates of food he and Kellan carry. I do the same, taking two giant bowls of popcorn from Kellan's hands.

Finn plays the movie he found about Christmas ghosts as Ash and Logan leave to collect blankets and pillows. I munch away on a sub sandwich Tristan prepared for me and the others lounge around with their own snacks and food, settling in. I fell asleep on Ash's chest long before I found out what the ghost of Christmas future wanted.

CHAPTER EIGHTEEN

Christmas day was fun and relaxed as the ten of us choose to stay on our floor, leaving all worries and problems behind for the day. Mikey had woken up first, spotting the presents Logan had wrapped and brought out for him. All of them were his, much to his delight. He got LEGOs, an art set with markers and colored pencils, a heavy winter jacket with a hat and gloves set, a remote-controlled airplane, his movie, and a few other toys. Logan had said that he and Jace had actually gotten more things for him, but they decided that Mikey would be more than happy with what they gave him, and they took the rest down last night for the few children in the pack who didn't have any presents. When I found this out, I was so proud of my guys and their charitable hearts. They also told me that there were two pre-teens that they had nothing for, since all of Mikey's presents were for someone younger, so

I offered to let some of my paintball gear go that Tristan had gotten me for my birthday. I had, of course, asked Tristan about it first, but he said it was no big deal and we could get more before we decided to play again.

As for the guys and myself, we had talked about it a while ago, and since I didn't really care about Christmas and getting presents, and with the hassle of having to move, we didn't exchange gifts. I already had everything I wanted, and that was my mates. Jace had also purchased new vehicles for most of the guys since their old ones were either totaled or not made for the snowy mountain weather, so we counted those as gifts, too, though they won't be here until after the new year. I thought it was gift enough to spend the morning and afternoon watching Mikey play with his toys and cuddling up with my guys with soft blankets and hot chocolate.

By the afternoon, though, Logan was impatient and wanted to get started on the rooms. I helped where I could, but the guys were better equipped for the heavy lifting while I helped make beds and unpack boxes. I especially helped in Logan's room where I had worked with him on the design. His walls were painted a dark gray, which had unsettled him a bit at first, but once we got the blue sapphire silk bedding and pillows on his round bed, he came around to seeing the bigger picture. The three main colors were gray, blue, and just a touch of white, like with the accent rug and the frame for the tall mirror to hang on the wall.

Logan has said that my room at the old house was atrocious and looked like a tween threw up in there, so he had chosen a different route for me. He said it was Moroccan theme, with gauzy tapestries hanging on the walls and from my new platform canopy bed, with matching low nightstands on both sides. Because I didn't have a favorite color, he went with gold and gemstone colors like ruby, jade, and sapphire. When we were done, it seemed like stepping into a whole new world. I absolutely loved it. Mikey's room was moved closer to ours, though we left a few rooms between us so we wouldn't wake him with certain bedroom activities. His walls were supposed to be blue, but Tristan had given him *his* original room, so his walls were now bright red, a color he was pretty happy with. Tristan waved away Logan's offer of painting his new walls, stating that white walls for perfectly fine for him; his bedroom décor was all red anyway, so the white offset it now, making it stand out more.

It was later that night that I found Logan sitting on his bed, looking forlornly out the window.

"Hey. You okay?" I ask, taking a tentative step into the room.

Logan turns me with his trademark smirk. "And if I said no?"

I frown and walk over to sit beside him. "Well, then I'd have to try to fix it."

"You don't even know what it is that needs to be fixed," he replies.

"True." I chew my lip, thinking over the day and wondering what could be wrong. Nothing seemed out of the ordinary, I don't think. Out of the corner of my eye, I see he has gotten started on his music wall. Logan has a mess of records, CDs, and other stuff, so the idea was to fill the wall to wall shelving with them.

"You started without me," I point out, gesturing to

the shelf.

"Yeah, but only the top shelves you can't reach, Shorty," he jokes. "Want to listen to something?" he asks but doesn't wait for an answer.

LOGAN

I need a song, any song. What song do you play when you want your girlfriend to bite you and drink your blood? Do people still play music when they...? For fuck's sake, Logan, get it together!

I pull in a deep breath and hold it for a few seconds. I flip through my collection of CDs and decide on a mixed one that I had Finn burn for me a while ago. If I wasn't a total dumbass, I wouldn't have forgotten my phone in the other room and could use the playlist on the iPhone dock. Seriously, man, this isn't your first time with a girl.

I smirk at the stereo as the first song starts to play. I release the air from my lungs as the music starts to soothe over me. Yes, music and Kitten. It's a perfect combination. I turn the volume up a little and let *Born* tell Kitten just how I feel about her in their song 'Electric Love.'

I turn and look at the gorgeous girl sitting on my bed, peering at me curiously like I'm a puzzle she can't figure out. She sees me looking her way and a soft smile forms on her lips, and her eyes look quietly excited. She couldn't be more stunning if she tried.

I extend my hand in invitation to her, and the beautiful creature doesn't hesitate to accept it. I pull her slim body into mine and wrap my arms around her. My hips sway from side to side, and I feel her inhale my scent. I smile down into her hair as she makes a contented little sound. I wonder if she even knows she does that. I could stay here, just like this, with her, for the rest of my days. I really thought we had lost her for good. I didn't think I'd ever get to hold her like this, to feel her in my arms, and the regret almost ate me alive.

We're both quiet, protected in our little bubble of bliss as we dance slowly to the music. As the song comes to an end, and James Bay's 'Let it Go' starts up, Kitten glides her slender hands up my back and over my shoulder blades, causing me to lose my breath.

"Is this okay, Logan?" she asks in a whisper.

I pull my head back to see her worried expression. "Everything is perfect, Crazy Girl." I can't help the grin that overtakes my face.

Kitten's eyes light up, and she graces me with one of her fan-fucking-tastic smiles. I hold her tighter to me and bring my lips to her jawline. "I didn't know it could be like this," I whisper.

"Like what?" she whispers back.

I release her but take up one of her hands with mine and step back to take a seat on the end of my bed. Without me having to ask, Kitten crawls into my lap, her slim arms going around my neck.

I take a deep breath and try to explain the thoughts rolling around in my head. "You see, before I was turned, I was…let's just call it…very open to female interaction." Kitten's face scrunches up cutely as she tries to understand what I mean by that. I mentally roll my eyes at myself for trying to explain to my mate why she is so special to me by beginning with 'hey look, I used to be a man-whore.'

"I grew up in France, not a particularly important person in society myself, but my father was. Women weren't much of a challenge for me. Sex was more of a game to keep me entertained than anything. I'll be honest with you, Kitten, there was a time, a long time, where I gave my body freely to any beautiful woman who wanted a go," I reluctantly admit.

Kitten's eyes reveal a hint of pain, but I see no judgment there, and that gives me encouragement to continue. "I wish I could tell you that becoming a wolf made me smarter or more selective in that regard, but it only made me worse. I had led a common woman away from an event my father was holding, and into the forest that surrounded his property for some privacy. We came across the wolves and the next thing I know, I'm alone and in an immense amount of pain in the dark forest." I close my eyes briefly and shake the memory off. It's been a long time since I've thought about it.

"Anyway, even after I learned what I had become and chose to leave home before anyone found out, I still tried to remain the person I was before. Believe it or not, I was a lot like Jace; just with less formality and arrogance." I smile ruefully at Kitten and shake my head. Kitten doesn't look disgusted, just curious. I take that as a sign to continue.

"I resented being a wolf. I went from having more money than I knew what to do with, men and women alike vying for my attention, invitations to the best events in all of Europe, to being some... nameless, homeless freak. Women still found me attractive, and as time passed, I realized that I wasn't even aging. And, while I had never allowed myself to have affections for any of my previous dalliances, it was becoming apparent that I couldn't even if I wanted to. There were no feelings to be had from spending time in a woman's company, no intimacy, even when I sought it out. Older women, younger women, married women or maidens, it didn't make a difference.

"Somewhere along the line, I grew disgusted with it all. Disgusted at myself. I continued to need a woman from time to time, as there *is* a physical pleasure to be had, but it was never the same. It wasn't until after the guys found me that I learned it's a wolf thing, and later, we all learned that the only person to change that for us would be our mates."

I blow out a breath and suck in some courage to look at Kitten.

She seems curious and a tad saddened by my confession. "I'm sorry, Logan. That sounds so lonely." She looks sad, and I realize that I'm a complete idiot. Here I am, trying to bond with her, and I'm running my mouth about shit that doesn't matter anymore.

I sigh deeply, "It was, and I was stupid for acting the way I did back then. It got better once I met the guys. I had them then, people who were like me, who understood me. Jace had just been turned around the same time as me, and came from a similar background as I did, and we worked through it. The point of telling you any of this is because it's all changed now. You changed everything. I can feel you, Kitten. You make me feel. Things I've never felt for anyone, pre- and post-wolf. It's intoxicating and exhilarating, and I'm just…happy."

"I'm happy too, Logan," Kitten replies with a soft smile.

"You're special to me; that's what I was really trying to say. Bond or no bond, mate or no mate, I am yours." As sappy as it sounds, it's true. I wonder if she'll even let me mark her now. I should have just bitten her, then told her she's stuck with me now. Nah, that seems like an Ash thing to do.

I feel Kitten's body shake before I hear her soft giggling. I groan and flop myself back on the bed as I realize I must have said that last part out loud. "Are you laughing at me right now?" I question her even as I grin despite myself. I can't help it, she looks happy, and I like her happy.

"No!" she says adamantly. "Not at you, but that does sound like Ash." I watch as her soft giggling turn into full blown laughter, and she falls onto the bed beside me.

I growl playfully at her and get up to toss her further up the bed. She squeals and I pounce on her, tickling her sides until she's breathless.

Once I figure she's had enough, I lay beside her again and shove a pillow under my head, relaxing as she catches her breath, cuddling into my side.

"I'm happy you told me more about yourself. I want to know everything about you, Logan. The good and the bad. It may be your past, but it's part of you and I…I love you. Every part of you."

My breath hitches and I turn my head to find she's already looking at me. She's biting her lip nervously like she's said the wrong thing. Crazy girl, those were the best words she could have ever said to me.

I roll over and throw my leg over hers. I press my lips

to hers until she opens for me. I taste of her until she has trouble breathing. "I love you, too, Kitten. And I always will." Before I can say anything else to screw this up, I place my mouth over her neck and suck on her skin. My canines shift down, and I bite as gently as I can. My eyes close of their own accord as I take in her blood. It should be gross, but she simply tastes like everything I've always wanted.

Kitten grips at my arm, and I let her have it. I distantly feel her press a light kiss to my wrist before I feel her teeth scrape over my pulse point. She bites down, and it's like we're both floating in a world of fire. Not burning, just soothing warmth cocooning us and taking us to a distant land. It feels magical, and heartbreaking, and fucking hell am I turned on!

I release Kitten's neck to see if she's feeling what I'm feeling. Her eyes are bright, and her face is flushed. Oh yeah, she's feeling it. I peck at her lips and smirk down at her. To my surprise, she smirks back. Her small fingers find the skin of my neck and she trails them over the exposed skin there. Lightning follows her movements and sends shockwaves throughout my body. I do the same to her and her breath hitches.

We lay like that for a long time. Her touching me and me touching her. As arousing as it is, I just want to revel in her touch for now. I remove my shirt and let her explore my chest before she tells me she intends to play a game. Only Kitten would feel like this and still want to play. She really is the perfect girl for me. I roll over onto my stomach as she instructs and I sigh contentedly as her hands smooth over my back. She removes all but one fingertip and starts tracing over my skin. It takes me a moment to figure out she's spelling something. Electric love. I laugh out loud, and she giggles. Turns out I picked the perfect song after all.

CHAPTER NINETEEN

This morning is all business as Remy wakes us up for breakfast as the crack of dawn. Last night was wonderful. After I played my game on Logan's back and he fell asleep, I decided to take a quick shower in his bathroom. It must have woken him up because he joined me shortly thereafter. He made love to me in the shower, then pampered me with brushing my hair and blow drying it for me. Afterward, he showed me just how talented the French are with their tongues.

"Daydreaming about me already, Crazy Girl?" Logan asks hotly in my ear, nipping at my lobe.

"No," I lie, sure my blush is giving me away, though.

"Sure you're not." He winks at me, whistling as he takes a seat across from me.

"I was lying in bed last night, trying to figure out the easiest way to accomplish the most, in the shortest amount of time," Remy starts. "There are some issues within the pack that require our immediate attention, so I thought we could forego the elaborate Alpha ceremony, and just do the blood exchange this morning."

"We do currently have the entire pack here," Albert agrees.

"I'm good with that." Ash puts in.

Remy makes sure all are in agreement before continuing. "The past two nights, the people from the camps have shifted to their wolves and piled into the ballrooms, but I'd like to find them more permanent quarters today. We can have them help with any rearranging of furniture and cleaning, so that part should go quickly. The real issue will be getting enough beds and bedding here before nightfall."

Jace raises his hand in the air. "I can take care of that. I'll need at least two men to come with me, though."

Remy nods a thanks to him. "I'll see that you have helpers. Next issue is food. There's no plan in place to feed the number of people who now reside here, because they simply didn't feed everyone here before. We also don't have enough cooks, serving sets, or cookware. This needs to be dealt with as soon as possible. Any ideas?" he throws out.

Tristan lifts the pen he was chewing on, offering his services. "I can use my contacts in the restaurant business and have the dishes and cookware here ASAP. I'll also ask around for more help in the kitchens, see if there's an aspiring chef or two among them. At the least, we can get a rotating schedule going. As for the food itself, once we've got a menu, I can start placing deliveries."

"That brings me to our next issue. With the delivery

of goods coming in, we make it easy for our enemies to gain entrance through the gates, and even into the house. There wasn't much going on here before, but we're talking what, a once a week type deal, Tristan?" Remy looks for confirmation.

"At the least," he agrees.

"I was going to check out what kind of security they were running anyway. I can set something up, even if we have to unload and reload at the gates. It's not perfect, but it will do for now." Ash shrugs.

"Yes, that will do for now. Until Tristan gets regular shipments of food arriving, let's look into purchasing our own delivery vehicles, and shopping at the bulk supply stores, so the humans won't ask questions," Remy suggests, gaining a nod from Ash, who will probably be the one to buy the trucks.

"I have a question," I speak up. Everyone looks my way, so I go ahead and ask. "What do people think this place is now? I mean, even if all the wolves didn't live inside the house, they were still here. So that's way too many people for one house or one family. You know, normally."

Albert looks up from where he's taking notes for us. "Actually, the property is listed as a private resort. The towns are far away, and you own the entire mountain, so nobody questions how many people are coming and going. Also, a lot of the camp wolves didn't leave the property often. They ate what they could catch and harvest," he explains.

"There's something I would like to bring up as well," Finn jumps in. "I was already going to tutor Mikey, but I'd like to educate the other children as well. My issue is with the adults. I realize that the outlying Ivaskov communities allow their members to work in society and explore different routes of education, and I'd like to offer that here as well. I know we'll have a lot of expenses heading our way, but the better educated the pack, the more they will be giving back in the long run. Not to mention they deserve to do what they love."

"I agree with that statement, and will sign off on the cost for anyone who seeks higher education, but they should be contributing what they can, even if it's just a couple hours in the kitchens a week, or babysitting the children," Remy states.

"I have no doubt that our members will appreciate that, and they will help out whenever possible," a man named Yarley speaks up for the first time. He's one of the commanders of the army Remy invited to join us.

"Thank you for supporting the idea, but the problem lies with enrollment, logistics, and everyone having the same address," Finn points out.

Remy sits back in his seat, thinking it over. "We could think about getting a bus system going, heading into different towns and into the city. That way more people will have access to shop on their own and do other things, like attending schools, possibly for work. Let's find out how many people are interested before we worry about the address issue; it may not be a problem if we spread them out in the schools. We could always say they are family members of the live-in staff."

Finn nods in agreement, and Remy moves on. "Now that the important things are out of the way for now, I want to talk about the soldier housing."

"Yes, that shit needs to go!" Logan demands.

"I agree with you there, Logan. No matter what we put in that location, it's going to look atrocious and become a security threat, so I was thinking I could draw up plans for a series of single-family home communities to be spread out on the property. Not only would that solve the appearance problem, but we would then have soldiers in several areas, making it nearly impossible to attack them all at once."

"A fine plan," Yarley agrees, the other two commanders also looking happy about that.

"Speaking of the soldiers," Logan speaks up. "Those uniforms have to go. They are ugly with a capital fucking 'U'. I'll design new ones, better ones that actually match, but in the meantime, they should burn those things," he says adamantly.

"Not possible." Charlie, another commander states with a shake of his head. "Once you become a soldier in the army, gray is the only color you're allowed to wear. It's all they own."

Jace turns to Logan before he can voice his outrage. "Do you think you can get them measured and get me a list of their sizes?" he asks.

"You know it." Logan answers.

"Good. Then I can take care of getting them new clothing. The former camp members will be needing it as well," Jace replies.

"That takes care of that then." Remy nods in approval. "Kellan, if you could see to the health of the pack, that would be a big help. I know born wolves are immune to some illnesses, but not all of them, and some of them have been in horrid conditions."

"I already put an order in for supplies. I'll be starting

with the children," Kellan informs us.

Reed raised his hand as he senses the meeting is about to be over. "I just wanted to add that, while the soldiers have shelter, someone ought to look into whether or not they have everything they need out there. Heating, beds, running water, and the like. There's no telling what's going on inside of those buildings."

"Good idea, Reed, thanks for pointing that out." Remy clasps him on the shoulder. "So, there are several things to be done, and I'd like to get these handled ASAP. Those of you without specific jobs, just jump in with one of the others. I'll ask the rest of the pack for volunteers after the ceremony. Any questions?"

Nobody has any, at least for now, so we finish up with our quick breakfast of eggs and toast and head down to the biggest ballroom.

Grandfather joins us with Mikey in tow, and he takes over leading the ceremony for us. My guys pledge to take the Ivaskov name as their own and to defend and guide the pack to the best of their abilities. In return, the rest of the pack pledges to obey and honor the Alpha family. It's short and to the point and I have a hard time believing that the larger ceremony Albert spoke to me about would have taken over two hours. At the end of it, though, there was a blood-sharing custom where each of my guys provided a drop of blood to every pack member, excluding me, as a symbol of their willingness to bleed for the pack. Each person then gave them a drop of blood back as a symbol of their willingness to bleed for the Alpha family and their children, which also allowed the guys to recognize them on a magical level that only Alphas ever obtained. I didn't understand that part of it, but I guess I didn't have to.

That was supposed to be it, but before announcing the ending of the ceremony, Remy gave a speech stating that their mate, me, will be given the same respect as them and that they would be ruling by my side, not in front of or behind me. They are so sweet to me. It was all over after that. They were supposed to be crowned, but no one wanted Uncle's tainted crown, and there are eight of them anyway. Ash told me yesterday that he didn't even want one, but when Logan begged him to make them, he reluctantly agreed and said he'd get around to it eventually.

With our volunteers in tow, we quickly got to work. I had started out with Logan, who was measuring people to get their clothes sizes. It went alright with the kids, but when it was time for the men, it became apparent that me helping wouldn't work. The men were afraid to get too close to me, and I simply didn't want to touch them, which made it more than a little difficult to get the measuring tape near them. Instead, Logan taught his helpers how to get the right sizes, and I took over making the list.

I was surprised to learn that we all have the same last name. I mean, I know the guys took my name, but I had thought that was because there are eight of them and one of me, and I couldn't possibly take eight last names. But nope, everyone took the Ivaskov name when they joined the pack or were born, according to Ray, who was a size medium. He said that was why our scents were so important. You could tell who a child belonged to or who a female was mated to by the scent they carried. I'm still figuring out the whole smelling thing and what each smells means to my wolf, so I have no idea if that's true or not.

Eventually, my hand started to hurt from all of the writing, so I handed over the list to Ray, and he took over that job. With a quick kiss to a busy Logan, I sought out another of my mates and came across Finn, who had set up a sort of office for himself. There was a line of people outside of his office, waiting to speak with him about job opportunities or school enrollment. When I went in to see if I could help, I saw that he was talking to each person one on one and trying to find the right classes at the nearest schools. Most of what he was doing was taking place on the computer, so I doubted I could help with much of that. Finn took the time to walk me back out the door, though, and gave me a kiss, telling me Jace could probably use my help.

I walked around for a while, trying to figure out where my golden boy might be, but I couldn't find him. Eventually, I remembered my cell phone and had to call him.

That's how I came to be out here, looking through the trailers and apartments with Jace. We only looked through a few after getting the permission of the residents first. They had running water and heat, but the apartments were only single rooms with a toilet and a sink. There wasn't much to them, just blankets to sleep with and personal items. Other than heating and a toilet, these guys didn't have it much better than the people in the camps. The trailers were a little better, with actual furniture and bedrooms and a small kitchen area, though everything was old and rundown.

"I don't understand why no one has replaced

anything. It seems as though everything in these trailers was bought around the same time," I confide to Jace.

"I don't think they get paid, so nobody has any money to buy new things when something breaks or falls apart," he tells me.

The man whose home we're in speaks up to answer me. "Alpha Jace is correct, Princess. We serve the army in return for meals and housing only; we do not earn money," he tells me.

"So you guys in the trailers were at least fed regular meals then?" I ask, thinking that's at least something.

But the man shakes his head. "Maybe many decades ago, when the barracks were first replaced and these news ones were bought, but by the time the trailers were brought in, Marcus was already siphoning most of the pack money for himself or his friends," he finishes bitterly.

I offer him a sad smile. "I'm so sorry you were treated in such a way, and by my own blood. It won't be like that anymore; we're going to try to fix the mistakes and make it better for everyone."

"Yes, my Princess. I do not mean to complain; forgive me," he says with a bow.

I share a look with Jace, then look back to the man. "What's your name, sir?"

The man falls to his knees so he can now bow so deeply his head rests in the snow. "Please, your Highness, I meant no disrespect. I am happy to have all you provide me," he begs.

I stare at the man in horrified fascination, but luckily Jace speaks up. "Please stand, or else my mate is going to start crying and, trust me, no one wants that."

The man stands cautiously, brushing off the snow. "Of course, Alpha."

Jace leans against the porch railing, relaxing his stance. "I'm not much for titles, never have been. The Princess was only asking for your name so she may know who you are, that's all," he explains.

"My name is Henry, Princess," he answers me.

"Hello, Henry. It's nice to meet you. I won't punish you for your opinions on my uncle; I don't hold any affections toward the man. I actually ordered his death," I add.

"Furthermore," I continue, "I was just going to tell you that if you have any issues, like if your heat goes out, or the water stops working, to let one of us know, or Albert, so that we can fix it. There's a lot to be done, and it will take some time to get to the point where we can start replacing items, but we want to make sure everyone has what they need and are not left in the cold. That's our priority," I tell him firmly.

"Thank you, my Princess. I will keep this in mind for the future. And I apologize for my unfair judgment of you. I will have to remember that you are your father's daughter and not your uncle's niece," he says with a grin.

I'm confused by his meaning, but Jace thanks him for letting us look around and ushers me back to the house. "Sorry, but if we didn't leave soon, we would've ended up in a thank you war, and we have other things to do today," he says.

Jace leads me up to our floor and finds two laptops for us to use, setting them on the coffee table. We take seats on the floor in front of them, and I stare at him, wondering what we're doing.

"Alright, so I'm just going to have to assume that the dimensions are the same throughout the barracks and the trailers because I don't have time to look through them all. Let me just text Remy really quick and we'll see where the children are going to end up and also ask Logan if there are any unusual-sized men in our ranks," he tells me as he pulls out his phone.

His phone beeps with incoming messages, and he sets it aside. "Alright, Funsize, looks like we can go with full-size mattresses for the barracks, extra-long twins for the trailers, and queens for the bedrooms in the house, with a few exceptions, given the height of some people."

"Okay," I say, still having no idea what we're doing.

He types at his computer and I push the button to turn mine on. It's Finn's, so the password screen appears. I don't know the password. I tap Jace on the shoulder and point to my screen. "Oh, right. Sorry about that. It's IloveKiTTen4L1fe. He's a bit of a dork that way." He rolls his eyes. "I'll get you to the right sites; just see how many mattresses they have available in their stores in the sizes we need."

For the next two hours, we clean out every mattress store within fifty miles of here. Jace eventually has to call some of the stores to arrange payment and schedule pickups, but most of the shops allow us to pay with his credit card that we pass back and forth. Between furniture store and department stores, we manage to find most of what we need. Jace told me that we could probably locate the rest once we went looking. Not every store has a website, I guess.

"Time to see if Ash came through with the box trucks or not," he says, taking out his phone again. After a short chat, it turns out Ash did come through, and the trucks were already here. He then texts Reed to ask him to meet us up here.

"What's up, dude?" Reed asks as he jogs in into the family room. "Oh, hey, babe, long time no see," he jokes, coming to me and giving me a long, passionate kiss.

"Just pretend I'm not here, go ahead," Jace drawls.

"Sorry man, you know how it is." Reed winks at him. "What did you need?"

"Do you think you can stay here with Kitten and get working on ordering the bedding and such while I go with Ash to pick up the mattresses? I figure by the time we're done getting those, you guys will have finished, and we can head right back out," Jace asks.

"Sure, no problem, man. Tristan has enough help down there now, anyway." He shrugs.

Jace comes to me and gives me a lingering kiss as well. "Be back soon, Doll. Do try and behave yourself," he tells me with a smirk.

"Okay, I will. Don't be gone too long," I say back, waving before he turns to leave.

Reed rubs his hands together, taking Jace's vacated seat. "Alright, alright, let's get this show on the road, ladies and gents."

I giggle at his enthusiasm and go back to some of the sites where I saw bedding available. This proves a bit more difficult because the only options they have is shipping it to our house or buying it in the store.

"We're going to have to go get these if we want them here tonight." Reed comes to the same conclusion as me.

"Yep," I agree.

"Grab your coat and that credit card, babe, and we'll

see what kind of vehicles are left," Reed instructs me.

Downstairs is organized chaos as Logan finishes up his measurement list and Tristan teaches a crowd of people about food prep. Remy is also there, speaking to a different group of men about what kind of construction skills they might have to help with the new building. I check in with Mikey before we leave and see that he's made a couple new friends, and they're playing in the living room with their new toys. Grandfather sits nearby, keeping an eye on them as he watches the news, and the reading guy is there as well.

"Everything going okay in here?" I ask Grandfather as I walk in.

He smiles as he stands to greet me. "Oh yes, they've been at it for a while now. Apparently being wolf shifters isn't cool enough for them; they have to pretend to be superheroes as well." Grandfather shakes his head in wonder.

"Okay, I just wanted to let you know that I'll be going out with Reed to find bedding. Jace is already out getting the beds. Do you mind watching him a little longer? Has he eaten lunch yet?"

Grandfather frowns at me. "They've had their mid-day meal, yes, but why are you going out?"

I frown back at him in confusion. "To get the bedding, I just told you."

"It's not a good idea for you to leave the property, my dear. You put yourself at risk and the others with you when you leave. I know you have not seen it yet, but there are those who will wish to keep you for themselves if they can get to you," he warns me.

Reed sighs behind me. "I didn't think about that. He

may have a point, Kitten."

"Then who will go with you? Won't you be in danger if you leave? You're an Alpha after all. More important than me," I point out.

Reed chuckles. "Because I'm an Alpha they will want to stay away, but besides that, not too many wolves try to mess with a changed wolf. We're stronger than them. I'll just grab a couple of the volunteers to come with me, no biggie." He wraps me in a tight hug and places a loud smacking kiss on my cheek. I giggle as there is a chorus of "Ewwww" from the boys.

"Okay, but hurry back," I tell him.

Grandfather puts an arm around my shoulders as I watch Reed leave. "Don't worry too much about him; he'll be fine," he consoles. "I see you've marked the last of your mates; any hope of getting started making tiny Ivaskovs anytime soon?"

I pull away from him in shock. "Grandfather!" I exclaim, not believing that he'd ask such a question.

He just chuckles and sits back down in his seat. "What? You can't blame an old man for asking. I'd like to see my great-grandbabies run around here soon. I didn't get the opportunity with you or your cousin. Katerina would have loved grandbabies, and great-grandbabies, too," he says with a wistful sigh.

I take a seat in the plush chair by the fireplace so I can watch Mikey and his new friends, Morris and Perry. "We haven't talked about kids, well, not really anyway. There hasn't been much time for it, and I don't think any of us are in a hurry," I tell Grandfather.

"Hmm, does that mean you don't want them?" he asks.

I shrug a shoulder. "I don't know. I don't even know what kind of world I'm living in anymore; what kind of world I'd be bringing them into. And we still don't know if it's a possibility anyway. Why try for something, only to be disappointed?"

He nods his head thoughtfully. "All of that is true. You and your mates have plenty of time for all of that; it will happen when it is supposed to. That's what your grandmother always said."

I agree with him there; we have plenty of time. Though babies are super cute and I would love to see what baby Kellans and Logans looked like, and the rest of them, too.

"How come there are children here? I thought it was difficult for wolves to have children, that they were considered precious and protected at all costs. And where are their mothers?" I have to ask.

"Wolf pregnancies are complicated. Most of what we know about them is just guessing and experience. Things have changed so much since The Suffering. Those boys there are half-bloods with wolf daddies and human mothers. Some of our males are still able to conceive with humans, but once they find out about the wolves, they tend to run and leave their 'monster' children behind. It rarely happens, as the relationships themselves can never last, so most don't even try it, and they have to leave the pack to do so as well," he tells me.

"So their human mothers didn't want them?" I ask.

"That's right. And since they are half-bloods they won't shift until puberty, unlike born wolves, who are literally born as wolves. We have some of those as well in the pack, but Marcus demanded to have a chance to breed any female who proved herself capable, so that's how the remote villages were started. They hide both our females and our young there."

"That's horrible." I shudder in disgust. No wonder there aren't any women around here.

Grandfather grunts. "It certainly was. I suspect that we will be seeing them soon enough, though. Now that our Alphas are mated, and there's a female ruler, there is no reason to hide, and they will want to seek safety with the pack again."

"If they are safer here, then they *should* be here. Could you let them know that they are welcome here? We can put all the children and families with women and girls on the floor right below ours. They'll be as safe as ever there," I tell him.

He smiles at me in approval. "Of course, my dear. I'll make the calls myself. You really are a lot like your father; you both have generous hearts and level heads."

I continue to watch the kids playing, not knowing what to say about my father when I still see him as the man who threw me away. A few people have spoken about him, and from what I gather, he doesn't seem like the type of person to do that, or at least they don't think he was.

"Wait. You said wolves are born as wolves. How is that possible?" I ask, a horrifying image of a baby wolf clawing itself from its mother coming to mind.

"When a female wolf gets close to giving birth, she'll shift into her wolf form and remain as one, until about after a week after her pups are born. The pups themselves stay wolves for at least six weeks, and can shift any time after that," he explains.

"Oh. That must be difficult then. Babies turning into little wolf puppies whenever they feel like it and all." Nursing must be very complicated, scary even.

Grandfather laughs. "It can be, yes. But as infants, they pick up on their parents' energy and learn to shift when they do quite quickly. It's the toddlers you have to watch out for. The stubborn ones can be hard to handle. Your father liked his fits when he was younger; he'd feel as if some great injustice had been done to him and remain a wolf for days at a time." He smiles at the memory. "All I wanted was for him to take a bath or eat his vegetables usually," he adds with a chuckle.

I laugh, too, glad that Mikey can't shift, but he's pretty easy- going as far as kids go. I know some of it has to do with his past and the punishments he received for acting out at home.

Grandfather and I talk for a little while longer, about everything and nothing really. Soon, though, I decide it's time to get back to work and leave the kids with him and the other man, who never looked up from his book.

We get the beds situated with the help of most of the pack, complete with sheets, pillows, and blankets. It's a heck of a lot of work, but it's worth it. Once the beds are made, though, it still doesn't seem like enough. I just keep telling myself that it will take time. I had told Remy of my offer to the women and children and how we might be needing space for them, and he agreed to keep the floor below ours empty for now, except for the few children we have already, until we see how many there are. He also suggested that their floor have security as well, and that would give us double the protection, so it's a win-win.

Tristan had managed to get his hands on a couple of box trucks, so he and a bunch of others had taken a trip to a club store to stock up on groceries and personal items. We may be eating a lot of macaroni and cheese and ramen noodles for a little while until we can get the rest of the stuff for the kitchen we need. But that's okay with me; as long as everyone gets fed, that's good enough for me. And Tristan makes fantastic macaroni and cheese.

CHAPTER TWENTY

I had been up on our floor for a while before the guys started to return. I had to put Mikey to bed, and I didn't want to leave him up here by himself, so I grabbed the Harry Potter book Finn and I were reading and read ahead to keep myself entertained. That, and because I was quickly becoming addicted to them. I read at an average pace, though, so I wouldn't get too far ahead.

Logan and Jace were the first ones back, and they were happy to grab the laptops and sit on either side of me while I continued to read and they shopped online for clothing for the men in the pack. I took a quick shower, and when I returned, Finn had the book and was catching up where I had left off. Logan must have gone to shower, too, as it was just Jace and Finn.

"How was your day?" I ask him as he sets the book aside.

"Long," he replies with a smile, bending down to give me a kiss. "I think we've found classes for most everyone that won't be too far out of the way. There were a few people who asked about nursing and cooking classes, but I told them that Kellan and Tristan could probably teach them better than any school. So that helped cut down some of the need. Others were interested in carpentry and mechanics, so I told them the same about Remy and Ash. If they're dead set on degrees, they can still go of course, but as it is, we'll have to spread the enrollments out so as to not draw attention to ourselves."

"That does sound like a busy day." I hug him to me and run my hands through his shiny black hair. He sighs and nuzzles my neck in thanks. "I bet people were excited. You did a wonderful thing today, Finn."

About that time, Remy strolls in, looking beat. He gives me a hard kiss on the mouth and messes with Jace's hair before he heads straight for the shower. Reed follows shortly after with Tristan right behind him, Kellan and Ash being the last ones in. Each of them gives me kisses or hugs before showering or snacking on the chips Tristan brought with him.

"And how was your day, Shadow?" I ask Ash, having already asked everyone else.

He snorts as he sits heavily on the floor in front of me, leaning his head back into my lap. I play with his long locks as he answers. "It was a fucking nightmare," he starts, craning his head back to look at Remy. "Did you know that they have no training facilities to speak of? Those shit trailers were placed where their field used to be, and the new barracks are where the training center was on one side and the other used to be stone barracks that matched the house."

"So where do they train?" Remy asks, his rumbly voice sounding tired as well.

"They don't. That's my point. This army that's supposed to scare the living shit out of all other armies hasn't trained since the fifties. They rely on their parents or other soldiers to show them a few things. Most of those men haven't ever touched a sword or a gun," Ash huffs, closing his eyes as I use my nails to scratch lightly at his scalp.

"What about the commanders we met today? What do they do?" I ask.

Ash snorts. "Apparently nothing. They're mostly secretaries and make the schedules for patrol and security. These people are lucky no one has come for them in a while; they couldn't fight their way out of a wet paper bag."

"You telling war stories again?" Logan asks as he saunters back into the room, shirtless. He catches me staring and winks at me before collapsing on the couch.

"I wasn't talking to you, Fucker," Ash responds.

"You know you love me, Fatass. Don't act like you don't," Logan calls out playfully. Ash just grunts, pushing his head into my hands as I momentarily stopped scratching his head.

"Are we sleeping out here again or in our room tonight? I'm beat, so I'm heading to bed either way," Reed asks.

"I'm going to stay up for a while and work through some of this list," Jace tells him.

"Yeah, I'll help you with that," Logan offers. Jace nods and tosses him the other computer.

"I guess it's rooms then," Remy answers the question.

"You ready for bed, babe? Or are you going to stay up, too?" Reed asks me.

"I'll come to bed. Goodnight, guys." I tell the others as I make my rounds to give them each kisses. They tell me goodnight back, and then I head off to bed with Reed. He still has his white cloud bed, but he chose to hang paintings up this time, including the finger-painting I did of the guys with the heart around them. And instead of the all-white furniture, he went with pale beech wood this time. I loved his other room, but the new décor seems more like Reed. Laid back and relaxing, just like him.

Reed turns the lights off and slips under the covers with me. I snuggle in, feeling the mating bond rise to the surface, the electric sparks buzzing softly along every surface of my skin touching his. I kiss his neck before finding his lips in the dark. He kisses me back with a passion that only Reed possesses.

* * *

Time flies as we keep busy with getting everything situated and organized around the house. I met with Philip, Perry's older brother, and Damon, Morris' father, because Mikey seems to be inseparable from the other boys now. We had gotten the other kids bikes to ride so that Mikey could ride his and the others wouldn't have to miss out. Now, it's hard to keep track of them as they cruise around for most of the day. Phillip and Damon are nice guys, though, and when my guys or I have things to attend to, they look after the boys. Also Albert and Grandfather, and pretty much everyone else. Grandfather pointed out that that's how the packs were, everyone looked out for each other, especially the children. I still worry about Mikey when I'm not around, though; I wasn't raised in a pack like and this pack has been through some things.

He was right about the off-site pack members, though. More and more families have been showing up, with moving trucks and all, asking to be allowed back in the pack house. I try to tell them that they don't need to ask, and I made the offer in the first place, but they do anyway. So now we have other women in the house, finally. Some of them look my age, but they're older, a fact I was a little disappointed in. There's only about ten of them and most seem nice enough, though a couple just come off a spoiled to me, but then again they are spoiled, so that makes sense. With few women around so many men, it's just the way it is, and I haven't taken the time to get to know them yet either. The only issue I've had with any of them were the two who laughed when I asked them to help me sort out the new clothing Logan and Jace had gotten. Logan was worried they'd all look like clones, so he got each person an entire wardrobe, but the companies who shipped the clothing didn't know, so it got all mixed up. I kept my anger at the women in check and explained that everyone around here helps out. Well, maybe I said that if they want to remain in my pack they have to earn it, but it's about the same thing.

The biggest difference and my most favorite change is the wolf pups running around now. They're all boys, but they are the cutest little things I've ever seen. There are a few bigger ones, too, so Mikey got more friends to play with. I had to tell him not to pet them and talk to them like he would a dog, but treat them how he would a person at first. He got the hang of it quickly and the boy he treated like a dog came around again after the slight insult. I have to keep after Perry and Morris about riding their new friends in wolf form, but Remy explained that boys are weird, and as long as no one is complaining, then it's fine. Two things I never thought I'd hear myself say are the two things I always have to say when I'm around the boys: You don't bite your friends, and you don't ride your friends like a horse.

Even with keeping the floor below ours reserved for children and families, we were able to move some of the soldiers inside the house as well. Of course, almost all of the rooms had to be converted to bedrooms, but we made it work. That made less room for common areas, but it became understood that we could go outside and run around if we needed space. Ash even suggested turning two of the smaller ballrooms into bunkhouses so we could get the rest of the soldiers out of the trailers and get those out of here. So now three-bed-high bunk beds are lined up in rows in those rooms. It's a bit cramped, but we make it work, and everyone pitches in where they can.

The next step for us is converting the basement into laundry facilities. As it is now, there are daily runs to laundromats and the washing machines we have here are working 24/7. And hot water? Nope, we don't have that anymore, not even on our floor. I'm not sure how we're going to make that possible again, but Finn is working on it.

Tristan spends most of his time in the kitchens. Not only cooking, but showing others how to prepare and cook food for the masses. With some of the ballrooms gone, dining space is limited to the small dining room and the bigger ballroom. Finn took over a big office room to start teaching the children, and I sneak away from whatever I'm doing to try to catch him with the kids during their recess.

Seeing him playing with the children makes me love him more than I already did. The wolf pups usually make their way outside with the rest of the kids, and they shift when their siblings do, running around as yipping balls of fur. They seem to like me, too, as they come up to me without reserve and nibble away at my shoelaces and whine for a good belly rub. Grandfather told me that they can sense that I'm their Alpha female, and that's why they act the way that they do. Why all the children act that way in wolf form. I told him that may be true; then again, I've always been good with kids.

Tonight is New Year's Eve, though, and I'm excited to get to run with the rest of the pack. I've been running with Ash and the soldiers he's training in the mornings, after my private yoba sessions with Reed, of course. Ash and his men stay human as they run around the perimeter, but I think it's fun to chase them as a wolf, so I do.

"You ready for this, Princess?" Jace asks as we head down to the backyard, or mud pit.

"Don't you call me that, too. It's hard enough to remember people are speaking to me when I get called that all the time," I tell him.

"Actually, if you'll remember, I called you that first. Long before I knew you were an actual princess," he reminds me.

I smile up at him. "That's right. I guess you were ahead of the curve."

"Always," he replies cockily.

"Oh my God." I gasp out, before covering my eyes with my hands.

Remy laughs behind, Logan joining him. "It's okay, Love. We haven't been taken over by flashers; these wolves just don't care about nudity. They'll be shifting soon," he assures me. Or tries to.

"I don't want to be naked in front of a bunch of people," I tell him nervously.

"Don't worry, you don't have to. I think the other females have chosen to shift inside the house once everyone else leaves. I'll wait outside the door for you; just bark when you're all ready to come out," he tells me.

"I guess that's a little better." I grudgingly agree.

The men file out, and I wave awkwardly at Maxine, one of the other women I've come to really like. She has two kids, Sway and Maxwell, and Mikey really likes them.

Maxine waves back, stepping closer to me. "Hey, there, Princess. Nervous?" she guesses correctly.

"Just about the naked part. I'm excited for the run. I run with my mates all the time, but never with so many other wolves," I tell her honestly.

"Oh, it's fun. I suspect you'll be in the back with our Alphas, so I'll probably see you at some point. I'm going to stick near the middle, back where the kids will be. Sway is always going off, trying to do his own thing, so I have to my eye on him," she tells me with a roll of her pretty blue eyes.

"He is a bit of a rebel, isn't he?" I joke with her.

"Gets that from his father, I assure you," she says with a shake of her head.

"I guess we'd better shift and head on out then. The

men are probably getting impatient," I sigh.

I slip my furry robe off and toss it onto a chair. I shift quickly, shaking out my fur then scratching an itch behind my ear. I give the other women a few moments to shift in privacy before looking behind me to check if they're done. Yep, all finished up.

I bark at the door, and a naked Remy opens it for me. I rub against his leg as I exit and sit next to him. Ash is on my other side, so I lean up to lick his muzzle. As my eyes turn back to Remy, closing the door, I catch one of the other females checking him out. Before I can think about it, I'm on top of her, snapping at her face with my teeth. Her head turns to the side, and she whimpers, so I let her go with one last growl. She gets to her feet and sulks away with her tail between her legs.

I grumble as I trot back to my guys, not caring if anyone thought I was mean. Remy is mine, and no one looks at him that but me. As if to reassure myself, I walk the line of all of my mates, rubbing against them and licking under their necks. Yep, mine. All mine.

Remy's red wolf comes to stand over me, bending his head down lick the top of my head, his chest rumbling at me in approval.

I finally turn my eyes to the rest of the pack, who sit patiently waiting for us. Remy takes his time showing me love, then backs away, taking a deep breath. He howls loudly, his voice carrying across the land and bouncing around the night. My responding howl mixes with the rest of the pack's. All eight of my mates chorus the next one, and that's the signal for those in front with Grandfather to starts running. The younger wolves yip in excitement, and I see Maxine up ahead with the pups, herding them to stay in line. I bark a hello, and she turns her head to see me, bowing her head and giving a short bark back.

The pack runs in groupings, the older wolves out in front, followed by the best fighting soldiers, other than my guys, the majority of the pack follows them, with more fighters, the families, even more soldiers, then us, the Alpha family running behind them.

Somehow, the guys seem to not only know where the wolves up front are going, but they're directing them from all the way back here. I howl when they howl, turn when they turn, and every now and again pounce on a rabbit. The last is not to the guys' liking at all, but it's fun. I don't know how long we run for, but my energy seems to build instead of drain. It's exciting being out here with the pack. We move as a team, as several parts of a whole, and I've never felt closer to them. I've also never found my guys to be as attractive as they are right now, either, and that's saying something since I have always found them attractive. The way they command the other wolves, the way they never break stride, their paws moving at exactly the same time, their fur brushing up against one another as they run side by side. It's infuriatingly sexy, and I find myself wanting them more than I ever have, all of them.

Eventually, we circle back to the house and the wolves shift back into men and flood the house. I, however, have only just run myself into a hot mess, so I issue a challenge to my wolves, getting their attention with a bark, then turning and raising my tail high, swaying my hips as I walk. Several turned-on growls meet my ears, and I know they're watching me now. I take off as fast as I can, heading for the orchards, wanting us to get some distance from the other people still milling about. They let me lead, for I know all of them could catch me if they wanted, especially the fast as lightning Logan. I weave through the barren trees, finding a nice spot for us. With a low howl, Remy orders the guys to surround me. Oh, this is fun. They play with me first, probably getting back at me a little. I try to guess which one tries to nip at my leg next; they're too good, and there's too many to keep an eye on at once. After a while I pout, huffing and sitting down. I don't like this game; I can't win.

Ash steps forward and nuzzles my neck, telling me it's okay and they were just playing. I nuzzle him back, and Reed starts in on my other side. They begin their slow seduction, and I'm soon lost in a tidal wave of love, lust, and passion.

And that's how I find myself waking up in the middle of an orchard, freezing my naked butt off, feeling irritable with lack of sleep. I cross my arms over my chest and kick out at a still-sleeping Ash. "Ash, wake up. Let's go get coffee. I need coffee," I demand. I am so not doing this again in winter.

"I apologize, Love. It was never our intention to fall asleep out here. Come here, I will keep you warm," Remy tells me, picking me up in his arms. I wrap my body around him, stealing his heat.

"It's okay." I sigh. "I fell asleep, too."

"Because we wore that fine ass out," Logan brags, with a slap to my bottom.

I yelp in shock, a little in pain as my backside stings. It's cold out here. "Hey!"

"Let's go inside. I, too, would like some coffee and some more rest," Remy says loudly, ensuring that the rest of my sleeping mates wake up and come with us.

Well, this is going to be fun, walking into a house full of people who know exactly what we have been up to. And we have the added bonus of being completely naked. I sigh heavily. Oh well, it was totally worth it.

CHAPTER TWENTY-ONE

REMY

"Fuck. This can't be good." I groan, scrubbing a hand down my face.

"War usually isn't." Maksim agrees.

"All this, just because we've accepted a few more changed wolves? Were they not aware that the eight Alphas of this pack are changed wolves or are they just ignorant all together?"

"In all fairness, I did warn you this could happen," the Russian reminds me. I shoot him a look, expressing how unhelpful he's being.

"Well, if they want to declare war on us, so be it. We won't strike first, so they'll have to come here," I state firmly.

"Is that a wise choice, Rem? These guys have come a long way in a month, but I don't know if they're ready for the real thing," Ash asks. He's got a point.

"The UK pack is small compared to ours. We'll at

least have the numbers, and the men will be fighting for their home and for their family; that might help tip the scales in our favor. Besides, I don't want this fight to happen if it doesn't need to. Declaring against us doesn't necessarily mean they'll come for us. They could just be taking a stand against changed wolves being granted entry into packs," Finn adds his opinion.

I nod my head. "That's true, but we need to be prepared, just in case. Tristan, can you place additional orders to the food suppliers? Make sure to add more non-perishables."

"I can do that, Rem," he confirms.

"Do we let the rest of the pack know? I mean, we don't even know if this is a real threat yet," Reed asks.

"I think we should hold off for now, see if any other packs declare for us or against us. There's a chance Finn is right and the UK pack is just getting pissy," Logan suggests.

I notice out of the corner of my eye that Kellan looks a little nervous. Since he used to go to war with Ash as a medic, it's out of character for him. "Do you have something to add?" I ask him.

"Not really about this," he answers. "Well, kind of about this. I think we should hold off on mentioning it to Kitten as well."

"Are you crazy? She'll rip our balls off if we don't tell her that someone has declared war against us. Can you imagine how she'll react if we wait to tell her we knew until they're knocking on the front door?" Logan questions. I agree that she'd be fairly angry about that.

"How exactly would we explain that she should stay indoors as well as the other women and children? She won't do it without asking why," Tristan says.

"Why don't you want to tell her? If anything, an angry Kitten will rally the troops better than any of us ever could. Angry Kitten gets things done." Ash directs his question at Kellan.

"I'm not suggesting we don't tell her until war is at our door; I'm just saying we can wait a little while. If you haven't noticed, Kitten hasn't been herself lately. She shouldn't be able to get sick, so I don't know what's going on with her, but something is," he says.

"She has been more tired than usual. She takes at least one nap a day," Tristan points out.

Reed's face scrunches up as he thinks about it. "And she's either starving herself or eating a meal fit for a family of six."

Thinking back over the past couple of weeks, I realize my brothers are right. Kitten has been acting strangely. We've had to keep her away from the television because she either gets angry at the commercials of old people falling and no one helping them up or bawling her eyes out at the commercials of abused animals and hungry kids. Even Mikey's animated films seem to set her off. She's also either been sleeping like a rock when we come in or ready to tear our clothes off, one or the other with no in between.

"Alright, I agree to hold off on telling her, for now. But only until we figure out what's going on with her, which will be as soon as this meeting is over." I put my foot down on this. I'm not keeping things from her; it's just not how this family works.

Maksim bursts into hearty laughter, holding his gut he's going at it so hard. Albert joins him, looking to my brothers and me and laughing harder.

"Is there something we don't know? Care to share? Or do you think a declaration of war and a sick granddaughter is something to be laughed at?" I grit through my teeth. The Russian's continuing laughter is getting on my last nerve.

My tone calms his laughter down into a shit-eating grin instead. "It's funny you say she's sick when we all know that she can't be sick. It must be something else, don't you think?" he asks me, the twinkle in his eye and his rosy cheeks making me want to punch him. If I knew what was wrong with Kitten, I would have fixed it by now. I'm not sure if she's just stressed out, or adjusting to having so many people around, or what. I think she just needs time.

"Shit," Kellan mutters as he stands abruptly, his face as white as a sheet, knocking his chair down behind him. In a flash, he's running from the room, the door slamming into the wall behind him.

"What the fuck?" Logan asks, standing as well. His worried eyes glance at me, asking questions I don't have the answers to.

As I follow after my panicked brother, I spare a glance back at Maksim. Both he and Albert are wearing matching, satisfied grins. I'm a tad creeped out by it if I'm being honest.

When the rest of us finally track Kellan down, back up on our floor of the house, my heart nearly stops beating. Kitten is standing in the middle of the family room, her hands clasped over her mouth, tears streaking down her face. Kellan sits on his knees in front of her, his head resting on her stomach, hands at her hips, fisting the material of her shirt. And he's crying. Great, wracking sobs, crying. I suddenly have no desire to learn what's wrong with my girl, not when the doctor of the family is on his knees crying.

Kitten notices us then, her light green eyes shining with tears, the gold lighting around her irises flaring wildly. She hiccups in laughter, smiling brightly at me. Then she says the words I never thought I'd hear.

"I'm pregnant."

ABOUT THE AUTHOR

Lane Whitt is a reader turned writer who found her niche with Reverse-Harem. As an Ohio resident, she spends her summers outdoors and winters inside freezing her butt off. She likes sticking her tongue out at people from the safety of her car, ice cream, and short walks on the beach (walking in sand is hard, ya know?)

With no formal training in writing, Lane Whitt takes pride in writing in plain English for those who speak plain English.

47126603R00170

Made in the USA
Middletown, DE
04 June 2019